"Hello . . . hello, is anyone there?"

"Don't hang up," a muffled voice ordered.

Instantly Christian's body stiffened. My God! It's him! "What do you want from me? Please leave me alone. I did what you wanted, I haven't called the police."

"I want to make love to you again." He coughed with a snorting sound. "Tell me you want me to."

Christian remained silent, stunned.

"Talk to me, you bitch. I saw you walk your son to school yesterday. I could have run you both over. Talk to me or next time I will."

Biting her lip, she nearly gagged on her words. "Want you to make . . . love to me."

His snorting sounds grew louder. "I'll . . . call you . . . I'll let you know . . . when."

PORTRAIT OF TERROR

Joseph Masiello

A DELL BOOK

Published by
Dell Publishing Co., Inc.
1 Dag Hammarskjold Plaza
New York, New York 10017

ISBN: 0-440-17031-1

Printed in the United States of America

August 1986

10 9 8 7 6 5 4 3 2 1
WFH

Dedicated to Kay . . . my wife

For any of the good that has come of my life . . . I owe you, the one person who has always been there—good times and bad. I have learned much from you and I am a better person, father, and friend because of you.

And I wish you sunshine on a rainy
day,
Joy when your heart is filled with
sorrow,
And, peace in the knowledge that
God has granted you another day.

And, P.S., I love you.

To Christopher George

Even though you are no longer of this world, I sense you in the energy that fuels each day, and in the warmth of the sun and the brightness of the stars.
I have never been able to say good-bye to those I have loved. So it is with you, my friend, it is not good-bye, but merely . . . until another time . . . another place.

chapter 1

Christian Day George glanced at the threatening sky before walking confidently toward the car waiting outside her home in Dedham, Massachusetts. The tree-studded suburban street had a feeling of peace and tranquility, although the town of better than thirty thousand secure suburbanites was a mere twelve miles from battle-scarred Boston.

Her blond hair, like strands of yellow silk riding a gentle breeze, danced on her shoulders. She moved gracefully, like an angel emerging from the darkness; the street light above, her halo. Her hazel almond-shaped eyes held an unmistakable intensity as she glanced toward the green Datsun 280ZX. She was the better side of thirty, vibrant, beautiful, a mother and a wife—an exciting collection of flesh and bone. The car's motor broke an almost eerie stillness as she opened the passenger door and gracefully slid her tall frame into the seat next to the driver.

Her husband, Ben, smiled broadly at her and leaned across to her as she met him with a kiss.

Their six-year-old son, Teddy, waved from the lighted bay window and was joined by Christian's widowed mother. Christian blew them a kiss as the car left the curb.

As they headed north toward Wilmington the sky loosed a torrential downpour, so fierce it echoed like a thousand tiny pebbles beating against the metal roof. Ben cautiously negotiated the exit marked Wilmington. Endless miles of unlit winding roads lay off the main route as they drove through the most rural area found in such close proximity to Boston.

The radio was playing. Willie Nelson was singing "On the Road Again."

"Ol' Willie didn't write that song with this weather in mind." Christian smiled wryly.

Ben glanced at her and put his arm around her shoulder as she snuggled close to him. A flash of lightning ripped through the black sky, followed by a near ear-shattering clap of thunder. Startled, Christian jerked into an upright position. Ben looked affectionately at her and chuckled.

"Sissy."

"Right." She smiled, clutching his arm.

The music on the radio was being drowned out by static and interference. Christian reached over and clicked it off. She grew tense at the not-so-distant grumbling in the turbulent sky. The rhythmic beating of the windshield wipers calmed her but still she leaned forward, straining to see through the downpour.

Passing cars became a blur as the downpour continued. Ben increased the speed of the wipers.

Death came riding through the night in a red 1982 Trans Am. Its occupants were four teenagers who hadn't heard that drinking and driving was out of fashion. The Trans Am rocketed across the slick road toward a horrified Ben and Christian George. Ben's hands frantically spun the steering wheel. The Datsun swerved, narrowly missing the Trans Am head on.

"Bastard," he shouted as he felt his car skidding off the road and shooting into the night. The occupants of the Trans Am rounded a curve and never saw them disappear.

Christian's scream mixed with the sound of shattering glass and crushing metal that pierced the night, then abruptly ceased. The Datsun, now a lump of twisted steel, lay in a gully some thirty feet below the road. But for the falling rain that hissed upon the exposed engine, the silence was deafening.

Ben George was in the driver's seat of the crumpled heap. His face was unmarked and his head hung limply over the broken steering wheel—its shaft driven squarely through his chest.

Christian, thrown clear from the wreckage, lay on her back unconscious some twenty feet from the wreck. The blond hair, pasted against her face by the steady rain, covered a gash on her forehead. Her soaked blouse was torn, revealing part of her full breast. A cool, hard rain beat down steadily, slowly reviving her.

Her eyes fluttered and opened. She lay there numbly for a moment. Fear gripped her as she tried to lift her aching body.

Slowly she sat up. Moaning and covering her face with her hands, she rocked back and forth. Lowering her hands, she stared at the twisted wreckage. Stark reality set in; she was alone and terrified.

A wild rabbit came between her and the car. It paused, seemingly to gaze at her, then popped into the woods.

Weakly, but with her whole being, she called out, "Ben . . . please . . . Ben . . ."

Christian was taken to Wilmington General Hospital—a small hospital compared to most—located far off the main drag amid acres of trees and rolling hills. They placed Christian in a private room in this subpar institute of healing.

The X rays, blood test—the entire examination was now completed. Diagnosis: minor contusions, slight concussion, shock. She lay bathed, gowned, in bed, in a hospital, in the middle of nowhere, sedated into sleep.

It was early the next morning when a small gathering, acting more like a doom squad than hospital personnel, gathered in the room of Christian George. They were murmuring among themselves as she began to wake. A nurse was busy administering an I.V. solution, a doctor was taking her pulse, and a priest, the symbol of death in any hospital, waited patiently for her to speak.

She felt someone holding her hand as Dr. Harrison, a graying gentle man in his late fifties, spoke softly to her.

"Mrs. George, Mrs. George."

The horror of the night's events was instantly made real by the gray light of day.

"No, no, God, no," she begged, pleaded, snapping her eyes closed.

The priest and nurse both glanced at Harrison. His breath deepened and his lips became a thin penciled line as he shook his head and gently reassured her.

"Mrs. George, you're safe now. Please try to understand . . . you're going to be just fine. Mrs. George . . . open your eyes."

She responded slowly and was so filled with a terrible, agonizing apprehension that she began to tremble badly. The doctor and nurse looked reluctantly in her direction while the priest,

Father Travers, a kindly man in his middle forties, wore a death mask.

Christian looked to the priest, their eyes locking. She struggled to ignore the finality of his consoling look, as she heard herself speak, almost involuntarily.

"Ben . . . he isn't dead? Please tell me he isn't . . ."

"God has taken him, Mrs. George," Travers murmured.

She shook her head, refusing to accept what she knew was true.

"No . . . no, not now. He can't be dead. He was all right; I saw him."

"Please, Mrs. George, don't despair, he is at peace," consoled Travers.

A wave of hysteria, bitterness, engulfed her. *"No! No! You've made a mistake. I want to see him. Damn you, he's not dead! Where is he? He's not dead!"* she raved, pounding on the bed with the sides of her clenched fists.

Harrison nodded to the nurse who was standing by with a syringe. The doctor stepped forward, holding Christian on one side, Travers held the other, as the nurse injected a struggling Christian with sweet oblivion.

For the better part of two days, Christian floated, a million miles from the pain and torment of consciousness and reality. Each time reality dragged her back from her drugged garden of tranquility to this small room filled with vivid, agonizing memories that she tried desperately to blot from her mind, she screamed until they returned her to that quiet place inside her head.

Finally she woke but it seemed she hadn't slept at all—her head throbbed with a dullness—when she suddenly felt someone touching her body. Her mind flashed to the scene of the accident, desperately trying to grab onto something as the car tumbled down the embankment. The nurse sprang backward, warding off the unexpected clawing hands.

Visibly shaken, and with a quake in her voice, the nurse stared incredulously at Christian while trying to calm her.

"Mrs. George, please, it's . . . it's all right. I'm just waking you for breakfast."

Trembling, she came to her full senses. "I'm sorry . . . I'm sorry . . . I thought . . ."

Cupping her hands to her face, she released the pent-up emotion and began to weep.

The nurse moved forward to Christian and cradled her head to her bosom, softly patting her back.

"There, there, you're doing fine. You just have to give yourself a little time, that's all."

She was trying to control her sobbing as Dr. Harrison entered the room. He walked directly to the side of her bed and cast an inquiring look toward the nurse.

"She seems a bit upset, Doctor." The nurse shrugged sympathetically. "Will you need me for anything?"

"No, no, that will be fine, thank you."

Satisfied, the nurse turned and left the room.

Harrison stood there quietly as Christian made an effort to compose herself. As she lowered her hands from her flushed face, he gently took one of them and sandwiched it between his own.

"Mrs. George, I realize how difficult this must be for you."

She remained silent. Unable to stop the tears from flowing, she stared painfully at him.

"You know you have to think about your little boy. He needs you very much."

Her speech was broken by involuntary gasps for air as she calmed, feeling more composed. "Ben . . . did . . . did he . . . suffer?"

"No, no, he didn't. He really never knew what happened."

Wiping the tears from her reddened eyes, she nodded almost thankfully.

Harrison bent over her, moving a lock of blond hair, inspecting the gash on her forehead. "It's fortunate that it didn't require stitches."

As he straightened, Christian seemed to study his face. Harrison's eyes had been shifting in thought; then his gaze came to light on the anguish in her face.

"I wish there was some other way I could phrase this . . . to make it easier for you," he stammered. "Your mother has made arrangements for your husband's funeral. Do you feel up to attending?"

For the first time her mind did not reject the thought: *Ben's dead!* Shakily, she nodded affirmatively.

"Mrs. George, if you don't think you can . . . it's all right.

The most important thing now is for you to get well enough to go home to take care of your son."

Her mind was suddenly filled with thoughts of Teddy. She desperately wanted to hold him, to let him know everything would be all right.

"Does he know . . . how is he?" she asked, her voice quaking.

"Your mother told him." Harrison smiled warmly. "He asked when you would be home so that he could take care of you."

Harrison took some tissues from a box on the table and handed them to Christian. "If you're sure you're up to it, the funeral is tomorrow at ten A.M. I'll release you about eight o'clock and make arrangements with your mother to be here with your clothes."

"Please . . . I'm fine. Discharge me today."

Harrison studied the intense, tired face before him. "It would be better for all of you if you used today to regain your strength and get a good night's sleep . . . don't you agree?"

She felt too weak to belabor the point and reflected that maybe it was better. She would have one more night to pull herself together.

"I'd rather not, but if you say so, Doctor . . ."

It was nearly nine in the evening when a slim nurse came into the room with the evening sedation—two 10mg Valiums and one Dalmane capsule.

"How are you feeling, Mrs. George?"

There were dark circles under Christian's eyes. The strain showed in her face as she answered. "Fine . . . I think I'm just a little tired."

The nurse extended her hand, offering the pills to Christian. "Just take these; you'll have a comfortable night's sleep."

She accepted them and eagerly gulped them down, grateful for the peace of mind the three tiny pills would bring her. "Thank you," she whispered.

"Is there anything else I can do for you, Mrs. George?"

"No, no, I'm fine."

The nurse fluffed her pillows, lowered her bed from the sitting position, and, with a reassuring pat on the head, left.

Christian closed her eyes. She never felt more alone in her

thirty-four years of life. Near tears, she softly murmured a prayer for her son and the soul of her dead husband. She dreaded and longed for the morning all in one breath. The funeral would mean saying good-bye to Ben—though how could she find the courage to do that so soon? It was too soon. But Teddy would be waiting for her, her precious Teddy.

It was two A.M. and the chief nurse, Mrs. Merguson, a hawk-faced, extremely thin woman, was quietly making her rounds along with the rest of her staff. Directly across from Christian George's room, a figure lurked in the shadows. He watched a nurse open the George door, go in, take her vital signs, and, satisfied, leave the room. He hesitated for a minute or two and then slowly crept across the dimly lit corridor. Taking a deep breath, he looked around to be sure he was undetected and went in. Shutting the door behind him, he quickly took a chair and jammed it under the knob. The glow of a small light outlined her sleeping form. He moved quickly, quietly, to her bed. For a moment he just leered at her helpless, sleeping form. His face started to perspire, his mouth grew dry as he hovered over her, removing the covers from her body. His eyes were wide and hands shaking in anticipation as he reached for her gown, pulling it over her head. He could hear his heart pounding as his excitement soared. As she lay there, the sight of her nude body with the slim waist and firm, ample bust nearly took his breath away. He straddled the shadowy, white softness upon the bed.

Strange sounds—an almost inhuman snorting—and the feel of the cool air against her nude body began to awaken Christian. The man's glazed eyes widened as he paused in midair then plunged downward. The strong evening sedation made her feel as if she were moving in slow motion. She brushed the gown from her face as the feel of a sharp, painful intrusion between her legs registered in her semiconsciousness. Her eyes opened and she glimpsed a man's outline. Her mind was clouded with the wheezing, snorting echoes that were coming from the shadowed face above her. He was grinding deep within her as she protested and struggled in vain.

"No . . . no, God . . . please no."

He reached under his shirt and pulled out a chloroform-soaked rag and shoved it harshly over her nose and mouth, while thrusting against her helpless form. She tried to fight back. Her head began to whirl as her efforts to push him off diminished and her cries were muffled as she sank into a darkened world of dizzy nothingness. He rasped at her still form as she lay unconscious.

"Nice baby . . . nice baby . . . you know you belong to me. See, I'm not going to hurt you. I just want to fuck you . . . come in you . . . come in you . . . come-come-come . . ."

He leaned over, sucking, fondling her breasts, and, placing his lips on hers, forced his tongue into her mouth. Still pumping inside her, he licked her eyes, her face.

"You love it . . . you love me to fuck you," he whispered hoarsely.

He exhausted himself and swung from the bed. Quickly he pulled her gown back in place and flipped the covers back over her. He rushed into the bathroom and, with a cruel smile, discarded an oozing contraceptive into the toilet and flushed it. Hungrily he took one last look at Christian.

"Whore, I'm not finished with you!" he said venomously.

chapter 2

It was five-fifteen at Wilmington General Hospital. Kitchen workers were busy preparing the morning breakfast for the hundred eighty-seven patients there. Mrs. Merguson was at her desk checking over the patients' charts. There wasn't a sound in the corridors except for the quiet shuffling of an occasional nurse attending to her duties.

Suddenly all hell broke loose, as blood-curdling screams echoed off the walls and down the corridors.

"AHHHHHHHH . . . AHHHHHHHH . . . AHHH . . . AHHHHH!"

Mrs. Merguson sprang to her feet, stumbling on her chair in her haste to race toward the cries. The corridor quickly filled with nurses and orderlies scurrying toward Christian George's door. They burst into her room.

She sat rigid in the middle of her bed, hysterical and screaming, "I've been raped! My God, you let him rape me . . . he raped me . . . NO . . . NO . . . NO . . ." She was nearly convulsing while pounding her fists into the mattress.

Don Spencer, a strapping orderly in his late twenties, rushed into the room and helped three nurses restrain Christian while another pushed a needle into her arm. As the sedative spread quickly through her system, Christian's ravings slowed to a slurred drawl.

"Please . . . please help me. A—a man, he raped me," she half whispered.

Dr. Milton Schneiderman, a man in his middle forties, bespectacled and balding, entered the room at a brisk pace, glanced quizzically at the slumping patient and the starched nurse, then motioned silently with his head for the nurse to follow him outside. Schneiderman looked at the nurse through his slightly watery eyes.

"It seems I can't leave this floor for an instant. What the hell is going on here?"

"We don't know, Doctor. It looks as though she's had a nightmare. She keeps insisting she's been raped."

"Raped! Christ, what next! I want to see her chart."

"Yes, Doctor, right away."

As the nurse hurried down the hall, Schneiderman reentered the room. He strode to Christian's side and looked at the nurse closest to her.

"Did you give her a sedative yet?" he asked irritated.

"Yes, Doctor, just before you arrived."

"Fine. You can all go back to your stations."

Schneiderman waited until the last person left and closed the door before he spoke, with a cool detachment. "Relax, Mrs. George, you're going to be fine. Do you feel like telling me what happened?"

The medication had its effect, for she was feeling very lightheaded, but she understood what Schneiderman had asked. Almost calmly now, almost matter-of-factly, she related what occurred.

As Christian was finishing her account, they were interrupted by the floor nurse, who came into the room, handed Schneiderman Christian's chart, and left.

Christian looked at him almost pathetically as he stood to the side examining the information in his hand. The last sentence she uttered before falling to sleep was "Doctor . . . do—do you believe me?"

With a note of indifference in his voice, he replied, "Yes, yes, of course."

He left her room and went to the head nurse's station. Mrs. Merguson was busy at work, seated at her desk, when he interrupted.

"I want the George woman to remain heavily sedated throughout the day and checked on every half hour. If she has another outburst like this, I want her put in restraints." He handed Christian's chart to her.

"Doctor, Mrs. Day, the lady's mother, has made arrangements to be here this morning to take her home."

Schneiderman replied sternly, "Mrs. George isn't ready to go home. . . . I'll call her mother."

A crowd hovered at Benjamin George's graveside at Holy Cross Cemetery. The sky was overcast. The grass was wet from a fresh rain and the chill of the early hour added an extra dimension of sorrow to the already gloomy morning. Mrs. Day had young Teddy by the hand. Their eyes were fixed upon the old priest who was to deliver the eulogy.

The priest looked skyward as he began. "Lord, hear our prayers."

He had no sooner uttered the words than a tremendous clap of thunder broke the now-eerie silence. The priest and those gathered about the grave were visibly shaken. The priest hesitated, then continued. A master at his craft, he evoked the deep-seated emotions that reminded all who were gathered there that "life is not eternal—and someday you die." Most wept for Ben George. There were others who were moved to tears by the sobering realization that they, too, would someday lie in a wooden box and be lowered into the earth.

When the procession left the funeral site, Mrs. Day and her grandson remained alone watching over the man who was so dear to both of them.

There was one other standing there. Father Travers had waited until the services were over before approaching Mrs. Day and Teddy. Her gray hair was blown softly by the wind as she held young Teddy's hand. They both stared solemnly at the flowered coffin, their backs to Travers.

"Mrs. Day," the priest quietly uttered.

She and the boy turned to him. "Yes . . . yes, Father?"

"Mrs. Day, my name is Father Travers. We have talked to each other several times by phone."

She extended her plump, wrinkled hand, and the priest shook it gently. "Oh, yes, Father. God bless you for taking care of our Christian while she's in that hospital. Well, she . . . she . . ." Weeping, Mrs. Day stopped in mid-sentence and glanced at her grandson. Although smaller than most youngsters of the same years, Teddy was extremely bright for his age and blessed with his father's gift of gab, blue eyes, and black hair. He looked up at the priest as he spoke sadly.

"Grandma always told me that when I heard that big noise up there that it was God clearing his throat. Is that really true?"

Mrs. Day looked down at little Teddy and was filled with love for him. The priest smiled at her and looked at the boy.

"Teddy, I want you to listen to your grandmother. I can't really tell you if that's the case every time—but today I have a feeling that was the good Lord himself telling us he heard our prayers for your dad." He paused, then continued. "Teddy, when your mother is well, would you like it if I came by your house and talked to you some more about it?"

"Yes . . . yes, I'd like that."

The priest blessed Mrs. Day and Teddy. "Mrs. Day, if I can do anything for you—anything—please call me."

Dabbing her eyes with the handkerchief, she nodded, watching the priest walk away. She felt as though it were the end of the world as she and Teddy stood silently alone there.

His eyes fixed on the coffin, Teddy whispered, "Grandma, do we have to leave Daddy here? He's all by himself."

Tears filled the old woman's eyes and were spilling over as she answered. "Your daddy will never be alone again. God has taken him to heaven."

She knelt on the wet grass, looking straight at the boy as she pulled him gently to her, holding him snugly against her bosom. Teddy put his arms around his grandmother's neck, tears streaming down his face.

The day after the funeral, Christian sat passively, numbly, alone in her room. When her mother told her that her husband had been buried while she slept, she wept. They were tears of frustration and loneliness. She thought of her son and became obsessed with the thought of leaving the hospital to go to his side.

As she lay on her side, her back to the door, Father Travers entered, undetected. He stood by the side of her bed, her sniffing the only sound to break the stillness. He softly laid his hand on her shoulder as he spoke.

"Mrs. George . . ."

She slowly turned to the priest. "Hello, Father."

"Mrs. George, my name is Father Travers. I want to let you know that your son and mother are doing just fine."

"Were they here? Why couldn't I see them?"

"No, no, they weren't here. I attended the services for your husband and I saw them there. Your son's a fine boy; you must be very proud of him."

"Yes . . . yes, I am."

"Mrs. George, would you like to talk?"

"No . . . no, thank you, Father." The warmth in his eyes and voice only seemed to stir the resentment she felt. "I don't think so," she added bitterly.

"The Lord works in mysterious ways, Mrs. George. There are many occasions we find difficult to understand. I know this is a trying time for you, but please, don't let your faith be weakened by this. Instead, allow your faith to give you the courage you need to get through this."

"Father, my husband was taken from us, from a little boy who needed him very much. On top of that, I was raped in this hospital . . . and no one will believe me. You know, Father . . . you're right. I don't understand, so please . . . please, don't talk to me about God's mysterious ways. Not today, not now." She turned her back to him, pushing her head into the pillow.

The better part of an hour had passed when Dr. Harrison entered, accompanied by another man. "Mrs. George, I'd like you to meet Dr. Spellie. I'll just leave you two alone . . . to sort of get acquainted." Harrison left the room.

Robert Spellie was a slender graying confident-looking man. He was of medium height and possessed steel-blue eyes that flashed with alertness above his high cheekbones. His manner was casually probing as he extended a hand to Christian.

"Mrs. George, I'm happy to meet you. Dr. Harrison has related your experience of the other night to me. I'm going to try to help you. Let's talk a bit about what happened."

Panic swept through Christian as she thought, My God, a psychiatrist! They think I'm crazy! There was a slight tremble in her voice as she spoke. "Are you a psychiatrist?"

"Yes, I am."

"Do you think I'm crazy . . . that I made the whole thing up?"

"I really don't know what to think yet, Mrs. George. Try to relax and tell me everything as best you can."

In relating to Spellie her account of what happened, Christian's bitterness and outrage came through.

Spellie studied her for a moment. "Mrs. George, you haven't once mentioned any concern about the possibility of your becoming impregnated by this . . . rapist."

Christian stared at him incredulously. "Doctor, I'm on the pill."

"It is important that we be completely honest with each other," declared Spellie. "So, very frankly, I must tell you that there is no evidence supporting your allegation of being raped the other night. Is it possible that you were just, say, having a nightmare?"

"No, Doctor, I was not dreaming! I was raped!" she responded adamantly.

"The entire staff related that they didn't hear any disturbance. Didn't you call out?"

"I can't remember," she softly uttered, suddenly puzzled.

"Mrs. George, doesn't it seem reasonable that if a man had been in your room committing such an act that you would have cried out?"

Christian remained silent and was now glaring at Spellie.

"Mrs. George, please believe me, I want to help you. I know you find it extremely difficult, but if we're going to get to the bottom of this, I have to ask questions."

"What I find *extremely difficult,*" she responded icily, "is the fact that no one here will believe me. I was raped, I tell you . . . not dreaming, not imagining, raped!"

"I'm not saying I don't believe you. I merely want you to realize that it is not unusual for the mind to play tricks, especially under traumatic stress. It can provide a temporary escape from the unbearable reality at hand. For instance, in your case, having to face your husband's funeral might have triggered a subconscious reaction. Do you understand what I am saying?"

His words fanned the flames of exasperation, anger that was growing inside of Christian. "Damn you! Why—why won't you believe me!" With her heart pounding, she took a deep breath, trying to control herself. Her eyes flashed and she wrung her hands in agitation.

"Yes, I certainly do understand what you are saying, Dr. Spellie. You are telling me that no matter what I say, not one solitary person in this hospital will believe that I am telling the truth—that I was actually raped!"

Spellie gestured for Christian to calm down. "Please, Mrs. George, getting upset like this won't help."

"You're absolutely right, Doctor," she interjected. Flinging the covers from her legs, she exclaimed, "All that can help is for me to leave here and go home!"

As soon as Christian's full weight was on her feet, her knees buckled. The power of her anger could not offset the weakness and trembling she felt in her legs. She offered little resistance as Dr. Spellie helped her back onto the bed. She lay there limply, seething, and turned her face from him.

"Mrs. George, you are in no condition to go anywhere at the moment. Why don't you rest for the time being . . . I'll be back."

Right after his disturbing session with Christian George, Spellie joined Schneiderman in the staff room. There was a tone of detachment in Spellie's voice as he spoke.

"Of course, if she had been raped, that would certainly explain her present emotional state. Milt, did anyone hear . . . see anything?"

"Bob, I've spoken with everyone who was on duty. No one heard a sound, and each time she was checked she was sound asleep. The woman must be fabricating the whole story—or else she was hallucinating."

"The pelvic examination . . . what did that show?"

Schneiderman squirmed in his chair. "I found no evidence of dried semen."

Spellie studied him for a moment. "How about loose pubic hair, blood, fingernail scrapings, the vaginal vault . . . abrasion, secretions . . . chemical tests? What were the results?"

"I only conducted an external." Schneiderman held up his hand, like a cop stopping traffic. "Now hold on, Bob, before you comment. I know the examination was very cursory, but for Christ sakes, the woman was obviously off her trolley. She was so disturbed at that point that I felt an internal examination would only add needlessly to her psychological upheaval."

Spellie was shaking his head in disgust. "And I'll bet you've bathed her since then, haven't you? We better hope to hell she doesn't contract syphilis, gonorrhea—that is, *if* she did in truth have a visitor. By the way, I don't suppose she was given any antibiotics just in case, was she?"

"No," answered Schneiderman, taking off his glasses and pressing his thumb and forefinger to the bridge of his nose. "We'll keep an eye on her, although I'm positive the woman was never touched." Lowering his hand, he looked directly at Spellie. "I had a meeting with the administrator this morning. He wants this mess cleared up—some outside help, discreetly, quietly. I advised him you had a brother-in-law who could possibly be of some help."

Spellie smiled wryly. "Lane Garrett? He's expensive."

"Bob, Jonathan Prendergast has been the administrator here for eleven years. He wants this resolved without it getting out. He'll pay. The hospital doesn't need this kind of publicity."

Two days had elapsed since Dr. Spellie's visit. It was nine P.M. The night nurse had just entered Christian George's room with her evening sedation. For the last two nights, Christian had held the three tiny pills under her tongue, careful not to swallow them. When the nurse had left, she had quickly wrapped them in tissue and disposed of them in the trash basket. She had stayed awake each night, fearful that her unwelcome visitor would return. In the morning, she would wait until breakfast had been served before falling asleep, exhausted.

The dawn had just begun to filter into Christian's room. Betrayed by exhaustion, her eyes were shut, and she was very close to sleep. She pictured herself and Ben dancing. She was wearing a wedding gown; they were deliriously happy. Her thoughts switched to their home as he playfully chased her around the kitchen till he caught her—she cupped his face in her hands, they kissed tenderly. Again the picture changed, this time to the three of them—her, Ben, and little Teddy—walking in the Boston Common. It was winter and the pond was ringed with snow, the icicles hung from the leafless branches of the glistening trees, and Teddy was sliding down a hill on a piece of cardboard that Ben had found for him. She was at peace. She slept. The melody of a song kept coming to her. She searched for the words.

A sound breaking the silence in her room penetrated her subconscious. She forced her eyes open. Struggling, she tried to see through the sleepy haze. As her vision partially cleared, the outline of a blurred figure appeared inside her room, near the door. She screamed hysterically and grabbed for the water pitcher that was nearby, on the table. The blurred figure reached for the door as the flying pitcher came crashing against it. Christian scrambled from her bed. Stumbling, she rubbed her eyes as she ran for the bathroom. She quickly entered and slammed and locked the door. Her shouts could be heard throughout the corridors.

"Help me! Please, someone help me!"

Her room quickly filled with the floor nurses and orderlies. With considerable coaching from the head nurse, Christian finally relented and came out from behind the locked door. She was pale and trembling.

"He was here . . . the man who raped me; he was here again." A short, stout nurse stared at her as she continued. "Someone do something . . . find him," pleaded Christian.

The nurse, the short, stout one, was wiping off the front of her uniform. She looked at Christian in surprise as she explained, "Mrs. George, it was me you threw the water pitcher at. I only came in to check on you."

"No, no . . . it couldn't have been you. I—I was so sure that it was him . . . back again."

Mrs. Merguson walked up beside her, clasped her gently by the arm, and led her back to bed. "Mrs. George, it's going to be all right. I'll station someone right outside your door. You get some sleep; we won't let anyone in here."

Several hours later Dr. Spellie entered her room.

"Good morning, Mrs. George."

Christian was in a sitting position, leaning back against the pillows with her eyes closed. Hearing Spellie, she turned to face him. The intensity had gone from her eyes; she was listless as she responded.

"Good morning, Doctor."

"Mrs. George, I've talked to the head nurse and she tells me you had another bad night. She informs me you insist the man was back again."

"I—I thought it was. I couldn't—I opened my eyes and saw a figure near the door. I thought it was him."

"Don't concern yourself with it."

Christian's gaze followed him as he strode to the side of the bed. She blinked in the morning light as the psychiatrist stood with his back to the window.

"I know what you have been going through and how much you want to go home, and I—"

Christian softly interrupted. "No . . . no, Doctor, you have no idea what I have been going through. With or without your consent, I'm leaving this hospital."

"Mrs. George, no one here has any intention of keeping you here against your will. We want to resolve this situation . . . any injustice you feel that has been inflicted on you. That is first and foremost in our thoughts. Secondly, newspaper publicity, perhaps a lawsuit . . . it would all be very distasteful. On the other hand, if such an act has actually occurred, it would be imperative that we take measures to ensure it doesn't happen again."

Christian paused in reflection. "Doctor, believe me, I have no intention of bringing suit against this hospital. What proof do I have? Who the hell would believe me!" she flared. Softening, she continued. "Please, no more. I've just lost my husband. I have a little boy who needs me very much. I just want to go home . . . and forget."

"Mrs. George . . . would you be willing to cooperate with a friend of mine?" asked Spellie, hesitating. "He's a private investigator."

"An investigator! No! Doctor, I don't want to drag this out. I want it ended . . . over; I want to go home."

"Mrs. George, you tell me you were *raped* . . . that a man came in this room and violated you . . . that feeling, I am confident, will not go away until we get to the bottom of this. I assure you it will be done with the utmost discretion."

Christian did not respond.

"Mrs. George, do you want this man to get away with this, or are you trying to tell me that you now realize it was a figment of your confused state of mind? If that is the case, I understand."

Spellie waited patiently for Christian's response.

"Call your investigator friend, Doctor. You're absolutely right. The filthy scum that did this to me should not get away with it." She stared coldly into Spellie's eyes. "You assured me it will be done with the utmost discretion. Doctor, I assure you, if I or my family are harmed in any way by this investigation—newspaper publicity, whatever—by the time I finish with this hospital, a dog won't check in here."

chapter 3

Spellie was standing at a pay phone and just completed dialing a number. It was answered on the second ring.

"Good afternoon, Garrett International."

"Hello, Linda. This is Bob Spellie. Is the slave driver still overworking you these days?"

A cheerful note of recognition replaced the businesslike tone of the young woman's voice.

"Why, hello, Dr. Spellie. He works all our fingers to the bone, but we love him anyway. Hold on, I'll buzz him."

Within a few seconds the silence was replaced by a very genial, deep, resilient voice, as Lane answered.

"Bob, how's it goin', pal?"

"About the same, Lane."

"That's just like a shrink." Lane laughed, thinking out loud. "Can't ever get a straight answer out of you guys."

Spellie's good-natured laughter mingled with Lane's.

"So, Bob, what's up?"

"I need to see you. If your schedule permits . . . tonight, tomorrow."

"Schedule? What the hell are you talkin' about, schedule? You want somethin', you got it . . . just ask."

"Why don't we make it for dinner . . . say, eight o'clock at Michael's."

"I'll be there. See ya, pal."

"Thanks, Lane."

Lane Garrett had launched his business as a private investigator in one room, over a Chinese laundry, and slowly, over a period of twenty years, it had become one of New England's most successful agencies. In his early forties, trim and always meticulously attired, he spoke with confidence and authority. His short combed-back dark hair, graying at the temples, added to the distinguished and professional image he projected. Yet, in a way, Lane remained a diamond in the rough. For all his success and acquired expertise in his business, his speech still reflected a limited formal education.

At eight-fifteen Lane was sitting in Michael's, a posh restaurant. Spellie was opposite him with his back to a giant gold-frame mirror. The maître d' hovered about them, giving Lane a sharp look of disapproval when he ordered a bottle of Miller Lite, while Spellie ordered Château Lafite Rothschild.

The wine steward soon appeared with the fine Bordeaux. He removed the cork and gently poured a small amount. Spellie sniffed it, rolled it caressingly along the glass, then tasted it, letting the red wine linger on his tongue while nodding his head in approval. The key-bedecked man ceremoniously placed the bottled brew before him. Lane, mimicking Spellie, savored his just-sipped beer and stared at the wine steward.

"There's nothing like a fine bottle of beer," he said to the departing steward.

Lane glanced at Spellie with a wry smile. "This joint is nothin' but an overpriced McDonald's. And some of these yoyo's they got workin' in joints like this act like they're doin' you a favor waitin' on ya. Why, for Christ sakes, if they had to make an honest livin', they'd starve to death."

Spellie laughed and after a moment began his account of what had transpired at the hospital. He stopped only once, when the main course was served.

Finally he ended with "This situation is delicate, to say the least."

Lane put his fork down solemnly. "What exactly are you askin' me to do . . . run a polygraph on her?"

"No, I don't want to alienate her. The administrator at Wilmington, Jonathan Prendergast, has authorized me to . . . well, hire you. I want you to take the case, Lane. Conduct a full investigation . . . very discreetly, of course."

"I don't know, Bob. This sounds like one for the law. You people could wind up in a real jackpot. I rarely turn down business, but as your friend, I gotta tell ya this could blow up in your kisser. Call the law, Bob. Let them handle it."

"I need you on this, Lane. To use your terminology, we are in a jackpot. There wasn't so much as a smear done on the lady."

Lane sipped his beer while eyeing Spellie intensely. "Bob, are you on the hook . . . are you the guy that blew the examination?"

"No, Lane, but that hospital means a great deal to me. We've just filed a new Certificate of Need that will allow us more beds and equipment. If the state gets wind of this, true or not, there won't be a chance in hell it will be approved."

"Bob, I was married to your sister for a good many years before she died. I loved her . . . and I love you too, pal. This case ain't my bag, but you want me to take it, you got it."

"Lane, I believe the woman is being untruthful . . . and we have to prove that. It's important . . . well, to all of us connected with the hospital."

Lane absently sipped at his beer. Finally he set the glass down and stared at Spellie. "What if the lady is tellin' the truth?"

"Lane, no matter how it turns out, I want a lid kept on this situation. If it turns out she is telling the truth—and I doubt she is—we'll just have to take corrective measures to see that it doesn't happen again."

"I'll need a list of every male employee that worked that night—and I'll need it like yesterday."

"I'll attend to it first thing tomorrow," Spellie replied.

It was early the next afternoon. Dr. Spellie was seated beside Christian George's bed. "Mrs. George, Mr. Garrett informs me that he spoke to you this morning. I'm sure you'll find him to have the utmost discretion."

"After meeting him, I feel better about Mr. Garrett handling this situation. But right now all I want to do is leave here."

"I understand Mr. Garrett will be taking you home."

"Yes," replied Christian, "he felt it would give us more of an opportunity to discuss this—this situation."

When Spellie had gone, Christian stepped from the bed, feeling a slight weakness in her legs. She paused for a moment to regain her balance and reached for the beauty case her mother had sent.

She moved before the mirror to apply her makeup. She was brushing her hair when Father Travers entered the room.

Christian, seeing his reflection in the mirror, turned to him. "Hello, Father."

"Mrs. George, I heard the good news—that you're going home."

"Yes, Father." She beamed.

"I shall pray for you and your little boy. We're all in God's merciful hands—may He help you both to find happiness."

Christian felt pangs of guilt in remembering how abrupt she had been with him during his last visit. "Father . . . about the other day . . ."

"Mrs. George, I understand." Smiling gently, he continued. "You know, I have occasion to visit your area. The next time I'm out that way, perhaps I could drop by and see you and Teddy."

"By all means, please do; we'd like that."

Lane Garrett, waiting for Christian, was in the corridor talking to Spellie. "Did you get that list of all the male employees that worked that night?"

"You'll have it by midmorning, Lane. I'm putting it together myself. I don't want anyone getting wind of what we're doing."

An orderly wheeled Christian out of her room in a chair and paused at the head nurse's station. She signed the release papers and they were on their way. Lane, Spellie, and the orderly accompanied Christian down in the elevator, which opened onto the lobby floor. They proceeded to the entrance, where Lane had parked his car right outside the door.

Spellie smiled as Christian deeply breathed in the fresh air. "Mrs. George, even though I'm leaving you in good hands, I want you to know you can call me at any time."

Christian stood for a moment by the open car door. A soft breeze feathered her face and fluffed the sunlit hair upon her shoulders. It was like a warm welcome back into the world. She felt free and alive once again.

It's over, she thought as she settled into her seat. As the car began to move away, she sat back and looked out the window. Her gaze lighted on the small mirror outside on the car door. Christian watched the reflection of the hospital grow smaller with the distance. To her it seemed the gray facade had become the headstone for a nightmare of horrors.

Lane was the first to break the silence. "Mrs. George, if it's all right with you, I'd like to call you Christian. Since I'll be dropping by your house, it might seem more natural to your son and anyone else that might be there. Why don't we just say I'm an old friend of your husband's, okay?"

"That's fine with me, Mr. Garrett."

"Call me Lane, please."

"All right, Lane."

Lane drew Christian out about herself and her family: where Teddy went to school, how he got there, how friendly they were with the neighbors. He asked whether, if necessary, there was a man in the neighborhood they could call on for help. Looking at her and feeling her warmth, Spellie's belief that she was lying haunted Lane.

Soon they pulled up in front of Christian's split-level home. The shutters that Ben George had painted the day before the accident were propped against the side of the house. Christian swung open the car door and hurried toward the front door. Lane followed close behind, carrying her makeup case and a plastic bag containing some of her things. She opened the door and climbed four steps to the living room foyer, calling out softly, "Is anyone home?"

Christian's mother, Lois Day, was at the kitchen sink. She pivoted and ran toward her daughter, her voice rising. "Christian. Teddy! Teddy . . . your mother, your mother's home!"

Mrs. Day kept hugging her daughter, kissing her, patting her face. "Honey, Christian . . . baby . . . are you okay?"

Teddy excitedly called to her from the hallway approaching the living room. "Momma, Momma!"

He ran into her arms. She held him, dropping to her knees on the carpeted floor, kissing his face, eyes, head. Mrs. Day wrapped her arms around her daughter and her grandson for a few grateful moments.

"Momma, are you okay?" blurted Teddy.

"Oh, yes, honey, yes," she whispered, soaking in the feeling of warmth from her little boy.

"Daddy's in heaven. Do you know Daddy's in heaven?"

"Yes, I know, sweetheart."

"Grandma said we're all gonna see him again when we go to heaven. Are we, Momma . . . are we?"

Christian was trembling, holding back her tears, as she continued to cling to Teddy, kissing him, loving him.

"Yes, baby . . . someday."

Slowly she released the boy from her embrace, her hands upon his arms. She turned to speak to Lane Garrett. The plastic bag was propped against the makeup case at the top of the stairs. Lane was gone.

chapter

4

Lane blinked several times trying to adjust to the brightness of the sun after leaving the darkness of Zito's restaurant. The eatery, a scant block from Lane's office, was his favorite. Almost daily he would order a bottle of beer, followed by a bowl of beef stew.

He began walking toward his building, a thirty-story edifice located in the heart of Boston's financial district. Millions of tons of towering concrete shaped into man-made stalagmites. In ten square blocks were the powerful and the rich, the hookers and pimps and hoods.

Lane entered his office building, went to the elevator and, hurrying within the shutting doors, pressed the button marked four.

He stepped from the elevator at his floor, walked past the glass reception window, through two huge walnut doors, and entered the office. He paused before his secretary, Linda, a flat-chested girl in her twenties with long dark hair.

"What've ya got for me, honey?"

Linda smiled broadly at him and said, "Good morning, Mr. Garrett. There are a few messages for you. Uh, first a Mrs. Flint called. She wanted to talk to you before making an appointment—wouldn't say what it was in reference to. She left her number." She handed him a small slip of paper and glanced back at her pad. "Dr. Spellie dropped by to leave you a list; he said you'd know. I put it on your desk. Mr. Zimmerman phoned to thank you for locating his son."

"Thank me? The kid's a monster. Someday Zimmerman will

call me to get that kid lost again." Smiling, he walked to the door marked LANE GARRETT.

Lane's offices occupied a large suite, complete with conference room, three separate offices for his operatives, a reception area, and a spacious office of his own. His domain was simple but tastefully decorated. There were two blue highback overstuffed chairs facing a medium-sized desk, a matching convertible sofa against the wall, and a number of plants carefully placed around the room. The indirect lighting shone from the ceiling and through the glass cases mounted on three of the walls. The cases contained an assortment of tools used in his trade—walkie-talkies, binoculars, handcuffs, and a collection of strange-looking electronic equipment, tape recorders, bugs, and bug detectors.

The nucleus of his staff was Ernest Hampton, a heavyset, short man who wore thick glasses and was a superb investigator as well as an electronics expert; Thomas O'Brien, three years out of law school and brilliant enough to have gotten bored immediately with corporate law; Gina Cataldo, a streetwise undercover expert who possessed an engaging personality and good looks; and Dennis Raskin, an ex-FBI agent who had invaluable connections in some very high places.

Lane spotted the list of hospital employees Spellie had left for him. He studied the names carefully then double-checked them. There were nine in all. Six of the men were kitchen help, one was a janitor, and two were orderlies. He rubbed his chin and squinted while shaking his head disapprovingly from side to side. He reached for the phone. It rang several times before the other end answered.

"Hello, Wilmington General Hospital."

"May I speak to Dr. Spellie, please?"

"Just a moment, sir, I'll connect you."

"Hello, Dr. Spellie here."

"Bob, it's me, Lane."

"Hi, Lane, did you get the package I left for you?"

"Yeah. I did, that's why I'm callin'."

"You haven't found anything already, have you?"

"Yeah, I found out you better stick to bein' a shrink, because you make a terrible detective."

"What do you mean?"

"You didn't give me a complete list." Lane opened a fresh pack of cigarettes and lit one.

"No, you're mistaken. Everyone who was working here that night is on that list."

"I don't think so, Bob—unless you're runnin' that place without a doctor in the house."

"Lane, you can't think it's a doctor?"

"Look, unless it's a doctor that had one of them Danish operations, I want his name."

Spellie protested reluctantly. "Lane, is this really necessary?"

"Bob, if you really want a complete investigation on this, don't tie my hands."

"You know I do, Lane. The doctor's name is Milton Schneiderman."

"Gimme whatever you can on 'im." Lane put his cigarette in the ashtray, picked up a sharp pencil, and started to write.

"Schneiderman has been with us for about six months. He's single and transferred here from a hospital in the Midwest. He seems to be a dedicated doctor."

"And there's no one else," probed Lane.

"I was going to call you. I just learned that an X-ray technician worked that night."

"What's he doin' there at night?"

"He only helps out when we get overloaded. He's a med student at Harvard, Brian Summers. I'll find out what I can on him."

"You got anyone else hidden away you haven't told me about?"

"No," assured Spellie. "You've got everyone now."

"Okay. Bob, I'm gonna need the personnel files on all of these people."

"Sure, Lane, I'll photostat them and have them to you by morning."

"Thanks, pal, I'll be in touch."

"Lane . . . wait, don't hang up."

"What is it, Bob?"

"It's Schneiderman. One of the nurses told me she was looking for him between two A.M. and three-thirty on the night Mrs. George said she was raped. The nurse wanted to go over the sedation charts with him. He didn't show up at the front desk until close to four in the morning."

"Where did he say he was?"

"He told the nurse he had dozed off. He said he was tired, just having completed working forty-eight straight hours."

"Well, Bob, did he work forty-eight straight hours?"

"Yes, he did, Lane, but I just thought you ought to know."

"Don't concern yourself with your Dr. Schneiderman. It's probably like the man said, he was tired. I'll call you later this week."

"All right, Lane."

Lane found Dr. Milton Schneiderman a very interesting prospect. A knock at the door interrupted his thoughts. It was close to five and he assumed his secretary had come to advise that she would lock up before leaving.

"Come in."

The door opened. It was Gina. She had been with him nearly six years, and in the last two their relationship had developed into something more than just an employee/employer one. A tiny, gorgeous female, she greeted him with a warm smile, staring at him brazenly with her coal-black eyes as she walked into his office.

"Hi, boss," she said huskily.

Lane could never resist her obvious charms. He returned her smile. "Hi, baby, want a drink?" he said teasingly.

"Yes, I could use one. That lab you have me working in has got me exhausted. That chemist we're trying to trap is a very rambunctious guy. Between stealin' little company secrets, all he wants to do is play grab-ass."

Lane smiled, "Did he catch you?"

"Yes"—she scowled—"and I don't think he'll want to catch me again."

This time when the knock came at the door, it was Linda advising Lane she would lock up before she went home. Lane bade her departing figure good night. He poured Gina and himself each a drink and reached into a mini-refrigerator in the corner of the office for ice cubes to drop into the liquid pick-me-ups.

Lane spent the next hour going over the Christian George case with Gina. They'd had several more drinks when he declared,

"I'll be right back. I wanna get rid of some of this booze I've been guzzlin'."

He walked through his darkened outer office to the area immediately outside the big double wooden doors. He soon returned and let himself back in with his key. As he entered the doorway to his office, he noticed that the lighting was dimmed. He stood just inside his office door. The overhead lights were out. A small lamp on the desk was the only light in the room. The couch—a sleeper—had been pulled out. Gina was standing by it. She was completely naked.

Afterward they lay in each other's arms, neither saying a word. Lane reached to the corner of the desk where his cigarettes were. Still not speaking, he lit one for both of them.

Her head on his chest, she breathed his name. "Lane."

"What?"

"Do you go . . . do you go out with other women?"

"Yeah."

"Do you love me?"

"I like to be near you. I like you around. If that's love, then I love ya."

"And you still go out with other women?"

"Sometimes."

"Lane, why did you have to tell me?"

" 'Cause you asked me."

"Lane."

"What?"

"You're a prick!"

He smiled warmly at her. "Well . . . nobody's perfect."

chapter 5

It was eleven-fifty P.M. on a dead-end street in Dedham. Only four houses graced a darkened road. A man, hidden by the shadows of the trees, was seated in his car. Pausing only to wipe the nervous sweat from his face, he stared at the green split-level home across from him.

Inside most of the house lay in blackness. It was quiet. A dim ray of light spilled into the hallway from Christian George's room. Knowing her mother and son were both alseep, Christian stood before her window at the rear of the house, gazing out at the starlit sky. In the solitude of her empty room and at peace with the cover of darkness, she closed her eyes and thought of her husband. She reminisced of the happiness that had been theirs when Ben was alive, but resigned herself to the knowledge that he was no longer of this world.

Her steps were silent as her shoeless feet moved across the carpeted floor to Teddy's room to watch him sleep. In his small hand he still held a toy soldier he had been playing with. The wallpaper was covered with cartoon characters. She glanced at the chest full of toys in the corner and at the clown face on the lamp upon his bureau. He was sleeping with his friends. She marveled, thinking of his wit and sensitivity. He was dwarfed by the huge double bed. She moved to his side. Looking down at him, she was filled with love. She leaned over and, ever so softly, kissed him on the forehead.

Outside in the car, the man, now wheezing hoarsely, muttered to himself. "You know you're mine. Why did you go away?

You're mine, damn you . . . mine." He started his car and, looking back threateningly at the house, drove away.

Dennis Raskin, a slender man in his late fifties and sporting a crew cut, sat in Lane Garrett's office across from his boss. Raskin, the former FBI agent, was dedicated to Lane and, accordingly, used his resourcefulness to the utmost. He was a master at his craft and dispatched most of his assignments quickly and quietly. His manner was unpretentious and efficient.

Lane had given him the list of the eleven male employees who worked the night of Christian George's rape. Raskin wasted little time in securing a preliminary report on each of the suspects. With cigarette in hand and fresh coffee raised to his lips, Lane thumbed through the reports. He peered across his desk at Raskin, took a long pull on the cigarette, and spoke as he exhaled.

"Dennis, what's it look like to you?"

"If she was raped, and let's assume she was, Lane, it could be any one of them. If we want to keep this quiet, we can't ask too many questions, but I think we can figure that whoever did it has done something like this before. And he got away with it. Lane, this one is going to take a lot of spade work. First, we have to find out what makes each one of these men tick, then I believe we'll know who, if anyone, did it."

Lane spoke, almost angrily, projecting his disturbed frame of mind. "We gotta take some shortcuts on this one." He tossed his pencil onto the desk. "Everythin' goes on this one, taps, surveillance, undercover—the works. I want this cleared up, one way or the other . . . and fast."

Lane felt Raskin's steady, unsettling stare.

"I know, I'd like to dump this case right now," Lane flared. "Turn it over to the law before we even get started. Christ, it's not like I don't have enough static from the D.A.'s office already. I have to take on a goddamn case that could really get us in trouble."

Lane stood by the window as if watching the traffic below. Raskin waited. Finally Lane walked calmly back to his desk and sat down as if nothing had happened.

Raskin smiled. "Lane, if you're finished, why don't we get down to business and put this case to bed?"

"You're right, Dennis. I took it on and we both know I won't let go until it's cleaned up. Some of your friends owe us—call in other markers that are comin' to us from around the city. Let's nail this guy."

"Nail what guy?"

"The guy that raped Christian George, that's the guy!"

"Lane, maybe I missed it, but I don't recall us showing that the woman was actually raped."

Lane snubbed his cigarette out in the large glass ashtray. "Dennis, the lady was raped."

"Enlighten me, Lane. How do you know?"

"Dennis, I been in this business twenty years . . . and my gut tells me the lady is levelin'."

It was two-thirty P.M. Young Teddy George was in school and due home in forty-five minutes. Christian's mother was busy in the kitchen preparing the evening meal. Christian was seated at a picnic table in her backyard, reading the *Herald.* The phone rang and Mrs. Day answered it.

"Hello."

"Hello, is Christian there?"

"Yes, just a moment, I'll get her."

As Christian came in from the backyard she asked, "Who is it, Mom?"

"I don't know dear; they didn't say."

"Hello."

"Is this Christian?" The man's agitated voice seemed muffled.

"Yes . . . yes, it is."

"Why did you leave me?"

She answered cautiously, "Who—who is this?"

"You bitch, you know who this is," he hissed.

Christian answered, her voice trembling, "Please . . . I think you have the wrong number. Who do you want?"

His voice burst forth with hate. "Every blond hair on your head . . . every inch of your body . . . is mine. You slut, you whore . . . you're mine."

Her whole body shook, her voice rose cracking, stammering, "Please . . . oh, God . . . please don't do this."

Mrs. Day, witnessing the conversation and watching her daughter's anguish and distress, snatched the receiver from her hand, as she angrily barked into the phone, "Who is this, damn you, who is it?"

The man rasped and raved on. "You interfering old bitch . . . put her back on the phone . . . she's mine," he screeched.

Mrs. Day, though bristling at the sound of this lunatic's voice, tried to patronize him. "Please settle down. You have the wrong number. Tell me who you are trying to reach."

Calmly, icily, he answered. "Don't you get in my way . . . don't call the police . . . I know where the kid goes to school. You remember this. She's mine. She was mine in the hospital . . . but next time she's going to be awake. She's going to love every minute. You tell her . . . you hear!"

The man slammed down the phone. Mrs. Day stood there with the phone still at her ear, dazed. The sound of the dial tone seemed to bring her back to her senses as she slowly returned the phone to its cradle. Her mind raced as she recalled Christian's account of being raped. Mrs. Day's drawn face reflected shock and fear as Christian questioned her.

"Mom . . . Mom, what is it? What did he say?"

Almost not believing what she had heard, she repeated slowly, "He said . . . you were his. Teddy . . . he knows where Teddy goes to school. . . ." Her voice trailed off. "He said not to call the police."

"Teddy! I'm going up to the school and get him. Call Lane Garrett and ask him to meet me here."

"Christian, call the police."

"No! Please, Mom . . . just call Lane."

Christian glanced at the clock. Ten to three. She had only ten minutes before the Capen School let out its charges. She burst out the front door and raced down the stairs to the street. Breathless, almost panic-stricken, she arrived in front of the school a few minutes before the final bell rang. Nervously she paced just outside the huge wire-meshed fence that opened into the schoolyard. She saw Teddy and called out to him. "Teddy! Teddy!"

Lunch box swinging at his side, hair ruffled and smiling, he ambled over to her. "Hi, Mom, how come ya came to meet me today?"

Without replying, she leaned over, hugging him and kissing him on the cheek. Not fully realizing her actions, she continued to hold him till Teddy put his hands to her shoulders and pushed away from her. He looked up at her and whispered somewhat indignantly, "Hey, Mom, all the kids are lookin' at us."

She quickly understood his embarrassment, as she nervously glanced around to find several children and a teacher looking at them. Playfully she tapped him on the jaw with her closed fist. "I guess I just got carried away by your good looks, tiger."

As soon as he received Mrs. Day's harried phone call, Lane Garrett raced from his office to the George home. He was waiting for Christian as she and Teddy came in the front door. Rising from his seat in the living room, he smiled at her. "Hello, Christian."

Teddy looked from Lane to his mother.

"Hello, Lane. I want you to meet my son, Teddy. Teddy, this is an old friend of your daddy's . . . Mr. Garrett."

Lane held out his hand to shake that of the young man.

"Did you used to work with my dad?"

"Well . . . sort of."

Mrs. Day took Teddy by the hand. "C'mon, Teddy, let's get you out of your school clothes."

Christian looked at Lane, not quite knowing how to broach the subject.

Intuitively he guided her. "Is there someplace we can talk?"

Rubbing her palms nervously together, she replied, "We could go out into the backyard."

"Fine, that would be fine."

"Would you like something to drink?" she asked distractedly.

"Whatever you're havin' is all right with me."

"I'm just going to have a soft drink."

He smiled. "That's plenty strong enough for this time of day."

They made their way out to the yard and seated themselves across from each other at the picnic table. Christian related to Lane what had transpired on the telephone, and as she repeated the ugly words and realized their meaning, a sudden apprehension seized her. Whoever this madman was, he now loomed as a threat to Teddy. Her voice cracked, but it didn't lessen her conviction. "The police, Lane, I want the police brought in on this matter!"

"Christian, believe me, I can handle this. Please try not to worry."

She rose from the picnic table, wringing her hands together.

Her face was ashen and her eyes shone with a fierce intensity as she rapidly spoke. "You know, Lane, everyone tells me not to worry. You, Dr. Spellie, Father Travers—everyone. This man raped me in a hospital filled with people. He knows where we live . . . and now he threatens me with the knowledge he is watching my son. Don't worry! You all say don't worry! Well, I am worried! I want the police brought in and I want them here today!"

Lane slowly lit up a cigarette, stood up, and extended the pack to Christian. She practically snatched the package from his hand.

"Will you sit down for a minute?" he asked quietly as he lit her cigarette.

"Lane, my mind is made up; I want the police called."

"Christian, believe me, I'll play it any way you want to. Please sit down; I just want to go over this with you."

They both sat at the table as Lane continued. "I gotta let you know what's in store for you if you go this route."

Irritated, she responded, "Lane, from here on in, I'm looking out for Teddy and me. The hell with that hospital and the embarrassment this will cause them."

Lane leaned across the table and, looking directly into her eyes, his voice just above a whisper, spoke. "Christian, do you really think the hospital is my main concern? Do you?"

"Well . . . maybe you didn't deserve that. I just feel with the police helping, we have a better chance of catching this man."

Lane took a long pull on his cigarette. "Whether the police enter this case or not, I'm in it until we nail this bum. So, before you take a step that you can't take back, will you hear me out?"

Having vented her anger and frustration, she was regaining her composure. "Yes . . . yes, Lane, I'll listen."

"Christian, I've seen a hundred rape cases go down. They get messy—ugly. That courtroom scene leaves a lot of scars, the kind that are inside, that never heal. The guy that commits the rape is made out to be some poor soul that was led on by an evil lady. His defense attorney will ask some pretty raw questions. It will be in the newspapers. He'll try to make you out a whore." Christian flinched. "Your son will hear it in the schoolyard. Your friends, neighbors, the guy at the corner store, all of a sudden they look at you kinda funny. I don't want *you* to hafta go through that number. Honest to God, I don't want to see you hurt anymore. You gotta give me a shot at doin' it my way—it's the best way for you and Teddy."

"Please, Lane, don't say any more." Christian thought for a moment. There was a note of desperation in her voice as she spoke. "Lane, can you do it? Can you catch him?"

"You believe me. I'll land on this guy so hard he'll never know what hit 'im."

"What about Teddy? How are you going to keep this man away from him?"

"First of all, I don't want you to be alarmed or frightened. I'll have constant surveillance on your activities until we clear up this matter. Meanwhile, you can be a great deal of help to me."

"How, Lane . . . how can I help?"

"I'm positive you've got somethin' trapped deep down in your mind that, if you let go, could help us identify this man. If you feel up to it, I'd like to give you some sodium pentothal and ask some questions."

"Sodium pentothal . . . is that like truth serum?"

"That's what many people call it. Christian . . . if you don't feel comfortable with the idea, I want you to know we'll find this man with or without it."

"I'll—I'll try anything. Where do you want me to go?"

"Leave the details to me. When I have it arranged, I'll contact you."

"That man . . . he said he knew where Teddy went to school," she blurted, to remind him of her main concern.

Lane took a sip of the cold drink and looked her straight in the eye. "Christian, I want you to listen to me. Carry on your normal activities and leave the rest to me. I'll have someone watchin' over you night and day. You gotta believe me when I tell you no one is gonna harm you or your family. If this bum calls again, try to be calm. Remember everythin' he says. Listen for noises in the background. Anythin' that comes over that phone can be important to us. Patronize him, try to draw him out in the open. If he's willin', set up a meeting with him. I'll take it from there. I've been in this business twenty years. I've never let a client down—and I'm not startin' with you."

He reached across the table and, placing his hand on top of hers, continued. "I'm not about to have this bum make me look bad. You can put this in the bank—I'm gonna nail that guy. Are you gonna be okay now?"

Her voice was low but assured. "Yes, I'm fine."

"Can I get out that way?" he asked, pointing toward the back gate.

She felt better, safer than she had in days, and couldn't resist teasing Lane. "You're a fine detective, you can't even find your way out of my backyard."

For a brief moment, all of Christian George's problems were left behind as they both laughed.

chapter 6

Lane Garrett had called a meeting of only his most trusted operatives: Ernest Hampton, Gina Cataldo, Dennis Raskin, and Thomas O'Brien. They joined Lane in the conference room, seated around an oval rosewood conference table. With closed door and instructions to Linda that they were not to be disturbed, they proceeded with the business of the morning. They carefully went over each and every case that would be handled by Garrett International. The final case they discussed was that of Christian George. Lane directed his first question to Dennis Raskin.

"Dennis, have you got a rundown on the eleven people in question?"

"Lane, I think we can safely cut the list of suspects to five. We can almost discount the six men in the kitchen. Two of them are over sixty. One just returned to work from a hernia operation, the dishwasher has one leg, and the final two—they have been living together for over fifteen years—both gay. That leaves us the X-ray technician, the doctor, a janitor, and two orderlies."

Lane lifted his coffee cup. "How about background, Dennis? Any of 'em got any prior arrests? Suspected of anythin'? Hate their mother or father?"

After each question, Raskin shook his head negatively.

Lane continued. "Cheat on their wives? Been in a mental institution?"

Dennis's response remained the same, negative.

Frustrated, Lane continued. "Speeding tickets? Pick their nose? For Christ sakes, Dennis, there must be somethin'!"

Dennis spoke almost apologetically. "I went the full route on this one—local, state, federal. If any of those five men have anything we should know about, it's not on record."

Lane looked around the conference table. "All right, let's kick it around."

Gina was the first to respond. "Personnel files. Family background, habits, associations, environment, full circle. How about if I cover those areas—and break out the information as it comes in?"

Lane slurped his coffee. "You got it, do it."

Ernest Hampton sat there taking in every word. He was considered by most a genius in the electronics field. The same people said that he had taps on half the phones in Boston. Ernest enjoyed his work. He especially liked the tough jobs because he worked for the challenge first, the money second. He looked at Lane and spoke matter-of-factly.

"I can take care of their phones, their houses or apartments, cars—whatever you want."

"I don't think you have to bug the houses or the cars, Ernie, not yet," stated Lane. "Why don't we just start off with their phones? That should get us rollin'."

"Okay, just the phones. Do you want pictures?"

"Yeah, yeah, Ernie, but you don't hafta go overboard . . . a small layout on each one. You know, the regular stuff."

Ernest nodded in agreement.

Dennis had a frown on his face. Lane noticed the very distinct look of disapproval. "What is botherin' you, Dennis?"

"You have a license on your wall to protect. If Ernest is ever caught dropping a line on someone's phone, you can kiss that good-bye. I just don't think we have to go that far on this one."

"He knows where she lives, Dennis, where her son goes to school. He's called her there—at home. The man's a real sickie; we need him fast. Believe me, we need those phone taps." Lane smiled at Raskin. "You worry too much."

Dennis Raskin nodded in resignation.

Thomas O'Brien, counsel for Garrett International, reveled in the confidence bestowed on him. A tall dark-haired, blue-eyed man in his twenties, O'Brien dove into his work with unhesitating dedication.

"Tom, get me the info on their financial holdings. Research the title on any property they got and stand by, in case Ernie takes a pinch on this one."

By the end of the day, Ernest Hampton had successfully tapped the phones of four of the five suspects. None of the four had been a problem. He looked at the last of the five residences whose phone he would tap. This one would be the toughest.

Briefcase in hand, he entered the sprawling six-story building that stood before him. Where once it had been the home of high-tone society, it now was a lower-class tenement. Locating the stairwell, he descended the concrete steps. He quickly glanced around the basement for the door leading to the electric and telephone circuits, fairly confident the door wouldn't be locked. Score one for him—the lock had disappeared long ago, leaving only a gaping hole in the door. Ernest pushed it open with his foot and hurriedly slumped down to avoid hitting his head on the low-slung steam pipes overhead. He whisked a flashlight from his back pocket. The beam of light slid along the wall, past rows and rows of electric meters. It stopped on a huge gray metal box fastened to the fieldstone wall. Ernest opened it. Before him was an incredible mass of telephone wires attached to hundreds of small screw-type poles. He searched for an apartment number beside each set of poles. *Damn,* no numbers. The telephone company had its own code for locations in the building.

He clipped onto the first set of wires before him. Using his test phone, he listened. There—a dial tone. He dialed the apartment of Carlos Garcia, the janitor at Wilmington General Hospital. The phone rang twelve or fifteen times before Ernest disconnected his clips.

Ernest took the creaking elevator to the sixth floor. The place had a musty smell and some of the paint had begun to peel from the wall. He came to the door he had been looking for, 642. He knocked loudly several times. No answer. He glanced up and down the dingy hall and took a strip of thin plastic from his pocket. He placed it between the doorjamb and the door. Skillfully, he worked it until it was against the beveled spring lock. He forced the plastic strip against the lock and the door jarred open. He went quickly inside and closed the door behind him.

"Hello . . . hello," he called. No one. He turned on the light next to the door. The telephone was on the table next to a tattered chair.

There were two ways he could tap a phone from the inside. The first was by attaching an "inline" to the wiring. An inline, an inch-long plastic device, is equipped to send out automatically any conversations taking place at the line of interception. Its frequency was matched to that of another that is hooked up to a tape recorder. Or he could use the second method, called a "drop-in." A drop-in merely replaces the speaking part in the mouthpiece of the telephone.

Ernest Hampton opted for speed—a drop-in. He quickly unscrewed the mouthpiece, removed the small perforated disc, and then replaced it with an almost identical twin. Next he quickly checked the rest of the apartment for extension phones. The bedroom was the last place he looked. When he switched on the lights what he saw made him shudder. The walls were covered with mutilated pictures of nude women. Some photos had eyes ripped out. All of them had some body parts missing. There was an ice pick in the bust of one, a knife in another. Wounds and missing limbs and the walls were smeared with red paint.

He shut off the lights and opened the apartment door a crack. No one coming.

Gina had been assigned a man to tail, an orderly by the name of Don Spencer. She followed him to a local club where she positioned herself at the bar across from him and boldly eyed him. It didn't take long for him to receive the signal. Spencer looked at dark-haired Gina and concluded that this was definitely a young woman on the make. He walked around the bar and, coming up behind her, tried his John Wayne approach.

"Hi ya, little fella . . . the name's Don Spencer," he drawled.

Gina turned to him with a full smile. "Hi ya . . . me Jane." She laughed. "Gina Cataldo."

"Gina . . . Gina, that's a nice name. Mind if I join you?"

"Please, please do."

He sat on the stool beside her. "What do you do, Gina?"

"Insurance. I work for an insurance company. How about yourself?"

"I'm a stockbroker."

As she listened to him discussing various stocks, she found herself becoming attracted to him. Oh, he was lying about what he did for a living, but what the hell? That didn't matter. She had expected it. The main thing was that she'd already gotten to first base. He was perhaps in his mid-twenties, sandy hair and inviting hazel eyes. A pretty good-looking dude, she thought.

They talked aimlessly and were on their fourth drink as he asked, "Dance?"

"Love to."

The music was slow as they got to the dance floor. He was taller than she had realized. He pulled her tightly to him and kissed her softly on the ear. The music stopped. He held her close, looking down at her as she eased her way out of his arms. She returned to the bar feeling a bit light-headed as he sat down beside her.

"Feel like another?" he asked.

She smiled a lazy, warm smile, her teeth gleaming in the dim light. Her tongue flicked her lips as she spoke. "Don, I've had it. My roommate is at her parents' home and I have to pick her up."

He lifted her hand and gently kissed it, saying "It was fun; let's do it again."

"I'd like that," she murmured encouragingly.

Don Spencer made a note of Gina's telephone number and walked her out to her car. He opened the door for her and she slid in, rolling down the window. He had a look of mischief about him as he leaned through and kissed her lightly on the lips. As they parted, he had a slight smile on his face that piqued her curiosity.

"A penny for your thoughts," she prodded.

"Sold." He grinned. "Do you really have a roommate?"

"Doesn't everyone?" She smiled.

chapter 7

Lane Garrett had just pulled his Lincoln to the curb outside Christian George's home. They had an appointment with Dr. Henders, a personal friend of Lane's. Henders had agreed to administer the sodium pentothal to Christian at Lane's office rather than his own.

Christian was inside watching out the window as Lane drove up. "Mom, I'm leaving. See you a little later." As Lane and Christian headed north from Dedham, toward Lane's office, Lane tried to keep her mind occupied. To distract her, Lane told her about the case of a woman who claimed her vacuum cleaner was following her. She laughed so infectiously that he could not help but laugh with her. The more she laughed the more he embellished the story. By the time they pulled into the parking garage on Washington Street, Lane's face was red from laughing, tears trickling from the corners of his eyes. He parked his car, then took a handkerchief from his pocket to wipe his eyes.

Struggling to control himself, he said, "I haven't had a laugh like that in God knows how long."

"Neither have I." She sighed.

Lane looked at her warmly. "You should do it more often . . . it becomes you."

There was a moment of silence. She broke it lightly. "Maybe I can retain you to make me laugh," she quipped as a smile crossed her face.

"Our laughin' rates are very reasonable." He winked at her. "C'mon, let's go see what the good Dr. Henders has in store for us."

As per Lane's instructions, Linda had ushered Dr. Henders

into Lane's private office. He was seated in a soft upholstered chair, reading a magazine, as Christian and Lane entered the room.

"Lane, nice to see you."

"I'm glad you could make it, Frank. I hope we're not inconveniencing you in any way."

"No, not at all. I'm glad I can help."

Lane introduced Christian to Henders.

"Why don't we take a seat," suggested Lane as he sat on the couch with Christian beside him.

Henders swung one of the large blue chairs around to face them. "Mrs. George, I might just explain, briefly, what we're going to do here today. Have you ever had sodium pentothal before?"

"No, no, I haven't, Doctor."

"Well, Mrs. George, it's used frequently as an anesthetic. The amount that you will receive today will keep you on the brink of consciousness. You will have no aftereffects, nor will you remember anything. The drug is sometimes used to bring to the conscious that which is locked in the subconscious."

"Will I talk about *anything* while I'm under the influence of the drug?" worried Christian.

"May I interrupt a moment, Frank?"

"Certainly, Lane, go right ahead."

Lane talked to Christian as if the doctor were not present. "Christian, I'm gonna be askin' the questions. I won't ask you anythin' that would embarrass you, nothin' about your private life. As a matter of fact, the only questions I will ask are Why didn't you call out that night? and Do you remember anythin' about the man? That's it. That's all I'll ask, okay?"

"Yes, Lane."

He stood up smiling. "Why don't you just lie down, get comfortable, and we'll get this over with and have some lunch."

As she lay back, Lane placed a throw pillow under her head. Henders opened his medical bag, swabbed her arm with alcohol, and removed a plastic cap from the needle he held in his hand. He leaned over, pushing the sharp point into her arm. She flinched. The doctor removed the clamp attached to a plastic tube leading to the bottle he held above her.

"You okay?" asked Lane.

"Yes, yes, I'm fine."

On one knee beside her, Lane took one of her hands and held it. He teased a smile from her as he spoke gently. "Did I ever tell you the one about the lady whose vacuum cleaner was followin' her?"

She smiled faintly. "It—it sounds . . . very . . . familiar."

Lane looked questioningly at Henders.

"You can proceed any time you like, Lane."

Lane stretched to the corner of the desk and turned on the tape recorder. He started to pull his hand from hers, only to find she was holding it tightly. He left it in her grasp.

"Christian, it's Lane. Can you hear me?"

Her voice was distant. "Yes, yes, I can hear you."

"You're in my office. You know no one can hurt you, don't you?"

"Yes. Yes, I know."

"Christian, can you picture your room at the hospital?"

"Yes, I can see it."

"Did you see the man come into the room the night you were raped?"

"No . . . didn't see him."

"Were you sleeping?"

"Yes."

"Christian, what woke you up?"

"Cold . . . no covers . . . he was on top . . . of me."

"Can you remember anythin' about him?"

"His noises . . . he made noises . . ."

"What kind of noises did he make?"

"Horrible . . . horrible noises."

"Can you describe what kind of noises he made?"

"I—I can't."

She was visibly upset, but he soothed her before continuing.

"Christian, why didn't you call out?"

"He—he put smelly cloth . . . over my mouth . . . I tried to . . . push him away . . . my head . . . my head dizzy . . . fell asleep."

"Do you remember anythin' about the man, Christian?"

"Yes . . . cold hands . . . strong . . . so strong."

"Can you remember anythin' else, anythin'?"

"No—no, can't . . . remember."

Lane looked up at Henders. "That oughta do it, Frank. It's not much . . . but it's somethin' we didn't have before."

Christian's hand relaxed, releasing his as he stood up.

Henders leaned down and slid the needle from Christian's arm as she dozed off.

"How long will she be out, Frank?"

"It'll only be a matter of five or ten minutes. She might feel a bit light-headed for the first twenty, twenty-five minutes." He picked up his black medical bag.

Lane extended his hand to Henders. "Frank, I appreciate your comin'."

"Lane, if I can be of further help, please don't hesitate to call me."

"Let me show you out."

"That's not necessary, I can find my way. It's best if you stay by Mrs. George." Henders left, shutting the door behind him.

Lane turned to Christian and stared at her. The sunlight had filtered through the window and was touching her blond hair as she rested peacefully on the couch. He shook his head slowly from side to side, saying "Christian . . . you're one beautiful lady."

Her hazel eyes opened slowly. She looked at him. "Is it over? Are . . . we finished?"

"Yeah, it's over. But I wanna tell you, I did all the work while you slept."

"Next time . . . you take the needle . . . and I'll ask the questions," she teased. Despite feeling unsteady, she tried to stand and lost her balance. Lane caught her in his arms. Her head rested against his chest. A sudden rush of sensation caught him off guard.

"You shouldn't have tried to stand yet."

"I'm—I'm a little light-headed."

She felt so delicate in his arms that he held her as if she were going to break. He eased her backward and sat her down on the couch. She had made him feel awkward.

"Don't you pass out on me," he scolded. "I gotta bad back; I could never lift ya."

"I promise I won't faint, if you get me a black coffee."

"You drive a hard bargain, lady—but you got it."

Linda brought in their coffee. Lane relaxed and they talked

about nothing important for the better part of an hour—Teddy, her mother, her home, the weather. Finally Lane said, "Christian, I'm starvin'. How about you?"

"I'm so hungry I could eat a bear."

"Well, that's not exactly what I had in mind, but where I'm gonna take you, I don't think you'll be disappointed."

They walked around the corner from Lane's office building to Zito's. Joe Zito, the owner of the small, intimate cafe, quickly spotted Lane in the reservation line and showed him and Christian to a table. As soon as they were seated, he handed them a menu.

"Lane, my friend, what can we get you and the lady today?"

"Joe, I gotta tell ya, you make the best beef stew in the city. Lemme try that and gimme a bottle of Miller Lite. Christian, if you like stew, this is a must."

"All right, Lane, I'll try it."

"Can I get you something to drink?" Joe asked with a smile.

"Hmmm, I think a glass of white wine would be nice."

Christian was rather quiet during lunch and, as they finished their meal, Lane studied her pensively.

"You wanna talk about it?" He smiled.

"What?"

"Whatever's on your mind."

"Are you into mind reading?" she said, smiling.

"No, not mind readin', people readin'. After twenty years it's a look or a gesture, a word . . . it doesn't take much for me to know when somethin's cookin' in someone's mind. So, what's up?"

"Lane, have you found anything yet?"

"Christian, this is one of those numbers that just take time. We just started to gather the pieces of the puzzle. Today you gave me a few more. It's simple. Once we got all the pieces, we put it together, bingo, we got our man."

"You make it sound so simple."

He smiled gently at her. "Most of the time it is, but don't you crack to anyone about that—I'd have to lower my fees."

Christian, with the end of a cigarette, was making circles in the ashtray before her. "Lane . . . well, it's about Dr. Spellie."

Taking a long pull on his cigarette, he asked, "What about him?"

"I don't think he believes me. I . . . well, I had this feeling that he's having you work on this case . . . to prove, well, to prove that I wasn't raped. Am I right?"

Lane reached across the table to light her cigarette. She caught the side of his hand, guiding the flame to its tip. Her touch warmed him.

"Christian, it doesn't matter what anyone at that hospital thinks. It doesn't influence the way I'm conducting the investigation on your case. It's the facts in this case that will give us the answers—not the opinions."

Her eyes met his. Her voice was just above a whisper. "Lane, do you believe me?"

"Christian, I purposely used a doctor not connected with the hospital to administer the pentothal. I wanted it kept strictly between us. The reason I did that is because I did believe you, and after the test I have no doubts. Someone *did* rape you."

It was in the sleep-drugged hours of the morning that Christian George was awakened by her telephone. She groped for it without opening her eyes. Groaning and half asleep, she yawned her hello into the mouthpiece.

"Hello." Silence . . . "Hello . . . hello, is anyone there?" She was just about to hang up the receiver.

"Don't hang up," the muffled voice ordered.

Instantly her body became rigid. My God! It's him! She remembered what Lane had told her about the importance of staying cool and trying to gain his confidence. "Who—who is this?" She tried to hide the trembling in her voice.

"It's me. You know who this is."

She found herself being calm, even a little confident. "I'm afraid I don't know you. You must have the wrong number."

He became enraged. "Don't get cute with me, you whore."

"If you're not going to act civilized, I'm going to hang up."

"Don't you dare . . . don't you dare. You know you belong to me. If you ever hang up on me, I'll—I'll burn your house down . . . with you all in it."

She couldn't compose herself any longer. "What do you want from me? Please leave me alone. I did what you wanted, I haven't called the police."

"You looked beautiful in your black negligee."

Christian's heart pounded as she automatically looked at the sleeve of the black nightgown she was wearing. She tested him. "I don't own a black negligee."

"That's funny, it sure looked black from where I was standing in your backyard tonight."

She remained silent, stunned.

"I want to make love to you again." He coughed with a snorting sound. "Tell me you want me to make love to you."

She was nearly paralyzed with fear. She started to speak but couldn't.

"Talk to me, you bitch. I saw you walk your son to school yesterday. I could have run you both over. Talk to me or next time I will."

Biting her lip, she nearly gagged on her words. "I want you to make . . . love to me."

"That's better. You're all mine. Tell me you're all mine . . . tell me you want me to fuck you again."

She begged, pleaded, "Oh, please . . . don't . . . no, no."

"Say it, say it," he screeched, "or I'll blow up your house right now!"

She was petrified, near hysterics, sobbing. "I'm—I'm all yours . . . I want . . . you to . . . fuck me again. Oh, God . . . God . . ."

His snorting sound grew louder. He talked as though gasping for air. "I'll . . . call you. I'll let you know . . . when." One last gasp, then silence. He hung up.

With every bit of emotion drained from her body, she weakly flopped the phone back on the receiver. She turned on the small lamp by her bedside, groped her way into the bathroom, and opened the mirrored medicine cabinet. She uncapped a bottle and took out two pills, filled a glass with water, and gulped down the tranquilizers.

With her entire body shaking almost beyond control, she rummaged through her dresser drawers looking for something. She found it—Ben's gun. A .38 revolver. She pushed a button on the side of the gun and the cylinder fell sideways, exposing the six empty chambers. She opened the box of bullets next to the gun and loaded it. Her body began to quiet as she returned to bed. She shut out the light and lay there, her hand pressed to her bosom, clutching the gun.

chapter 8

On a rising mound in the center of the dew-soaked lawn stood Lane's two-story gray colonial house, white shutters bordering the windows. Directly behind the house, an endless lush green lawn led to a cement walkway bordering the Olympic-size pool. On the patio, metal tables stood beside beach and lounging chairs. A soft breeze blew through the protection of Lane's heavily treed six acres, causing the water to lap slightly against the sides. A huge barnlike cabana sat back from the pool. Upstairs in the imposing structure was Lane's hideaway, complete with an oversized Jacuzzi, redwood sauna, thick plush carpeting, small cocktail bamboo tables and chairs, indirect lighting, Hawaiian music, and a modest bar tucked in a corner, amid artificial palms.

Inside, the house was magnificently furnished—all the touches of a wife long since dead.

Lane's bedroom was upstairs. It was huge, with furniture to scale. A waterbed, raised on a platform three steps up from the floor, sat squarely in the center of the room, facing a breathtaking view of rambling gardens out the sliding-glass doors. The closed circuit TV built into the wall was hooked up to cameras that were scattered outside the house. The latest alarm that technology could provide assured him of complete privacy when he was there and security when he was not.

The phone was ringing. Lane reached to the table beside his bed and pushed a button on his speaker-phone. He lay there, not lifting his head from the pillow. "Yeah."

"Lane, it's me, Ernest."

"What time is it?"

"Six-thirty."

"Ernie, if you're not in the hospital, like dyin' or in jail, you're in trouble. Six-thirty!"

"Lane, I have to talk to you."

"I wouldn't get up this early if my lawn was growin' thousand-dollar bills. This better be good, pal."

Ernest Hampton's voice had a ring of urgency. "Lane, it's important. I have to see you . . . about the George case."

"All right, gimme an hour. Make it at the office."

When Lane arrived, he met Ernest in the lobby and proceeded to his office. It was just seven-thirty, and they were alone in the quiet office.

"What is it, Ernie? Whatcha got?"

Ernest set the cumbersome-looking case he had been carrying on the rosewood conference table. "Lane, on a hunch I added an extra tap to the list of five that we had. I think we hit bingo."

"Whose phone, Ernie? What other phone did you whack out?"

"Christian George!"

Lane smiled. "Damn it, Ernie, good thinkin'. She shoulda been on the list to begin with."

"I checked the other reels around five-thirty this morning."

"Anythin' on the others?"

"Might be. The X-ray tech's had a few calls but he's never there. His roomie keeps tellin' everyone he thinks Brian went back to his parents in Scarsdale, New York, for the summer."

"Did you check?"

"No word yet. He certainly isn't in Boston. The hospital or med school ain't seen hide nor hair of him since the George rape."

"I'll get a New York agency to check it out right away," Lane stated, pulling out an unopened pack of cigarettes from his desk. "Any other tapes show up anythin'?"

"Nothing significant. The Spanish guy, Carlos Garcia—his was completely blank. After I heard the George woman's tape, I went by his apartment. His car wasn't there. It looks like he didn't go home last night."

"How do you know?"

"It rained about three this morning—a shower. It was just enough to wet the surface of the road. His parking space in the rear of the building didn't have a dry spot on it. It should have been dry under where his car had been parked."

"Ernie, you shoulda been a detective. C'mon, play that tape for me."

"Lane, there's something else about Garcia."

"What?"

"When I tapped his phone, I had to go inside his apartment to do it. His bedroom is wall-to-wall nude pinups. He's mutilated all the pictures, cut off arms, legs, poked holes in their eyes. It's a real horror show."

"Christ almighty. Okay, Ernie, play the tape. Maybe it'll tell us somethin' about our man."

Ernest took the recorder from the case and plugged it in. The tape rolled.

"Hello . . . hello, hello, is anyone there?" It was Christian's voice.

"Don't hang up," commanded a voice.

"Damn it, he's putting somethin' over the phone to completely distort his voice."

"It's gotta be some type of filtering device," Ernest stated.

Lane's hope changed quickly to anger as he heard the caller's threats. He sat on the edge of the table, his hands gripping the wood tightly.

The two men listened even after the tape spun off the empty reel, neither saying a word. Finally Ernest reached over and shut off the recorder as Lane slowly paced up and down the conference room. It frustrated him to think what this man was doing to Christian George. He blamed himself. How could this happen? They had a twenty-four-hour surveillance on her house. How could this bastard be spying on her? He could have gone over the back fence.

"Ernie, this is no good. We gotta stop this guy—and fast!"

"Lane, I think we got lucky with him making that call. The man couldn't have been in two places at once—the hospital and her house."

"I gotta get that tape to Spellie. Ernie, unless I miss my guess, that guy has got some sort of physical problem. Did you hear the way he was gaspin' for air and snortin'?"

Ernie nodded. "Of course the voice is really distorted," he

declared, "but there's always the remote chance Spellie might recognize something about the voice."

"All right, Ernie, let's go over what we got. The guy has her telephone number and he knows where she lives. We know since she left the hospital he's followed her at least once. We know he's been at her home at least once—in her backyard! What the hell is the matter with us? We've been on her every minute of every day since she left that hospital and yet we don't see this guy. Ernie, it's like he's invisible."

"I don't know what the answer is. Maybe he's running around in some sort of outfit or uniform that makes him blend in with the surroundings—a milkman, some sort of deliveryman. Then again, maybe he varies it. He's doing something that's making us look right past him."

Lane was shaking his head. "This guy worries me, Ernie; he's clever and unpredictable. He's also one dangerous and sick son of a bitch. Keep checkin' those taps, Ernie. Check 'em twice a day, and I want you to find that spic, what's his name?"

"Carlos Garcia."

"Well, I want you to find *Mr. Garcia* and when you do, I don't want him to go to the john unless we know about it. When you locate him, call in and I'll send another man to relieve you."

"What about the X-ray tech?"

"Somethin's outta whack with this kid doin' a disappearin' act right after Christian was raped. Who the hell knows? Like I said, I'm havin' New York check him out. If he's not back home, then we'll go full blast on him too. I don't like the idea of him missing since the rape. He could be making Christian an exclusive project."

"How about the tapes? If I'm on Garcia, I won't be able to leave to check them out."

"I'll have Gina or someone else check 'em. Just make sure and gimme your locations before you leave this mornin'."

Lane had given Christian his home number in the event she needed him after office hours. He had an uneasy feeling as he glanced at his watch. Eight-fifteen. He picked up the phone and dialed Christian's number. He listened as it rang once, twice. On the third ring it was picked up.

"Hello."

"Hello, Christian?"

"Lane?"

He thought he heard a sense of relief in her voice as soon as she realized who it was.

"Hey, you sleepyhead, it's after nine. You just gettin' up?"

"No, I've been up for a while. My watch says eight-fifteen."

"Oh, sorry, I wouldn't have called this early. This Mickey Mouse watch of mine is either too slow or too fast."

"That's all right, Lane. I was up anyway."

"You get a good night's sleep?"

She hesitated. "Yes, fine, just fine."

Why doesn't she tell me about the call? he wondered. "I gotta be out your way later this afternoon, and I thought if you'd be home, maybe I could mooch a cuppa coffee."

"It's Teddy's last day of school. He'll be getting out early—noontime. I'll be home any time after that."

"I hope you make a decent cuppa coffee. I'd better warn you—when I get a bad cuppa coffee, I'm the grouchiest man in New England."

"Well, then, I'd better not take any chances; I'll have my mother make it."

"That's the way to play it safe. See you about three, three-thirty."

"I'll be waiting."

Ernest had just returned with coffee and set one in front of Lane on the conference table. Lane stared into the cup, and as he raised it to his lips, his mind raced: Why didn't she tell me about the phone call? Maybe her son or mother was by the phone . . . maybe she couldn't talk. No, damn it! She acted as if nothin' was wrong. Her voice, if I didn't know better, almost sounded cheerful. She's gonna try and cover this up. Why? He set the hot coffee down. "Thanks, Ernie."

"Lane, we'll crack it . . . we always do."

"I know we'll crack it, Ernie . . . but can we do it before the freak pushes the lady over the edge?"

Christian had no intention of sending Teddy to school—last day before vacation or not. She wanted to keep him by her. She was seated at the kitchen table opposite her mother. They were both nursing their cups of coffee, with Mrs. Day also reading the paper.

"Has Teddy been in for breakfast yet?"

"No, he's still playing in his room."

"He seems awfully quiet to me. Teddy!" She anxiously called again. "Teddy, come have breakfast."

Silence! Even the clocks seemed to have stopped. Christian jumped up and screamed her son's name. "Teddy!"

Mrs. Day quickly placed her hand on her daughter's. "Maybe he just fell back to sleep." But she didn't believe that herself. She, too, could feel he was gone.

Christian spun around, intending to race through the house, searching. Just at that moment there was a clicking noise downstairs. Christian and Mrs. Day gasped, holding their breath. It was the front door shutting. Christian edged her way across the living room. Hearing a footstep on the stairs, she instantly stood still. "Who is it? Teddy?" she half whispered.

"I was at the corner store," he said quietly, looking over and up at her.

Mrs. Day was perplexed. "But you don't have any money."

"Don't you know you're not allowed to go off on your own to the store or anywhere else?" Christian didn't mean to scold him.

Teddy glanced at his mother and back at his grandmother as if trying to decide whom to answer first. "I took the money from my piggy bank. I wanted to buy a candy bar. I—I always went to the store by myself before. How come I can't go now?"

Christian looked to her mother and back to Teddy. "Teddy, just for a while . . . Momma doesn't want you to go to the store alone, okay?"

"Sure, Mom." Feeling reassured, Teddy volunteered, "I thought I'd get a candy bar and share it with you. But you can have it all, Momma."

Christian affectionately squeezed his chin with her hand and smiled. "I have an idea: Why don't we share it?"

His eyes glistened and grew wide as a slow grin lit up his face.

Standing, she ruffled his black hair, put her arm around him, squeezed him, and sent him to the kitchen as the doorbell rang.

Christian made her way to the front door and opened it, to be greeted by a smiling Father Travers.

"Good morning, Father, this is a pleasant surprise."

"Good morning, Mrs. George. I was in the neighborhood and thought I'd stop by and say hello to you and Teddy. I hope it's not an inconvenience."

"Not at all, Father," Christian answered, asking him in.

He followed her into the kitchen.

"Father, it's a pleasure to have you in our home. Would you like a cup of coffee?" offered Mrs. Day.

"Thank you . . . tea would be fine if you have it."

"You'll have it in a jiffy, Father. Teddy, say hello to Father Travers."

"I remember you," Teddy blurted.

Christian interrupted Teddy as he was about to ask a question. "Honey, why don't you go play in the other room? Then later maybe your friend Bobby can come over."

"Okay, Mom," he said brightly. "See ya, Father."

Mrs. Day had just served the tea, saying, "Father, we have some fine apple pie, if you'd like some."

"No, no, thank you," he answered, patting his midsection. "Well, now, Mrs. George, how is everything coming along?"

"Each day seems to be a little brighter, Father," she lied, which made her feel uncomfortable to look at the priest across the table.

"Do you get out this way often?" she added, changing the subject.

"Wherever I'm needed and the hospital cases lead me," he replied.

The phone began to ring and Christian picked it up. "Hello," she answered cheerfully.

"Christian . . . it's me." The muffled voice cruelly cut into her. Her stomach knotted. "I saw the priest go into your house. I envy him, Christian. Maybe next time I'll come in myself. You bitch! You rotten whore! You're mine," he screamed, "all mine! I'll be coming for you . . . when I'm ready . . ."

There seemed to be a scuffle on his end of the phone as the dial tone suddenly blared in Christian's ear. The color had drained from her face. She slowly shook her head from side to side, trying to erase his voice—him!

Father Travers and Mrs. Day waited for her to respond. "It was him," she said quietly. "He's close by . . . he saw Father Travers come into the house."

Lane Garrett was seated behind his desk, phone in hand. He had just completed placing a call. "Hello, Bob?"

"Yes."

"Lane here. I need some information."

"I'm with a patient. Can you hold for a minute."

"Sure."

The intercom on Lane's desk began buzzing.

"Yeah, what is it, Linda?"

"Gina and Dennis are waiting for you in the conference room."

"Okay, tell 'em I'll be with 'em in a few minutes."

"Yes, Mr. Garrett."

Lane reached for his cigarettes by the large ceramic ashtray on his desk. He flipped one out of the pack and lit it with a Dunhill lighter Gina had given him. As he looked at the expensive lighter, he glanced at the couch. He smiled as his mind filled with a vision of their lovemaking. The smile suddenly faded as he pictured Christian lying there so peacefully, beautiful, his hand clutched in hers. The telephone was still pressed to his ear as he heard Spellie's voice.

"Hello, Lane. Sorry to keep you waiting. Now, what can I do for you? Ah, you're calling about the copy of the personnel files I promised you, right?"

"No, but now that you mention it, where are they?"

"Sorry, Lane, I've been so swamped, I haven't had a chance to get them yet."

"Bob, I gotta have 'em." Lane sighed. "I also called because I need some other information. It's important I get it right away."

"I'm listening."

"There are four names that I'd like you to check out for me."

"All right, Lane, who are they?"

"Dr. Schneiderman, Carlos Garcia, William Cunningham, and Donald Spencer. I wanna know what days they had off this week. Now, I'm assumin' they're all still on night duty. If that's changed, I'll need that information also. By the way," continued Lane, "you haven't heard from Brian Summers?"

"Who?"

"The X-ray technician."

"No, we haven't," mused Dr. Spellie. "Strange, too, since he didn't inform anyone he was leaving. You don't think he's the one?"

"I'll know better when I hear from New York. Now how about that info I need?"

"Lane, I can get it to you by tomorrow. Anything else?"

"Yeah, there is, Bob. I got a recordin' of the rapist's voice."

"You have what?" Spellie interrupted excitedly.

"I got a recordin' of the rapist's voice," repeated Lane. "I want you to listen to it and see if you can detect what type of disorder this sickie has."

"Lane, this sounds fantastic. Does it mean you know who he is?"

"We're gettin' closer, Bob, but nothin' definite yet. I was hopin' you might be able to identify his voice."

"I'll do the best I can for you, Lane. The problem is, I have a very tight schedule. The earliest I could meet you would be tomorrow night at seven-thirty at, say, Jason's?"

"Thanks, Bob. See you then." He snuffed out his cigarette and hung up.

Lane swooped up his pack of cigarettes along with the lighter and walked into the conference room. Dennis and Gina, sitting at the large table, stopped their conversation and watched him.

"Good mornin'," Lane said, and as they both answered, he noticed the dark circles under Gina's eyes. "You look beat, sweetheart. You musta followed that guy all night. Didn't you ever get to bed?"

Expressionless, she answered. "No, no, it wasn't that bad. I was in bed by ten-thirty, eleven. And alone too," she teased.

"All right, let's have it. Whatcha got?" asked Lane.

"He left his apartment and went to a disco. I followed him there. He seems a little on the quiet side. It took me almost an hour before he made his approach. We had a couple of drinks together, and toward the end of the evening danced a little."

Lane lit up a cigarette. "You can skip the social stuff. What else?"

"He doesn't seem to be your everyday rapist. Not the type. The only thing I can say for sure, he's got quite a line. He told me he was a stockbroker."

Lane took a long pull on his cigarette in contemplation. "He didn't get to you, did he?"

Gina played it down. "He's not exactly Mr. Universe."

"You be careful with this guy," Lane warned. "Rapists don't have it stamped across their forehead. They're all different. They only got one thing in common—they're all sick! And another thing, don't let this guy get you alone. Meet him in public places and stay where there's plenty of people. I don't want you bein' the next victim."

"Whatever you say, Lane, I'll play it safe."

Lane addressed Dennis. "Garcia, Dennis. Did you come up with anythin' on Carlos Garcia?"

"I spent most of the night with him making the rounds in the combat zone. He stuck mostly to the girlie shows, smut houses, and capped it off at an X-rated movie. The place made my skin crawl. I decided to wait for him outside. He never came out the front door. He was gone . . . must of left through the side exit."

"Did he know you were on him, Dennis?"

"I really don't think so, Lane."

"Where did the side door lead?"

"An alley that opened on Washington Street, beside the theater."

"What the hell made him go out there?" queried Lane.

"Lane, I've been around a long time—over twenty years with the bureau, and I've put in a few with you. Sometimes there just isn't any reason."

"Ernie was here this mornin'. He was in Garcia's apartment. Our spic's a real kook. He had nude pictures of women, all mutilated in some way or another. Dennis, did Garcia try to connect with any hookers?"

"That's a point that bothers me, Lane. The man goes to an area that specifically features that type of action. He goes through all the motions, but when he's approached, he shies away."

Lane shifted in his swivel chair. "You know, this case gets more interestin' by the hour. I wanna know more about this Carlos Garcia character. We also got us a young med student who's disappeared off the face of this earth. Just maybe he's left the school and hospital so he can devote his full time to Christian George."

"There's that possibility," commented Dennis, "but there's also the chance he's out on a real tear."

"Where'd you come up with that?" quizzed Lane.

"The only reason he worked at Wilmington General was to be near a Catherine Murphy. The nurse and Summers were a twosome until the night of the George rape."

"What happened then?"

"They had a fight about her seeing other men. I've checked it all out, Lane," confirmed Dennis. "She was two-timing him."

"Oh, fine! This kid could be runnin' around gettin' his revenge on other broads. I want that kid found." Lane glanced at the notes in front of him and continued. "Next is Don Spencer, the young orderly. Dr. Harrison tells us that on the mornin' of the rape, when Christian went into hysterics, Spencer was almost the first one on the scene. Gina here tells us that he's on the quiet side. Okay, maybe he is. Maybe he goes out with other women, feeds 'em a line, and is perfectly normal. And then again, maybe he's got this hangup about playin' 'bad guy' when it strikes his fancy."

Gina listened to Lane, realizing that he could be right. The thought sent a cold chill through her.

"We got the good Dr. Milt Schneiderman," Lane continued, "disappearin' durin' the hours that it is likely the George woman was raped. Nothin' on him . . . yet. And now we come to the main event—the rapist. He could be A, B, C, or D . . . or he could be none of the above. If that's the case, my two dear friends, then I'd hate to think it might be one of the patients. Christ, we have enough headaches without an added ninety-four male patients to check out. And, worst case, suppose this bum walked in unseen from the streets. Then where the hell do we start lookin'?"

chapter 9

Lane's black Lincoln sped along the Massachusetts Turnpike toward Dedham and Christian George. He had been so preoccupied that he almost failed to hear the news that blared forth from his combination quadraphonic stereo-radio. His mind suddenly locked in on the newscaster's voice: "Woman murdered in Boston Common. Police have announced the shocking discovery of the mutilated body of Michelle Carron. Miss Carron, nineteen, had been raped prior to her brutal death. The young woman, police said, was mutilated almost beyond recognition. The body was found floating facedown in the pond in the center of the Common's gardens about two A.M. Police say there are no leads at this time and appeal to the public for assistance."

The conversation he had had with Dennis Raskin crept into Lane's mind as he lit another cigarette. The theater that Carlos Garcia had attended was a scant three blocks from the place where the murdered girl had been found. Damn it, Dennis, why'd you hafta lose him! Lane thought angrily. It was a very concerned Lane Garrett who parked outside Christian George's home.

Christian met him halfway up the red brick pathway. They walked together around the house, through the rear gate and into the backyard. The coffee was in a Thermos on the picnic table, shaded by an overhead umbrella.

Lane took a sip of the coffee. "Hey"—he smiled—"this is great. Who made it?"

"My mother," she said, amused.

"So you decided to play it safe, after all."

"The way my luck has been going lately, I thought that was the best thing to do."

Lane subtly broached the subject that was on his mind. "This muggy weather kills me. I thought I'd never get to sleep last night. How about you, sleep good?"

"It doesn't bother me . . . I slept like a log. Lane . . . have you found out anything yet?"

Damn it! She won't tell me. I lost her. Why? Lane wondered. I gotta get her to come around. If she's lost confidence in me, we're up the creek.

"Yeah, we're makin' real progress," Lane answered. "We had a meetin' this mornin'. There's a couple of items I think we should touch on. First of all, he's already called once . . . and he'll probably call again. If the man has your telephone number, it's likely he has your address. The possibilities are very remote he would ever try to enter the house. Most likely, he'd try to see what's goin' on through a window, an open door, you know, like that. I've had a man keepin' an eye on things since the first day you came home. I think after reviewin' this . . . it was a mistake."

"What do you mean, Lane, that you shouldn't have anyone watching the house?"

"Christian, take a look around here," he said, motioning. "There are three houses that face this backyard of yours and one on each side of the backyard—plus the back gate. That's five different places of entry this man could come through. That's not even considerin' the front of the house. I've had one man watchin' . . . what I'm sayin' is, I'm gonna do better. For all we know, the creep might've been here already, but if he hasn't, he'll never get another chance." C'mon, Christian, open up. I told you I blew it. You gotta give me another shot, thought Lane.

She looked at him, taking stock of what he said. "Would you like more coffee?"

"Yeah . . . please."

She poured the coffee and put the Thermos down thoughtfully. "Lane, he was here. He called me last night and again this morning while Father Travers was here."

He breathed a sigh of relief. "Why didn't you call me? It's important! Why didn't you call . . . or tell me when I first got here today?"

"I'm not afraid anymore, Lane. I'm ready to stand on my own two feet. He made me say things last night . . . I didn't want to talk to you about them."

"Christian, listen to me," he said gently. "Whatever he made you say, they're only words. He probably intimidated you again by threatenin' your son . . . mother . . . you. I'm not gonna ask you what he made you say. Did you hear any sounds, noises . . . anythin' that could help?"

"He—he made that grunting . . . snorting sound. It sounded as though he had a hard time breathing, so I couldn't hear anything in the background."

Lane digressed. "As far as you standin' on your own two feet . . . great! But lemme tell you somethin'. If I thought you could help me in some way, I'd ask. Christian, no one in this crazy world is strong enough to never need someone. My helpin' you has nothin' to do with your standin' on your own two feet." He touched her hand. "You follow me?"

Her head was bowed, staring at the worn pine top of the picnic table. She raised her eyes to him. "I understand."

He patted her hand and smiled. "Listen, I gotta make a livin'; I'll hafta leave. I'll give you a call tomorrow, okay?"

"Lane," she said, troubled.

"What is it?"

"Last night on the phone . . . toward the end, his voice . . . I know it. I know that voice from somewhere."

"Christian, maybe it was from that night."

"No," she stated emphatically. "It wasn't from that night. I know that voice from another time." She paused, then added with conviction, "It was *not* from the night I was raped."

"Could it be someone that you know? A past acquaintance of yours or your husband's?"

"I don't know, Lane, I only know I've heard that voice before."

He stood up. "Christian, we're gonna put this together, and we're gonna nail that guy."

Her eyes held a twinkle as she spoke. "Do you think you can find your way out . . . this time?"

Dennis Raskin had busied himself with background checks on the neighbors that were in the immediate vicinity of the George residence. He labored over the information before him. Mr. and Mrs. Arthur Hamill: three children, dog, residents for four years —Mrs. Hamill, housewife; Arthur Hamill, insurance salesman. Raskin wrote "not suitable" on top of the paper.

He looked over several more residents again, marking the same notation at the top of the information sheet. He had nearly finished his survey when a look of satisfaction crossed his face. He studied the sheet carefully. George and Stephanie Dawson—sole occupants of the dwelling. George Dawson, retired; Stephanie Dawson, Red Cross volunteer.

Perfect, thought Raskin.

He proceeded directly to the Dawson home. Upon arriving he noted that the front of the George property could be seen clearly from there. He approached the door and rang the bell.

The door was opened by George Dawson, a balding man in his late sixties. "Yes, what can I do for you?"

"Are you Mr. Dawson?" quizzed Raskin.

"Yes, I am. What are you selling?"

Dennis flashed his identification, saying "Sir, I'm a private investigator. May I speak with you for a moment?"

The elderly man looked confused. "Private investigator? Why, sure . . . sure, come right in."

It was a modest Cape Cod–style home. Dawson led Dennis Raskin into a small but cozy den, where Mrs. Dawson sat reading. "Mother," he addressed his wife, "this man is a private investigator. He wants a word with us."

Stephanie Dawson, still holding her book, her head down, looked over the top of her glasses. "A private investigator—why, for heaven's sake, what would you want with us?"

"May I sit down?" asked Raskin.

As they both chorused "yes," he seated himself in a maple rocker and drew from his pocket a picture of a teenage boy. Showing it to them, he asked, "Have you seen this young man?"

Holding the photograph in her outstretched hand, Mrs. Dawson peered at it through her bifocals. "Looks like a nice young man . . . no, I don't recall seeing him." She handed the photograph to her husband. "You, George?"

"No, I can't rightly say as I have. What's he done?"

"He hasn't done anything, Mr. Dawson, except run away from home." If he told them whom he was really looking for, thought

Dennis, they'd probably throw him out. "His parents think he's somewhere in this neighborhood," he continued.

"I wish we could help you," replied the old woman, "but we haven't seen the youngster."

"Perhaps you could help us." Dennis waited for a response.

"How can we help?" quizzed George Dawson.

"Well, my firm would be willing to pay you three hundred dollars a week if you would permit one of our operatives to stay here. We think we could keep a satisfactory surveillance on the neighborhood from this vantage point. It could help us locate him."

"Three hundred a week!" exclaimed a very impressed Mr. Dawson.

"Yes, sir, three hundred per week."

"What do you think, Mother?"

"Well, if it might help . . . and we could certainly use the money," she replied.

"Glad to oblige," decided Mr. Dawson, holding out his hand to Dennis.

"Mr. and Mrs. Dawson, we'd appreciate it very much if you kept this in the very strictest of confidence."

"We will," they promised.

Dennis made arrangements for their operative to take a bedroom on the upper floor and left.

"What do you think, George?" Mrs. Dawson inquired thoughtfully.

The old man stroked his chin with a wrinkled hand, smiled, and squinted his eyes, saying "I got a hunch about one thing, Mother, they ain't looking for no young boy, and for sure, we got nothin' to hide. But for three hundred a week, they can stay as long as they want."

Ernest Hampton had combed the streets of Boston. He traveled from one end of Washington Street to the other, searching for Carlos Garcia. He didn't bother looking in any but the sleaziest of public gatherings. Finally he went to Garcia's apartment house and took the elevator to the sixth floor. He stood before the apartment door and glanced at the top left-hand corner. The fragment of Scotch tape he had placed at the top of the door had not been broken, so he concluded that Garcia had not been home since he had tapped his phone. Ernest quickly returned to the lobby and outside to a pay phone. He dialed a number.

"Good evening, Wilmington General Hospital."

"Hello," Ernest said, "may I speak to Carlos Garcia?"

"It's after visiting hours, sir."

"Ma'am, he's not a patient, he works there."

"Sir, I'm sorry, but employees are not allowed personal phone calls."

"Please, ma'am, it's very important. It's about his mother." If that snake has one, Ernest muttered to himself.

"Just a moment, please."

Ernest was upset with himself. Here I am turning the city upside down for this guy and he's at work, he thought angrily.

"I'm sorry," returned the shrill, high-pitched voice, "but Mr. Garcia did not report for work tonight."

"Thank you, ma'am."

"You're welcome, sir."

Lane Garrett had met Dr. Spellie at Jason's for dinner. During the leisurely five-course meal, Spellie advised Lane that Carlos Garcia, Dr. Milton Schneiderman, and Don Spencer were all off-duty the night Christian had had a backyard visitor. That was in addition to Brian Summers, who hadn't shown up for days. The only one of the five who no longer remained a suspect because of his working that night was William Cunningham, the other orderly.

As Spellie set his napkin on the table and prepared to leave, Lane placed his hand on his friend's arm and motioned for him to remain.

"One thing before we go. Bob, you know I'm not a patient man. In my line I can't afford to be—I gotta know when I'm gonna see those damn personnel files!"

"Maybe never," Spellie replied soberly. "They're missing."

"What!"

"The files *L* to *U* are missing . . . and, believe me, they weren't misplaced. Sorry, Lane."

"Christ, anythin' to make this case simpler," he swore in sarcasm. "I gotta have that info . . . I'll hafta go a longer route."

"Well, there's one consolation here, I should imagine," offered Spellie. "Somebody went to an awful lot of trouble to hide something important. It must mean you're on the right track."

"Some consolation."

They proceeded somberly to Lane's home. They sat by the pool drinking brandy while Spellie listened to the taped conversation between Christian George and the rapist. Spellie listened to it several times before offering an opinion.

"Lane, that snorting sound is caused by a type of hypertension. When he becomes highly excited, the breathing passage contracts, thereby creating a labored intake of air—the snorting sound. What scares me is his frame of mind."

"How do you size him up, Bob? How dangerous?"

Bob Spellie thought for a moment and frowned. "Lane, this isn't much to go on, but unless I miss my guess the man's a walking time bomb."

"Bob, I gotta find him!"

Dennis Raskin drove down the narrow, dimly lit road to Wilmington General Hospital. He stopped his car just outside the employees' parking lot and stared at the hospital against the outline of rolling hills and darkened skies. Lights burned brightly in the building, like eyes peering out at him. He stepped from his car. The stillness and the barren pathways, together with the rest of the setting, were eerie. Looking around, he walked slowly and quietly into the parking lot. He approached each car, taking note of its plate number. There were nineteen in all: two doctors, interns, nurses, orderlies, kitchen and clean-up help . . . And who else? he wondered.

Lane Garrett wanted to blast the crows out of the trees. He'd had a restless night as it was, without the black beasts' cawing waking him at six. He left his bedroom with his black silk bathrobe draped over his arm and put it on while descending the stairs to the kitchen. He started a pot of coffee and proceeded to drop two eggs into sputtering grease, while thoughts of Christian dominated his mind.

Lane popped two slices of bread into the toaster and filled a mug with steaming coffee. He placed his breakfast on a tray and carried it, barefoot, across the cool wet grass to the side of the pool. He sat there sipping the hot brew and as he began munching on the toast, he spotted a squirrel digging a hole in the lush green turf. "Hey," he shouted, sending the furry animal scampering up a tree. It perched high on a limb, bravely peering at Lane, who returned the leer. "Be careful, my friend, I'm bigger than you are," Lane warned it. The little animal didn't move, except to twitch its bushy gray tail, and continued to stare boldly at this human who dared to threaten it. Lane smiled. "So, you're a tough guy, huh?" He took a piece of his toast and tossed it to the bottom of the tree. His eyes then fixed on the water in the pool as it heaved steadily from its rush through the filter system. The sun had risen overhead, shining brightly on the clear, bluish-green water.

Having finished his meal, he leaned back in the lounge chair with coffee in hand and a fresh cigarette dangling from his mouth. He took a long drag and closed his eyes as the smoke came from his mouth, clouding the clean fresh air. In all his years in the business, a case had never troubled him so. None had ever affected him so very personally. His mind searched desperately for something . . . anything that would make this beautiful woman's world safe again.

He couldn't relax and finally, even though it was seven A.M., Lane picked up the poolside phone to call Bob Spellie at home.

"Hello," Spellie answered.

"Bob, I know it's early and I hate to ask you—but I gotta have someone I can talk to on the inside of the hospital. Someone who was there the night of the rape. There must be someone we can trust—one of the nurses, maybe."

Spellie could hear urgency in Lane's voice and he thought a moment before replying. "Well, there is one person I have confidence in: Virginia Merguson. She's been with us over nine years, the head nurse, nights."

"Can you set it up for me, Bob?"

"No problem, Lane. When do you want to see her?"

"Yesterday," Lane said. "I gotta see the lady as soon as possible."

"I'll give her a call and try to set it up today."

"Thanks, Bob. You know, I should make you my assistant."

"No thanks, Lane. I have enough troubles of my own."

Lane headed for the house. He looked at the base of the tree where he had thrown the toast. It was gone.

Dennis Raskin was in downtown Boston at the John F. Kennedy building located in the area known as Government Center. He was seated in the office of the FBI agent-in-charge, William Fulton. Fulton, a longtime associate and friend, was reminiscing with him about old times when Dennis abruptly interrupted. "Bill, I need a favor."

Fulton, a balding, fair-minded, dedicated agent, wasted little time in answering. "Name it, Dennis. If I can do it—you have it."

"I'll be candid with you, Bill. I'm working on a case for Lane Garrett that's got us stymied. Garrett's taken the case as a personal favor for a friend. It involves a real psychotic. We have reason to believe the man is connected in some way to Wilmington General Hospital."

"How can I help you?" offered Fulton.

"It's not going to be easy, Bill."

"Dennis, if it were easy, you wouldn't be here."

Dennis took two sheets of paper from his inside jacket pocket and pushed them across Bill's desk. "There are nineteen names and addresses on those two sheets of paper. They are owners of cars whose registrations I took at the employee parking lot of Wilmington General. The same cars were parked there three nights in a row. I'm assuming that's the entire night staff and general help. I need a background check on each one of them. You'll notice an asterisk next to a few names. They're the most important."

"That doesn't sound so difficult, Dennis."

Dennis continued, half smiling. "I also need a complete background on their families—sons, daughters, husbands, the works."

"I knew it wouldn't be easy," Fulton lamented. "Dennis, this is going to take a hell of a lot of work . . . how am I going to explain it?"

"We think the man is ready to kill someone, if he hasn't already. We really need help on this one."

William Fulton got up and walked around his desk, looking out the window at the magnificent view of the city. Scattered below were thousands of people that crowded the Quincy Market area. Hustling peddlers hawked their wares, while huge double-tandem trailer trucks unloaded fruit and produce. Hundreds of tourists inched their way through the throng, following the red arrows that led them to Boston's historical sights.

Fulton turned to his friend. "What the hell, I've only got another six months to go on this job. Let's try this in two steps. I'll get you the rundown of the 'Important' ones first, then the rest of the list, and, if that fails to turn up your man, I'll get you family backgrounds. How does that sit with you?"

Dennis, satisfied and ready to leave, walked over to where his friend stood and took his hand, shaking it warmly, sincerely. "Thanks, Bill . . . thanks very much."

Dennis drove his car out from the darkness of the underground garage into the bright sunlight. Leaving Boston, he proceeded to his stake-out across and down the street from the Schneiderman residence.

It was just after dark when Dennis left his car. Careful not to be noticed, he made his way to the rear of Schneiderman's car. As he passed close to it, with pliers in hand, he broke the red reflector that covered the bulb beneath. He continued walking, circling the block.

Nearly two hours later, Schneiderman left his house. As Raskin observed him, he noted his sagging silhouette and sluggish step. Schneiderman started his car and was soon on the expressway south, headed in the direction of the hospital. Dennis followed. Before him hundreds of red tail lights glowed in the darkness, except for Schneiderman's car, whose white light shone like a beacon through a broken reflector cover.

As they pulled into the hospital area, Dennis parked his car so that he could observe the doctor enter the employees' parking lot. As Schneiderman strode across the lot toward the main entrance, he was straight and erect, his walk brisk and light-footed. Dennis watched him skip up the stairs, amazed at the sudden transformation of a man who shortly ago had been dragging his rear to one now bubbling with energy.

There's no mistaking it. He's on something—an upper, thought Dennis.

As Schneiderman disappeared through the double doors, Dennis shook his head and took a log book from his glove compartment. While every detail was fresh in his mind, he made his entries and left.

Lane Garrett had received a call from Robert Spellie advising him that Virginia Merguson was expecting him in the afternoon at her home. Lane wasted no time in getting there. The big Lincoln turned into a potholed dirt street and pulled into the driveway at the end of Nardian Way. The white house was a small cottage-type dwelling set on the lake's edge. It had been winterized for year-round living. As he got out of his car and shut the door, a loud growling came from directly in front of him. The jet-black Doberman pinscher was straining at the chain he was hooked to, fangs showing and the hair on his back raised. Lane walked a wide berth around him toward the front door. He tried to humor the beast. "Nice fella, good boy, easy boy." The dog leaped at him, growling, snarling, as the chain stopped him in midair, bringing the huge animal crashing to the ground. Lane smirked at him. "I suppose this means that we're not gonna be friends." He knocked on the front door and noticed that the house was badly in need of repair.

Mrs. Merguson opened the door. She stood there, the skin sagging under her unflinching, sunken eyes—her coal-black hair pulled severely to the back of her head and tied into a tight bun. The stern mouth had no lipstick on it. A small hairy mole grew on her left cheek. She spoke without emotion.

"You're Mr. Garrett, I presume."

"Yes, ma'am . . . yes, Mrs. Merguson."

"Come in, if you wish."

If I wish! What the hell does she think I'm here for? thought Lane. "Yes, ma'am, thank you."

Lane followed her bony figure into a small room that he presumed to be the living room. He looked around and thought, Holy Christ!

The room was completely crammed with religious articles. A miniature altar, complete with a place to kneel, was in the center of the far end. There were several saints atop pedestals, with candles burning brightly in front of them. An antique stained-glass window, probably rescued from an old church, hung in front of her picture window. Soft choir music drifted across the room from her record player. She detected the look of surprise on Lane Garrett's face.

"When I'm not working, I spend my time with God. Sit down, young man," she ordered, indicating the worn fringed blanket used as a permanent throw cover for the couch.

Lane heard the Ave Maria playing softly in the background as he spoke with her. "Ma'am, did Dr. Spellie explain why I wanted to see you?"

"Yes," she replied, not offering any more than that.

"You were on duty the night Christian George was raped, weren't you?"

"Yes, I was working the night she claimed she was raped."

"Ma'am, believe me, we got every reason to believe she told the truth."

Her narrow lips barely opened as she stated, "If the woman was raped, it was God's will."

"Excuse me, ma'am, but I don't think that God wills it for some maniac to rape a woman."

"Mr. Garrett, nothing happens . . . unless it is the will of God." She emphatically repeated it as if trying to shut out his voice. "If the woman was raped, it was the will of God."

Lane called on all the finesse he could muster, for he thought that if he could placate her a little, maybe, just maybe, she'd soften up. "Ma'am, I must confess to you, I'm not a very religious man, so perhaps I don't fully understand the workings of God."

"You certainly don't." She sneered vindictively.

Lane looked at her and forced a smile as he thought: You old bitch, I'd like to strangle you. Hmmm, maybe that's God's will. "Ma'am, did you receive any phone calls askin' about Mrs. George on the night in question?"

"No." She pursed her lips, glaring at him.

"Do you recall any of the orderlies or anyone disappearin' for any period of time?"

"No."

"Were there any visitors that lingered after visitin' hours?"

"No."

"Did you notice any of the male patients in the corridors?"

"Certainly not!" she retorted, increasingly annoyed.

"Ma'am, what is your opinion of Christian George?"

"I have no opinion. I have my job to do and I do it."

"D'you object to my questions?"

"I object to the insinuations. I have been at that hospital for over nine years without a single blemish on my record, and now you come snooping around implying that a rape took place when *I* was in charge of the floor."

"Ma'am, we're talkin' about a woman bein' raped! Not a blemish on your record."

"Mr. Garrett, I know exactly what's going on."

"Oh?"

"You, sir, are doing the bidding of a woman with a pretty face, the devil's bidding at that. That's what it is. I've heard all about you private detectives," she added snidely.

Lane shuddered to think that this old witch might be the one to take care of him if he were ever in a hospital. "Ma'am, I wanna thank you for your time. You've been a great help." He rattled out the words insincerely as he got to his feet and made for the door. "I'll see myself out."

The phone was ringing in Gina's apartment. She reached for it as it penetrated her sleepy haze. She answered it with a husky "Hello."

"Hi," Don Spencer replied brightly.

Gina paused for a moment. It felt like the middle of the night. "Don . . . what time is it?"

"Wake up, sleepyhead," he said, laughing. "It's seven-thirty and it's a beautiful day."

"Oh, Don . . . not seven-thirty in the morning?"

"I'm just getting off work. I was wondering what you had planned for this morning."

A lazy smile crossed her face, hearing his voice and picturing his face. "You have to be some kind of a sadist, calling a girl at this time of the morning."

Spencer ignored the remark. "I go jogging every morning. I thought you might like to join me."

"Jogging . . . you mean like running? What are you on, spinach and vitamin pills?"

Laughing, he replied, "That and carrot juice. I usually run at Revere Beach. It's beautiful this time of morning. There isn't a soul around . . . it's really great. How about it, want to join me?"

Gina's mind flashed to a phone call she had received late last night from Ernest, letting her know he had followed Spencer to a nightclub where he witnessed an envelope being passed to Spencer. Spencer hadn't gone to work. What was he up to? She decided to find out. She agreed to meet him in front of Kelly's Roast Beef on the beach in an hour.

They had been running for several minutes. Gina had on a pair of tennis shoes, slacks, and an old winter pullover. Don had all the gear and paraphernalia synonymous with the American jogger.

The gentle sea breeze washed their faces with its fresh salty smell. Gina watched the ease with which a lone sea gull coasted in a circle over the sleepy waters. She wished that running along the sparkly sand could be as easy for her. As she eyed it enviously, the sea gull glided down from the peaceful blue sky and dipped its beak into the quiet sea, swooping up again to seek food elsewhere.

"Isn't this fantastic?" Don said in an even tone as they continued jogging.

Gina's breath was labored as she answered. "It's different . . . I'll say that."

Her large breasts bobbed up and down as she ran. Don glanced over to say something to her, lost his concentration, and stopped in mid-sentence.

Gina smiled at him. "You might find it easier to talk if you keep your eyes straight ahead."

Flustered and getting her meaning, he answered, "I . . . well, I just lost my train of thought."

She had a look of mischief in her eyes as she answered. "I have a feeling your train just switched tracks!"

"Does that make me bad?" he taunted.

She reached over and gently poked him in the stomach with her elbow. "Do you want to run . . . or what?"

He smiled softly. "Is this a multiple choice?"

They were running close to the water when Gina gave him a shove. He fell into the shallow water as he heard her laughingly shout, "No."

He scrambled to his feet, chasing her down the beach. Catching and tackling her from behind, they both went sprawling in the sand. He scooped her up and headed for the water, laughing as Gina implored him, "Don . . . Don . . . please, no . . . no."

She screamed as he threw her into a crashing wave. She came

up sputtering and splashing water in his direction. He ran toward her, meeting her in waist-high water. Holding her hands to stop her from splashing, he brought his lips softly down on hers. Her arms automatically went around his neck as he enfolded her, drawing them tightly together. The water swirled about them as their tenderness grew to excitement, but at the last moment she gently eased away from him, saying softly, "You taste salty."

"You too," he replied, gently stroking her cheek.

With her eyes slightly lowered, she murmured, "I think we ought to have some breakfast."

He kissed her lightly on the lips, took her hand, and headed for the car.

chapter 10

The stark single room was furnished with the barest necessities of life. An uncomfortable folding couch doubled as a bed, and across the bare wood floor to the corner of the room buzzed a small refrigerator with a hot plate set on top of it. Canned foods lined the inside of the peeling cupboards. Two dishes with hair-line cracks, a fork with dried egg permanently stuck between the prongs, a dull knife, and a small assortment of kitchen tools were all that was in the broken drawers below the cupboard. The bath-room, a community affair, stood outside the room. It was his clandestine place to be alone.

He walked out of his room toward the bathroom with a small dented coffeepot in hand. He pulled a string, lighting a globeless bulb that exposed an old chipped tub, a dilapidated wash basin, and a stained toilet. He turned on the water in the sink as the pipes clattered from the flow of water pressure, and filled the coffeepot. He passed into the musty hallway and across the faded tile floor, entered his room, and bolted the warped door. With the coffeepot atop the hot coils of his hot plate, he sat on the edge of his hard sofa bed. A lamp, a small radio, and a tape recorder rested on the four-legged splintered table next to him.

He clicked on his tape recorder. "I'm all yours . . . I want you to fuck me again." The words caused his penis to swell. He left the recorder on, caressing his groin as he heard her beg him to fuck her. Time and time again he had recorded just those words until he had filled an entire side of the cassette tape. Ob-sessed, he listened to her repeat the words over and over and over again. His eyes shifted from a faded picture of a woman to that of another beside it—that of Christian George. She was standing before a chain-link fence in front of her son's school. He had been close by the first time he had called. It had taken all his strength not to rush to her and pull the restraining clothes from her breasts. Now he wanted to suck at them. Instead he watched her from his car as she practically ran up the hill, and he followed her flowing body so he could take her picture. His eyes absorbed her photo, trying to bring her to life within the dirty, dingy room. "You'll never leave me again. You know you love me . . . why are you running away? . . . you're mine." He jumped to his feet and stood before her picture. His eyes were riveted to her face and body, his hand now fondling and pulling at his penis. "This is for you," he whispered to Christian. "The next time you'll be on your knees begging me to put it between your lips. You will . . . you know you will." He groaned.

Steam poured from the coffeepot, turning its last bit of water into vapor.

The postman rang the bell at Christian George's home. Mrs. Day called to him as she came down the steps from the living room. "Coming, I'm coming." She opened the door.

"Hi, Mrs. Day. Parcel for Mrs. George," he said, handing her the small package.

"Thank you, have a nice day" was her reply. Closing the door behind her, she glimpsed at the package and noticed there was no return address. "Christian, Christian," she called.

Christian came to the foot of the stairs, brushing her hair. "What is it, Mom?"

"It's a package for you, dear."

Christian tore off the brown paper wrapping, taking a note from within. "Sorry to hear about your husband." It was signed "A friend."

She carefully lifted the contents from the tissue paper. It was a statue of the Blessed Mary with her hands outstretched and holding a roll of white paper set between them. A pencil was protruding from a slot in the side of the statue.

"Why, it's to hang up beside the phone, to take messages," remarked her mother. "What a lovely thought."

"I wonder who sent it, Mom."

Mrs. Day already had a hammer and a nail. She hung it next to the wall phone in the kitchen, then stepped back and cast an admiring glance at it.

Ernest Hampton stood before Carlos Garcia's apartment door. He reached up, taking the Scotch tape from the corner of the door as he thought: He still hasn't come home, tape's in one piece. Good, this time I'll be able to give the apartment a real going over. Glancing up and down the dimly lit corridor, he took the plastic strip from his pocket and worked it between the door and the jamb.

Behind him, and several feet down the hall, a stairwell door opened slightly. It was Carlos Garcia. He had walked up the last two flights, having stopped to talk to a friend two floors below. He saw a man open his door and walk in. Garcia, his hands sweating and his insides shaking, quickly retreated and sneaked out into the night—and waited.

Careful not to disrupt anything, Ernest Hampton methodically searched the apartment. As he looked for further clues to the man's whereabouts, he found a small-caliber pistol in one drawer, a switchblade and marijuana in another, a drawer full of pornographic material in another, on and on. He took a small camera from his pocket and photographed the gruesome bedroom walls. Having completed his mission and, making sure everything was left in order, he left the apartment, replacing the Scotch tape on the top corner of the door.

Garcia was around by the rear of the building. He had taken a large, brown paper bag from his car. It contained bloodstained clothes belonging to him. He walked over to the dumpster and, confident that no one was in sight, nervously cast them into the big steel receptacle. Then he got into his car and drove around to the front of the building, parking across from it. Garcia's eyes were glued on the front entrance to the building. He saw Ernest leave through the double glass doors and get into his late-model car. As Ernest pulled away from the curb and down the highway, Garcia followed him, staying several cars behind.

The car's digital clock showed eight-fifteen P.M., and Ernest was en route to meet Lane, Gina, and Dennis Raskin at Zito's. He kept thinking about the wall in Garcia's room and what a sick mind it represented.

Though Ernest was used to being the follower, not the followed, nevertheless it was an automatic reflex for him to be alert to the cars around him. However, Garcia, nervous about being spotted, dropped farther behind, even at the risk of losing sight of Hampton's car.

Unaware that he was being tailed, Ernest parked in the lot reserved for restaurant patrons.

Garcia, now convinced that he had been overcautious, began cursing himself for losing his prey. He spat out the window in disgust and hammered on the steering wheel with his fist. He was about to blare his horn angrily at the car in front of him when he spied Ernest entering the restaurant.

Ernest pushed open the door squarely set between two windows made up from a series of smaller blocklike glasses. Inside he spotted Lane, Gina, and Dennis already seated at their regular table, a red-and-white barber-striped tablecloth spread over it. And old Chianti bottle, colored waxes running down its sides, a candle lit at the top, stood in the middle.

Lane waved at Ernest to hurry and join them as Joe Zito was bringing their wine and food.

For years it had been Lane's practice for the four of them to get together once a week in a more social atmosphere. He would always foot the bill for these miniconferences. They ate, drank, and talked over current cases in a secluded area just off the entrance. Linda and the young lawyer, Tom O'Brien, were never asked to the evening affairs to keep the discussion as freewheeling as possible.

Ernest came over to their table as a record in the juke box slipped into place and began playing. He quietly slid into a chair as he heard Dennis talking.

"You can relax over the missing hospital files, Lane," Dennis assured him. "I took care of it with Bill Fulton."

"Missing files?" piped Gina.

"Yeah, personnel files . . . *L* to *U* at Wilmington General," explained Dennis.

"Oh, craps! Hell!" Gina spouted. "I was counting on getting the rundown on Spencer right away."

"What's up?" interrogated Lane. "You got something hot?"

"Only that there's just something about the man that doesn't seem to fit . . . I can't put my finger on it. I really need more background."

"All right, hold it a minute, I'm thinkin'." Lane signaled with his hand for her to be quiet. "Got it! I'll buzz Tiernan in the A.M. He'll get the dope on Spencer."

"C-Captain Tiernan of the Boston Police Force?" stammered Gina.

"No sweat, Gina . . . he owes me one," Lane declared as he turned to Ernest. "Hi, Ernie, you got Garcia for us?"

"Yes"—Ernest smiled—"I got him locked in my trunk."

"Forget it, pal," Lane consoled. "Have a drink."

"I could use one; make it Scotch and soda. I'm going to go crazy on you tonight." Ernest directed his attention to Dennis. "Dennis, I'll have the rest of the pictures you wanted by tomorrow night."

Garcia walked tentatively up to the front of Zito's and squinted through a diamond-shaped segment of the amber window block. Under the faded lighting, he examined the faces of the people with Ernest.

"I think they're going to prove some help to us," Dennis replied.

"Hey, Ernie, speakin' about pictures, I got a little present for you."

"What is it, Lane?"

"I just picked it up today. It's a mini-infrared camera. You know, one of them numbers that take pictures in the dark."

"Lane, I think I love you," Ernest said, smiling.

"I meant to bring it along. Guess it slipped my mind."

"That's all right, Lane, I can pick it up tomorrow."

"It'll take only a minute; I'll get it now. Give you a chance to try it out tonight."

Garcia sized up the man in the smartly tailored brown silk suit as he rose and left the table. By the time he realized that Lane was on his way out, it was too late for him to run. He immediately lit a cigarette and glanced at his watch in annoyance. As Lane walked by him, Garcia followed, relieved and satisfied that he hadn't been seen. An evil smirk crept over his face as he watched Lane briskly walk into a building's lobby and enter the elevator.

Garcia quickly slipped inside and peered up at the floor indicator. As soon as the light lit up for the fourth floor, he hurried to the building directory and scanned it for its occupants.

Damn, swore Carlos, there were three names listed in white lettering. Ralph Nelson Literary Agent, Northeast Engineering Employment Services, and Lane Garrett Private Investigator. That's it, that's it, he almost yelled out loud—a private pig!

His success made him feel cocky. He returned to the restaurant window to get a better look at Gina. As he stood there scratching his groin, he inadvertently got a better look at Dennis Raskin's face. There was real fuzz if he ever saw one.

Anger flared within him and he swelled with the urge for vengeance. Racing into the brightly lit parking lot, he spotted Ernest Hampton's car and scribbled down the license plate number. He crammed the crumpled piece of paper into the breast pocket of his dark pinstripe suit jacket, then found a spot for himself across the street from where he could watch the group.

Lane Garrett turned the key in his office door. He went directly into his office, got the camera, and left.

As Lane reentered Zito's, Gina yelled, "And you might as well bring Lane another drink too, he's paying."

"Ernie, here ya go, pal, have fun."

Ernest took the camera. "Lane, it's a beaut."

"Don't they have pictures of Garcia and those other people at the hospital?" Gina inquired.

Lane looked disgusted. "They run that joint on a shoestring. Pictures, you kiddin'! For Christ sakes, I could trip over this bum and not know 'im unless he had a name tag on. Ernie, you got Garcia on that roll you're having developed?"

"Yes, Lane, I have the whole hospital crew."

The waitress, Dottie, came over, set the drinks on the table, and accosted Lane. "Lane, I have a job for you."

"What is it, sweetheart?"

"I want you to find someone for me."

"Who is it, Dottie? I'll track 'im to the end of the world."

"I want you to find me a boyfriend," she said with a twinkle in her eye.

"You got me, what more could you want?"

"Yes, I know." She smiled. "But what I had in mind was someone good-looking with money and intelligence." With that, and a devilish laugh, she walked away. Lane had to join her in a hearty laugh.

They remained at Zito's until nearly eleven o'clock and left together. As the foursome paused in front of the small restaurant saying their good nights, Garcia eyed Gina hungrily. When she got into her small yellow sports car, he followed her.

It was a bright, clear Saturday morning. Mrs. Day had taken Teddy to the local ballfield. It had a park area set off to the side for younger children, with seesaws, swings, jungle bars, and a sandbox.

Lane and Christian were seated at her kitchen table enjoying a cup of coffee. A warm breeze blew through an open screened window. Soothing, almost inaudible music came from the radio on the table. Lane brought Christian up to date on the team's progress, then, sensing her distress, gave her an update on the case of the woman with the wayward vacuum cleaner.

Christian began laughing. Her eyes sparkled and there was a soft rose color to her cheeks.

"Sure, sure, go ahead and laugh. You civilians think detectives have it easy. And that we *are* easy. Just the other day an old lady said I'd do anythin' for a pretty face. She assumed that because I'm a private detective, I have all kinds of women—three or four of them a day, no less."

"You mean to say you don't?" Christian feigned surprise, then began laughing hysterically.

"You're just like the rest of 'em. You see this?" He pointed to his face. "What you're lookin' at is the acne-scarred face of a tragic, shattered man, deprived of love."

"What!" she piped incredulously, laughing so hard she couldn't catch her breath. "Lane . . . Lane, stop, stop," she begged, wiping her eyes. She continued laughing as she left the kitchen, saying, "I have to get a handkerchief."

Christian came back into the kitchen, dabbing her eyes with a small lace handkerchief. She walked over close to him and breathed suggestively. "Lane, I have a surprise for you." A sultry smile crossed her face.

His heart raced as she said it. She stood in front of him, dressed in white slacks and a black blouse that showed a trace of cleavage. He was almost reluctant to ask. His throat became dry; he found it difficult to swallow as he stammered, "Wh-what d'you have in mind?"

"Close your eyes," she said.

"What are you gonna do?"

"Don't worry," she murmured, "I won't hurt you."

He closed his eyes and felt her kiss him lightly on the forehead and gently put something in his hand. It was a small jar of Zits acne cream. "Why . . . why, you!"

She pointed at him. "Don't you say it. I have very sensitive ears."

He chuckled to himself as he lit a cigarette. "I gotta tell you, the last thing I expected when I closed my eyes was a jar of Zits cream." He took a drag from his cigarette as his voice changed to a more serious note. "You know, come to think of it, I got a beef with you."

Christian put a single finger to her lips. "Hmmm, beef, that's like an argument, right?"

"Yeah, yeah, that's right."

"Well, Mr. Garrett, what's your beef?"

"It seems like every time I get together with you, I lose my professional image. You got me tellin' these wild stories and laughin' all over the place. If this gets out, it could blow my whole image. Say, I might as well go the whole way. Listen, what are you, Teddy, and your mother doin' tomorrow?"

"We usually take Teddy to church on Sunday morning. After that we pretty much spend a quiet day at home."

"Look, I got this swimmin' pool at my house that's screamin' for some bodies to use it. Why don't I pick you all up about eleven and we'll eat at my place?"

"Well . . . maybe in a week or so."

"Listen, a week or so will be too late, the water'll evaporate. Besides, sayin' nothin' of you and your mother, Teddy would have a helluva time for himself."

"I—I don't know, Lane."

Lane faked his saddest expression and spoke dejectedly. "Well, that's okay, Christian . . . even if I am all alone in that big empty house. I just thought it would be nice to have a little company . . . for once. You see, no one ever comes to see me. I just sit by that enormous pool . . . alone, all by myself . . . nobody to talk to, no company . . . no friends. Just me, alone . . ."

"Uncle, enough. Give a lady a break, Lane."

"Then you'll come," he gleefully confirmed.

"Yes, we'd love to," she said, smiling.

She walked him out to his car. It was a beautiful breezy summer day. The neighborhood was peaceful and serene. A man in the Dawson yard across the street was mowing the lawn. Lane recognized his operative but remained silent. He opened the car door on the passenger side, got in, and prepared to slide across to the driver's side.

"I'll see you tomorrow, Lane." Almost as an afterthought, she added, "I'm looking forward to it."

chapter 11

Ernest Hampton was making the rounds in his recorder drops—the places where he had hidden recorders to pick up conversations of the bugged telephones. After listening to the tapes of several suspects, he had found nothing significant, except Dr. Schneiderman had gotten an abrupt phone call from a disgruntled female patient—no explanation, just the statement that she would find another personal physician. Carlos Garcia's recorder was the last to be checked. After taking the tape back to his car, he turned it on expecting to hear the quiet sound of a telephone that had not been used. Much to his surprise, he heard voices.

"Hello."

"Hello, it's me, Carlos."

"Hey, man," the male voice said, "what's happening?"

"I got this problem. I gotta split and I wanna lay in with you for a couple of weeks."

"What's comin' down, Carlos?"

"When I got to my pad last night, I saw this dude openin' my door and go into my joint."

"Hey, man, maybe the guy busted your place lookin' to steal somethin'."

"No, no, I followed the cat. He's a private pig. And I could tell the dudes he was rappin' with was fuzz. . . ." Garcia had no intention of letting on that he hadn't spotted Hampton as the law right from the start.

"That's crap, man," rebuked the voice. "Whadda ya mean, you could tell they was private pigs? You blow your mind on some bad stuff or somethin'?"

"If I says they was private pigs, they was!" Garcia's hot temper flared. "They stinks just like any other kind of heat an' I don't need a forty-five up my ass before I can smell 'em! Christ, one of 'em almost walked over me when he left the joint. Coulda made me then . . . prob'ly has by now."

"Hey, man, what do those people want with you?"

"Don't give me that *you* shit," Carlos flared angrily. "Remember that scene *we* had in the park the other night? And the scene *we* had in the hospital?"

"You're fucked up, man . . . you're really blowin'. No private pig is gonna stick his nose into them numbers."

"I ain't goin' on no *trip* . . . on shit. All I know is, I got someone on my ass and you're gonna put me up so's I lose him! You're in this as deep as me."

"Okay, Carlos, no hassle, be cool, man. Don't do nothin' crazy . . . easy, easy. I'll catch ya when ya get here."

The sound went dead. For a split second it seemed the world had stopped. The ticking of Ernest's watch sounded like a time bomb in the silent car. He looked at the recorder with frustration, as self-recriminations plagued him. Damn it, where the hell was he? I looked up and down the hall . . . he couldn't have been there. I blew it! A thought occurred to him. He dashed across the street and into his car. He spun around the corner on two wheels. Maybe I can still catch him. He wheeled into the parking lot behind the building, looking for Garcia's car. It was gone. Spinning the steering wheel, he sped to the front entrance and jerked the car to a stop outside the main door. He took the elevator to the sixth floor, saying to himself: Let him still be there. Let him still be there. Off the elevator, he bolted down the corridor to Garcia's door. He looked up, out of habit. The Scotch tape had been broken. What the hell am I looking at? he wondered. He knew Garcia had been there by the phone conversation. He knocked loudly on the door. No answer. He took out his piece of plastic and popped the door open, closing it behind him. Empty! Couch, table, pictures, everything gone. He rushed to the bedroom. Nothing but four bare walls. Everything gone—the contents of the apartment had vanished with Garcia. "I had him, and I let him get away," he yelled aloud, slamming his fist into his open palm. The words echoed back at him. He charged to the telephone on the floor, unscrewed the mouthpiece, and took out the bug. Angry with himself, he charged out the door, banging it closed so hard the wood jamb cracked.

Late in the afternoon, Ernest pulled into Lane Garrett's driveway. Ernest walked down a flagstone, flowered path, and up the steps to the front door. He rang the bell several times. When there was no response, he walked around the side of the house into and through a heavily treed section of land. Upon reaching the clearing, he looked across the acreage that was a mass of green grass from woods to poolside. Ernest called to Lane, who was seated at the pool. Seeing Ernest, Lane waved his hand, motioning him over. Ernest walked toward the pool: He reached the deck of the pool and walked to where Lane was seated.

"Hi, Ernie, this is a surprise. Sit down, I'll fix you a drink."

"Lane, I just wanted to speak to you for a minute."

Lane fixed Ernest a Scotch and soda. Ernest rarely ever came to his home unannounced. Whenever he did, it was a matter of dire importance.

He handed Ernest his drink. "Here you go, pal. In order for you to be here on a sunny Saturday afternoon, you gotta have big news, like the inside track on the lottery number tonight."

Ernest savored a sip of his drink. "Better than that, Lane. Looks like we got Carlos Garcia cold—on two counts."

"C'mon, give," Lane urgently coaxed.

"He finally showed at his apartment and used the phone. The main event we may have Garcia for is murder one, for the number done on the girl in Boston Common. The phone conversation places him and an accomplice there that night. Number two, and of more interest to us, Mr. Garcia is the sickie that raped Christian George!"

Lane lit a cigarette as a hard smile crossed his face. "Garcia, huh? It figures. Ernie, you're a genius. You know, Ernie, it almost seems too easy," Lane continued.

"If it will make you feel any better . . . it's not going to be that easy."

"What the hell are you talkin' about? You got it on the tape, didn't you? I know we can't use the recording for evidence, but we can squeeze the guy now that we know he's our boy."

"He spotted me going into his apartment. When I went back, his place looked like someone came in with a giant vacuum cleaner and sucked everything up. There's not a piece of silverware left in the kitchen drawer. The man's gone, skipped . . . faded right out of the picture. I blew it, but good."

Lane got up from his chair, pacing back and forth. "Someone must've seen him leave. Someone in that building must know that bum. Put a couple of our people on it. Have 'em check the Spanish-sounding names first. Make a couple of dozen pictures of 'im—make 'em eight-by-tens."

"Lane, what about the rest of the taps?"

"You can pull 'em. Whatever they talk about is none of our business now."

"You know, Lane, I never had Schneiderman pegged for this one. And not quite the X-ray tech either."

"Me neither, Ernie, but we had to touch all the bases. I figured it to be a toss-up between Garcia and Don Spencer. Though I would like to know where the hell that kid, Brian Summers, disappeared to."

"I picked Spencer," Ernie said.

"How come?"

"Well, like you said, Garcia in the picture made it seem too easy."

Lane took a drag from his cigarette. "Ernie, if we ever had an easy one . . . I'm glad this was it."

The shiny big black Lincoln pulled up by the lamppost in front of Christian George's home. Lane noticed that her compact car was missing from the driveway. He looked at his watch: Hmmm, ten-forty-five. Maybe they're still at church. No, no way, he thought, viewing his operative playing gardener across the street. He ambled up the pathway to the front door and rang the bell. Christian opened the door. She looked beautiful. Her blond hair was pulled back into a ponytail and tied into a bow with a length of black yarn. The yellow sun dress clung to her curvaceous body. The lipstick that lined her full lips glistened in the sun.

"Good morning." She waved cheerfully. "This is the first time I've seen you in your civilian clothes."

Lane, in departure from his usual dress of suit and tie, was attired in a light-brown short-sleeved silk shirt and dark-brown pants. He was, though, still carrying a .38 in an ankle holster.

"Good mornin'. This," he said, pointing to his clothing, "is my Sunday goin'-to-meetin' outfit."

Lane entered the house, following her to the kitchen. She

poured him a cup of coffee, saying, "I'm just getting Teddy out of his church clothes; we'll be with you in just a minute."

"Take your time, no hurry," Lane advised, tasting his coffee.

Christian was in Teddy's room when she called to him. "How's the coffee?"

"On a scale of one to ten," he called back to her, "it's an eleven."

She laughed aloud. "Mother will be pleased to hear it."

"Isn't she comin' with us?"

"No," Christian said, entering the kitchen. "She's already left. She had previous plans with a friend of hers."

Little Teddy trailed behind his mother, a pair of bathing trunks clutched in his little hand. "Hi, Mr. Garrett."

"Hi, Teddy. I hope you know how to swim."

"Sure I do," Teddy perked confidently. "I learned last summer. My dad taught me."

Lane's manner was casual as he continued the subject. "I bet he was one great swimmer."

"He sure was," Teddy said excitedly. "How about you, Mr. Garrett, are you a good swimmer like my dad?"

"Well, first of all, it looks like we're gonna be pals, so why don't you call me Lane?"

Teddy looked up at his mother; she smiled approvingly at him.

"Okay, Lane."

"I'll tell you a secret, Teddy. When I'm in my pool, all the little critters in the woods come to watch me swim. It's quite a sight—to see them holdin' their bellies, laughin'."

"C'mon," Teddy replied with an infectious giggle.

The threesome left Christian's house. Teddy carried his swimming trunks; a small duffle bag dangled from Christian's hand.

They all sat comfortably in the front seat of the Lincoln as it purred down the highway toward Lane's house, some twenty-two miles away.

They were halfway to the town of Easton, heading down on Route 24, when Lane noticed in his rearview mirror that a car seemed to be following them. He accelerated to seventy miles an hour. The car in the mirror kept pace. He slowed to fifty-five. The car, which was now partially hidden behind another vehicle, did likewise. Lane pulled over and far off the shoulder of the road.

"Is something wrong?" Christian inquired.

"No," replied Lane, opening his door, "I just wanna check the tires. Felt like one of 'em is a little low." He went to the back of the car and bent down as though looking at the rear tire. His eyes were fixed on the older model car approaching. As it neared where Lane was parked, it swung into the passing lane, placing itself beside another car and completely obstructing Lane's view. As the cars passed by him, the beat-up blue car cut in front of the one in the right lane of the highway, shielding the rear license plate. Lane continued to watch as it swung off at the next cutoff. He got back into his car.

"Tires are okay. It musta been somethin' on the highway."

They drove steadily toward Lane's house. His watchful eye glanced regularly into the rearview mirror, while Teddy chatted away like a magpie. Where the hell have I seen that car? thought Lane. He racked his brain trying to place it. It looked like a thousand others. He concluded that to be the case, but remained positive it had been following them. As they pulled into the driveway, Christian was taken with the beautiful setting.

"Oh, Lane."

Lane smiled at her. "It's the stepped-up version of your everyday cold-water flat."

"It's quite a step up," she remarked.

Lane showed them through the house, downstairs, then up.

Teddy asked him a hundred questions. He had to know what all the electronic gadgets were and how they worked. When Lane switched on a closed-circuit TV and gave Teddy an electronic tour of the grounds, the boy was very impressed.

Finally, Christian reminded Teddy of the pool and he went for it, running. Lane left Christian and Teddy there, saying, "I'm goin' into the house to get my trunks. Make yourself at home; you can use the cabana to change."

Lane had changed into his pale-blue boxer-style swimming trunks and took a matching terry-cloth shirt from a hanger. As he slipped into his sandals, he walked past the glass doors in his bedroom. He saw Christian by the pool and backed up a step, to stand watching through the glass doors, like a voyeur. She was standing by the steps leading down to the pool, wearing a black one-piece bathing suit that fitted her body snugly. Beautiful, he thought.

A little guiltily he joined them at the pool. "How's the water, Teddy?"

"It's just great, Lane, you coming in?"

"Not just yet; after we eat."

Teddy looked around and yelled, "Where's the food, Lane? What are we gonna eat?"

"That's a surprise; you'll see. It'll be ready in a short while." Lane looked at Christian. "Drink?"

"I'd love one. White wine, if you have it."

"Madam, inside the cabana lies every elixir known to man." He added, smiling, "And then some."

Lane returned with wine for Christian and beer for himself. She tasted the cool wine, closing her eyes as she turned her face up to the hot sun. Teddy was on a small water raft, paddling around the pool. Soft music was flowing from the speaker attached to the cabana.

"Lane?"

"Yeah," he answered softly.

"Do you know who it is yet?"

"This is Sunday; I never talk business on Sunday." Lane Garrett did not want to spoil the seemingly perfect day.

"You don't have to tell me his name, just if you know who it is."

"You're a pushy lady," he said kiddingly as he nudged her with his elbow.

"If you tell me, I'll drop the subject for the rest of the day."

He turned his head to look at her. Her eyes pleaded with him, waiting for an answer. He relented. "Yeah, I know who it is. We have his name . . . his face, everything except him, and we'll have him soon."

"Thanks, Lane." Her smile warmed him as she observed him. "When you get him, I want you to ask him one question. Why? I want you to ask him why he did it."

Lane sat up straight in his chair and lit a cigarette. His gut ached for her, wishing he could take it all out of her head. He gazed at her, inches from her face, and spoke softly. "Christian, don't keep askin' yourself why. This man's a real sickie, and with people like that, there's no rhyme or reason for their actions. There is no 'why.' I think I know how to get this subject off the agenda for the rest of the day."

With her head tilted to one side, she asked, "How?"

Without warning, Lane stood up, swept her up in his arms, and tossed her into the middle of the pool.

She came up sputtering, smiling. "Lane Garrett, I owe you one."

He squinted at her and thought of how firm her body had felt in his arms. The flat stomach and firm breasts, the body of a girl . . . not woman, girl, he thought. He dove off the diving board, joining Teddy and Christian in the pool.

"C'mon, Teddy, let's get him," Christian shouted.

They cornered him at the end of the pool, beside the diving board.

Lane protested feebly. "You gotta gimmie a break."

They both jumped on him, pushing him under the water. He buoyed up, water spurting from his mouth. "You're drownin' me . . . give a guy a break."

Christian laughed as Teddy grabbed him around the neck from behind. Lane winked at her as he let the boy drag him under. When Lane popped up again, the three of them were startled by a voice above the pool.

"Hey, Lane, Bing sent me up with your stuff."

The three inhabitants of the pool looked up. There was Butch, the local cab driver—all three hundred pounds of him—chomping on a cigar that appeared to be a foot long.

"Thanks," Lane said, wiping the water from his eyes. "Set it right on the table over there."

Butch set the two shopping bags on the table and disappeared as quickly as he had appeared.

"Chinese food, mmm," Christian exclaimed, peering into the bag after climbing out of the pool.

"Where did this come from, Lane?" questioned Teddy.

"A pal of mine owns a Chinese restaurant. I had him send the food up to us."

"Lane." Teddy was tugging on Lane's swimsuit.

He looked down at him. "What is it, pal?"

"Lane, I don't know if I like Chinese food."

Lane reached into one of the shopping bags, probed around the large assortment of containers, and took from it two huge hamburgers wrapped in aluminum foil. Lane handed them to Teddy.

"Shame on you. You think your pal would let you down? I ordered these just in case you didn't like this other stuff."

The restaurant had sent everything—silver, plates, wipettes. Lane did not have to go into his kitchen for a single item. As it turned out, Teddy devoured a good portion of the shrimp in lobster sauce, with heaping mounds of pork fried rice. They swam most of the day, resting in between and basking in the hot sun.

Christian helped Lane put all the dishes in a container to be returned to the restaurant later. Their day ended as the sun melted down behind the graying sky.

On the way back to Dedham, Teddy fell asleep, his head resting on his mother's lap. Christian's fair skin glowed from the day's sun. Lane glanced over to her, holding out a pack of cigarettes. She took two, lighting one for Lane. She reached back with cigarette in hand and carefully put it into his mouth. He could taste the sweetness of her lips still on the tip as he took a long drag. She looked out the window at the reddish sky as the last ray of light began to disappear. Holding Teddy in her arms, she laid her head back on the soft headrest. A Sinatra tape was playing. He sang a few lines of "My Way" along with the inimitable Frank.

Lane spoke softly, not wanting to wake the boy. "Tired?"

"No, I was just thinking about today. It was beautiful. Thank you, Lane."

"I got a confession."

"What is it?" she smiled lazily.

"I never enjoyed that place as much as I did today. You see, that's the kinda place you hafta share with someone before it's any fun." Lane caught himself getting sentimental. "Hey, you know, that sounds like it could make a good soap opera."

She knew what he'd said had embarrassed him, so she tried to console him with a poor Bogart imitation. "You know, sweeeetheart, that joint would make a swell place for underprivileged kids."

As they pulled up to the front of Christian's home, the lights were on in the house. The compact car was in the driveway; Mrs. Day had returned home. Teddy was still sleeping as Lane turned off the motor. He turned the key still further to keep the electrical system on so they could enjoy Sinatra's version of "Pennies From Heaven." They both watched Teddy sleeping peacefully.

Lane lifted his eyes to Christian and said, "We could always wait until he wakes up."

"That could be morning," she replied, smiling.

Deadpan, he replied, "I'll go in and get the blankets."

She laughed softly. "I'll have to wake him up."

"Do you want me to carry him in?"

"No, don't bother, Lane, he has to get out of those clothes, anyway."

"Christian . . . I had a helluva day. Let's do it again."

She teased him. "As long as you provide the pool and the Chinese food."

She shook Teddy gently. He woke up, rubbing the hazy sleep from his eyes, smiling contentedly at her. "We home, Mom?"

"Yes, honey," she said, stroking his brow. "Do you want to say good night to Lane?"

He sat up bleary-eyed and uttered, "Good night, Lane."

"Good night, Teddy."

He turned away from Lane, then back to him. "Lane?"

"What is it, pal?"

"Will you take us to your pool again?"

"You're gonna be in that pool so much this summer you'll think you're a fish."

"Really, Lane?" he said excitedly.

"Teddy, I promise you, your pal Lane will never tell you a fib . . . really."

Without a second thought, Teddy put his arms around Lane's neck and kissed him on the cheek. "Thanks, Lane."

Lane was quiet, touched by the boy's spontaneous response. Christian swallowed hard as she forced herself to speak. "It was a wonderful day. Will you call tomorrow?"

"Yeah," he said softly, "you're at the top of my agenda."

Teddy and Christian got out of the car and walked to the door. At the doorway, she looked back to see the tail lights on the Lincoln disappear into the clear summer night.

chapter 12

The small house was a speck of white in the night shadows on Nardian Way. A flickering light against the shaded windows was the only sign of life in the darkened house. Inside, Virginia Merguson knelt at her makeshift altar. Several lit candles were placed around the room, their reflections dancing on the ceiling and walls in the old house. The black Doberman pinscher lay at the entrance of the room watching his mistress chant prayerlike words to the crucifix before her. The candles glistened in her deep-sunken eyes and reflected off her pasty face as her chanting voice reached a shrill, fevered pitch, piercing the black night.

With arms outstretched toward the steel crucifix, her voice, now low, whispered, "Lord . . . hear me, Lord. He is an evil man. Strike him down. Strike down his wickedness, his lust . . . his contempt for you." Her voice was rising and intense. "Point Your almighty finger at Lane Garrett and wipe him from this earth." She placed a small rag doll on a tray before the altar, dousing it with lighter fluid. "Lord, this is his likeness." She dropped a lighted match on the tray and instantly the rag doll ignited and crackled in the flames. "May he burn in hell!" she shrieked. "Do this, Lord, do this for your humble servant."

Strange sounds ushered from her throat as she wailed chants in a high, rasping voice. Her voice could be heard outside in the chill of the night. Suddenly she was joined by the howling of her dog.

A young boy of fifteen was passing the house on his way home. Petrified, he gawked at the house. Listening for a moment, he shuddered. "What the fuck is that!" Then he broke into a mad dash toward the end of the street.

Ernest Hampton was in his workshop located behind a locked door in the basement of his home. The room was completely surrounded by thick fieldstone, with the exception of the only means of entrance, the steel, alarmed door. It was packed solid with electronic equipment. He was like a mad professor as he surveyed the incredible amount of stock he had garnered in over fifteen years in the business. He had two tape recorders side by side and placed a cassette tape in each of them. He switched on the one to his left. The tape began as he listened to the voice of Carlos Garcia. Next he listened to the muffled voice that called Christian George. He played them again and again and again. The tone and quality were very much alike. Ernest strained to distinguish the voice as that of Carlos talking to Christian even though it was distorted by something covering the mouthpiece. Ernest thought to himself: That's right, Mr. Garcia, you can talk through an echo chamber if you like—we know who you are now.

Gina had finished her peach Melba and was watching Don Spencer enjoying his strawberry shortcake. She was too deep in thought to be aware of the restaurant noises around them or of the trio playing in the background. Funny how fast she agreed to meeting him when he called her earlier, in the morning. She smiled a little, remembering the tingle she'd felt at the sound of his voice, asking if she'd like to make a day of it. He'd been quick to explain that what he meant by that was for the two of them to go candlepin bowling, and afterward spend an evening dining and dancing.

As she studied his handsome face munching on dessert, Gina searched it for some evidence that would substantiate Captain Tiernan's report. It didn't jibe. The report had shown he was a drifter with all hell breaking loose at every job he'd held. You'd never know it to look at him—what a charmer.

Don Spencer had hardly stopped his contented chewing when he asked Gina to dance.

They danced for almost two hours to slow renditions of Willie Nelson songs. He held her so gently in his arms. Her troubled mind returned once again to Tiernan's report—specifically the part that stated Spencer's last job was as a custodian at a private finishing school around the time two young women had been assaulted there.

"I'd like you to come home with me," Don breathed into her ear. "So we can talk," he added softly.

"I'd like that," she replied.

His apartment was immaculate. Everything, right down to the centerpiece that was exactly in the middle of the waxed table, was in its proper place. He fixed them both a drink as they sat on the couch and listened to his stereo.

"Gina, I want to tell you something."

"What is it, Don?"

"I'm not a stockbroker!"

Damn it, I liked him better when he lied, she thought. "Well, if you're not a stockbroker, what do you do for a living?"

"I just met you, Gina; I hope I can trust you."

"Don, trust me, my lips are sealed."

"I'm an undercover cop."

Her mind raced as she smiled at him: That's a great story. Captain Tiernan would get a real kick out of it. "Don, that sounds exciting. Is it dangerous?"

"Well, yeah, I guess it is. That's why once in a while, I have to get away from it—you know, to sort of relax. I haven't been out on a date for almost six months."

"How about your girl . . . you do have a girl?" she asked, kicking her shoes off.

"No, no, I don't. With the kind of job I have, it's pretty difficult to carry on any type of meaningful relationship."

She looked at him as he was speaking. Wow, has this guy got a line! she thought. Her eyes fixed on his full wet lips. The man's a doll. He pulled her to her feet and they danced. She felt herself surrendering into his arms. Reluctantly she broke away and returned to her drink. She actually had butterflies and almost stuttered as she inquired, "What type of assignment do you have now?"

"I'm working undercover, that's about all I can say."

"Where, doing what?"

"Gina, it's sort of an important case . . . I really can't tell you."

She stared at him, silent.

"Gina, don't be upset."

She smiled. "I'm not upset. May I have another drink?"

He placed a soft melodic record on the stereo and coaxed her from the couch. The music was slow and she felt a little light-headed from all the drinks. He's taller than I realized, she mused as he pulled her tightly to him. She could feel his lean, muscular body tense as their bodies came together. She moved her hand from his shoulder to the nape of his neck, his own hand sliding softly from her waist to the smoothness of her behind.

She could feel his arousal . . . pressed even closer against her. He kissed her softly on the ear. To her surprise, it sent a shiver through her body. As she looked up at him dreamy-eyed, he brought his mouth down softly on hers. She placed her two hands on the back of his head, her feet on his, and held him to her. Effortlessly he lifted and carried her to the bedroom. Tenderly he laid her on the bed. Lying down beside her, he kissed her, touching her face lovingly. Slowly he unbuttoned her blouse, kissing every place where the buttons had been. The last button was over her navel, where he rested his warm, wet lips. His hot tongue filled the small space in her tummy. He kissed all the way back up to her hardened nipples. He took off her bra, softly kissing her milk-white breasts. She helped him undress, and, feeling more inflamed than ever, she tore the rest of her clothing off. He hovered over her with most of his weight on his outstretched hands, kissing her, pushing softly against her. She could stand it no longer.

"Oh, Don . . . Don . . . yes," she moaned.

With both of her legs pressed against her chest, he entered her with one swift motion. It nearly took her breath away as he plunged inside her. His size was startling. He entered her again . . . again. His stroke quickened as she writhed.

"Don . . . I can't . . . wait for . . . you . . . I'm com . . . comin'."

He put his hands behind her back, forcing her legs down, placing her in a sitting position on top of him. He burned and swelled deep within her. He felt a sucking sensation as he began slowly moving in and out, again and again. He reached up and caressed her warm breasts. Then, holding her by the shoulders, he lifted his head and sucked on her taut nipples while driving deep into her. She raised herself excitedly up and down . . . up and down, faster, faster . . . faster. The mounting thrill sent little chills sweeping over the wet skin of her entire body. She felt the depth of sensuous lust suddenly soaring to mingle with the divine. Her tightening forced him to explode in climax with her. For a long moment they froze, then Gina fell exhausted on him. Still pulsing slightly within her, Don wrapped her in his arms and gently began rubbing her back.

She snuggled her head against his chest, relaxing in his arms. Neither spoke a word. She just lay there within his warmth and thought: You can tell me all the lies you want, I love it.

His breathing was heavy. She looked at him. He slept. She covered him with the sheet, went into the bathroom, and got dressed. When she came out, she wrote him a note.

"Don, I'll call you tomorrow. Gina."

She went outside, hailed a cab, and went home.

Dennis Raskin sat in a recliner before the television in his home, staring at the screen. It just didn't mesh, he thought. Nineteen didn't go into eighteen. His mind counted the cars in the parking lot again. Nineteen. It just didn't go. He remembered asking Dr. Spellie how many employees usually work the night shift. Spellie's answer had been eighteen at most. Where the hell did the other car come from? Maybe a car was disabled there for a few days? Maybe Spellie was mistaken in his count of workers. Maybe someone was missing from the work schedule that should have been on it, thereby causing Spellie to get an improper count. Maybe . . . maybe . . . maybe. No matter, they had finally nailed it on Garcia.

Dennis's wife was in front of him shutting off the television.

"Wh-what are you doing?" Dennis asked, confused.

She turned around with an understanding smile. "You're watching the test patterns, dear." She moved over to him with a warm expression on her face and kissed him lightly on the forehead.

Christian George was lying in bed, her head propped up by the two pillows pushed against the headboard, a book in her hand. She'd read the same page for the past thirty minutes without getting beyond the first line. The thoughts of today, at Lane's, prevented her from concentrating.

She leaned over, putting the book on her night table, and turned off the small lamp. She closed her eyes, picturing Lane. How he stood by the pool after he'd thrown her in, with hands on hips, the black hair on his chest slightly graying, and laughing as she bubbled up from under the water. She heard Teddy telling Lane "Daddy taught me how to swim," and her thoughts were suddenly of Ben. The three of them had been at the lake last summer, where Ben had spent countless happy hours teaching little Teddy how to swim. She found herself comparing the two—Ben, a quiet, simple man; Lane, outspoken and complex. She twisted and turned in her bed. She could not sleep.

Without switching on the light, she fumbled for her cigarettes and lighter. Finding them on the night table, she lit a cigarette, the smoke swirling into the darkened room. She got up, with cigarette and ashtray in hand, and walked slowly to the drapes. The night was clear as she stood gazing out her window. The thought of Lane touching her hand while saying good night made her feel warm, secure. There! What was that? She thought she'd seen a man's outline tucked behind the bushes in the backyard. With her heart racing, she tapped out her cigarette, her eyes glued to the bushes. A movement again! Someone's there, in the yard! She could almost see him now. His bent figure seemed to be hovering with his back to the fence. In a panic, she bolted to the top drawer of the dresser and snatched out Ben's loaded .38. She thought of calling the police. No! The newspapers . . . the newspapers would print the whole story. I'll call Lane. No—no time. What to do . . . what should I do? she wondered frantically.

Straining her eyes out the window, the gun clutched in her trembling hand, she spied the intruder once more. Like a bad dream, he would not go away. She rushed to her mother's room, waking her and motioning for her to follow. Passing Teddy's room on the way, they closed his door.

The two women stared out the window. Christian, with her voice quivering, whispered, "There, over there against the fence, see him?"

"Yes, yes." Her mother gasped. "Give me the gun, we can shoot him from here."

"Mom, don't be crazy. You just can't go shooting people because they're in your backyard."

"The bastard is not a person, he's an animal," the older woman hissed.

Christian mustered all the courage she had as she said, "I think I can sneak up on him through the rear gate."

"Christian! You'll do no such thing."

"Mom, I don't want him to get away. I'm going out there. I can't stand living with this over my head any longer. We can hold him and then call Lane. Are you going to help me or not?"

Her mother looked upward. "Jesus help us." Then to Christian, she added, "What do you want me to do?"

"I'm going to slip my way along the fence. He won't see me from where he is. When I'm almost in front of where he's hiding, you throw on the floodlights."

"My God, Christian, what then?"

"I'm going to make him lie on the ground until Lane gets here."

Mrs. Day was shaking her head as she kissed Christian. "Christian, for God's sake, if he moves toward you—shoot him."

"Just remember, as I get to the bush, throw the lights on."

At the Dawson home, Charlie, Lane's operative, was seated in a chair, facing the front of the George house. His feet lay resting on the edge of the bed, his arms folded across his chest—sleeping.

Christian slipped out the front door. She was barefoot and felt the grass, wet with dew, beneath her feet. She held her breath and opened the rear gate without making a sound. She pressed herself against the fence, slowly inching her way to the bush. Halfway there, she thought. She was shaking badly; the adrenaline pumped her heart to a tremendous pace.

Her mother stood watching from the kitchen window, her hand shaking on the switch. "God help her, she can't do it all by herself," Mrs. Day prayed. "She's nearly there. That's close enough!" Mrs. Day threw the switch, lighting up the yard.

The startled man, crouching behind the bush, leaped to his feet. Christian held the gun pointed at his head, her hand trembling.

"Don't move. If you move, I'll shoot you. I really will." Her own voice surprised Christian. It wasn't hers—it was too convincing.

"Easy, lady . . . easy. That thing could go off."

Mrs. Day came up from behind, crashing down on the man's

head with Teddy's baseball bat. He slumped to the ground. Christian and her mother stood there shaking and looking at him. Boldly Mrs. Day poked him with the bat. "Praise the Lord. We got him, Christian, he's out cold."

Christian ripped the belt from her dark-blue robe, tying his hands securely behind him. Mrs. Day followed her example and bound his feet. She took the handkerchief from her pocket and wrapped it around his mouth, tying it behind his head, saying "We don't want him waking the neighbors."

They both raced into the house and up the stairs, shutting off the lights.

"Mom, you watch him while I call Lane."

Mrs. Day looked out the window, watching his motionless form.

It was two-fifty A.M. when Lane heard his phone ring. He pushed in the button of the speaker.

"Yeah."

"Lane, it's me, Christian. We got him . . . we got him," she blurted excitedly.

Like a shot, Lane was on his feet. "Easy now, easy. You got who?"

"We got the man who raped me. We knocked him out with a baseball bat and we got him tied up in the backyard!"

"Christian, you and your mother stay in the house; I'll be right there." Lane struggled into his pants, put his sockless feet into his shoes, grabbed a shirt and his gun, and ran out the door.

Lane's speedometer read ninety-five miles per hour as he hit the cutoff to Christian's house. With the tires squealing, Lane jumped out of the car before it could finish its rocking motion from the sudden stop in front of the house. He shot up the front steps to the open door where they were waiting for him.

Christian hugged him, almost crying. "Oh, Lane, thank goodness."

"Where is he?" Lane asked hurriedly.

"Tied up in the backyard."

"All right, you two stay in here."

The floodlights flicked on as Lane knelt beside the man, noticing the large goose egg on his head. The man was awake. Lane called out to the women, "I'm gonna take him down to the station."

Christian watched as Lane untied the man's ankles and pulled him to his feet. She heaved a sigh of relief seeing him draw his gun as he marched the gagged man out the yard to his car, putting him in the passenger side of the backseat. Christian and her mother gaped in awe as Lane pushed him to the floor before getting into the driver's side and driving off.

Lane had barely gone two blocks when he stopped the car to untie the man's hands and remove the gag from his mouth.

"Jesus Christ, what the hell happened?" he yelled.

"Lane, those two broads are holy terrors. I don't know where the one with the gun came from. And the old one, wow! I saw her just as she came down on me with the damn bat." He groaned, rubbing the large bump on his head.

"Jack, are you okay?"

Jack was Jack Reardon, one of Lane's investigators. His assignment for the past six days had been to watch the rear of the house.

"My head feels like it's gonna blow up. Guess I'll be all right. It could've been worse. I thought she was gonna blow me away. That lady really came on . . . scared the shit outta me. I never got a chance to tell her I worked for you."

"Thank Christ you're still with us. Better let me drive you home."

"Nah, Lane, really. My car's about a block from here. I'll be okay, just drop me off there." He paused. "What are you gonna tell Mrs. George and her mother?"

"Christ, Jack. I can't tell 'em they beaned the guy that was there to protect 'em. That would really croak 'em. I'll hafta think of somethin'."

As Jack got out of the car, he said, "I probably won't be in tomorrow."

Lane grinned. "Some guys will do anythin' to get a day off."

Christian and her mother all but dragged Lane into the house upon his return. They fired questions at him as he sat at the kitchen table.

"Is he the man who attacked Christian?" "What's his name?" "What's going to happen now?" "Will I have to go to court?"

Lane held up his hand. "Easy, easy . . . first of all, that is *not* the same man who attacked Christian."

Christian, with a note of anguish in her voice, sighed. "Well, Lane . . . who was it?"

"You girls were very foolish to pull a stunt like that. You shoulda called me. That man you caught, I'm told, is a very dangerous fugitive. He's wanted for bank robbery in three states."

Christian flinched. "You mean we caught a bank robber?"

"Listen . . . please listen," Lane implored. "Yeah, you caught a bank robber . . . but you two coulda been hurt. You got no license takin' shots like that."

"Will the newspaper people be here?" worried Mrs. Day.

"No, at least we got lucky as far as that's concerned. A friend of mine down at the station said he'd keep a lid on it. As a matter of fact, they're drivin' this bum to New York tonight and handin' him over for extradition to California. Once they finish with him, I got the word of the captain, an old pal of mine, that this will never reach the local press."

Christian poured Lane a cup of coffee.

"Now, ladies, let's get to current business. The only time I want to see that gun is if I gotta search the place. You two are outta the police business for good. Fired. Get it? If you see anyone or anything in your backyard, you are to go to that phone and call *me!* Do we all understand that?"

Christian and her mother both nodded in agreement.

Lane's voice softened. "The man who attacked Christian is named Carlos Garcia. We're very close to makin' this guy. It was a gutsy thing you did tonight. But you were mighty lucky . . . so please, please don't do it again. Besides, it makes guys like me look like a bum. You realize if this got out I'd be ruined. People would say who needs Lane Garrett—we can get Christian and her mother and maybe save a few bucks."

"What are you talking about, Lane? We'd charge an enormous price, wouldn't we, Christian?" her mother retorted.

"I knew it, I knew it . . . you *are* after my business," he accused, pointing at Mrs. Day.

"You're lucky I'm an old woman, I'd give you what for. But one in a night is 'nough for me. I'd best be getting to bed. Christian, you lock up."

Lane got up and took Mrs. Day by the shoulders, kissing her on the forehead. "You did a helluva job tonight."

"What kind of language is that to use to an old lady!" she snapped, feigning indignance. Then, smiling amicably, she added, "Good night, Lane."

"Good night, sweetheart," he replied.

As Mrs. Day went down the hallway, Lane turned to Christian. "It's gettin' late, I'd better go. Are you okay?"

"I'm all right, Lane. Even though it wasn't the man we were looking for, I feel better knowing he wasn't just some drunk."

"Christian, that was a very dangerous thing to do."

"I—I just wanted it over with, Lane. I won't do it again."

He took her by the hand. "C'mon, walk me to the door."

They stood at the foot of the stairs, in front of the door, within the darkened foyer. He held her to him, patting her softly on the back, her hands resting on his arms. His face was just touching her cheek. He spoke gently to her.

"Christian, I don't want anythin' to happen to you. I'm gonna see you through this thing. Just don't lose your head. Take it easy, and don't do anythin' foolish. There's a long life ahead of you, and there's gonna be a lot of happy times. You'll forget this thing. In a few months it'll be just a bad memory. You gotta do me this favor and hang in there. Remember that I'm with you. Do you know what I'm tryin' to say?"

She remained silent.

"Do you?"

She turned her face to his and, with slightly tearstained cheeks, she whispered, "Yes, Lane, I understand what you're telling me."

He took a handkerchief from his pocket, drying her eyes. "We could fall asleep here," Lane said softly.

She sniffed as she replied, "I'll get some blankets."

He smiled. "You're stealin' my lines again."

"I know, I know," she said, dabbing her nose with Lane's handkerchief. They stood inches apart yet bonded together by tenderness of the moment. Like two starry-eyed high school kids saying good night after the prom, neither wanting to leave the other.

"It's late," he said reluctantly.

His handkerchief was clutched in her hands, resting between her breasts. They spoke in whispered tones.

"Will you call me tomorrow?"

"Yes," he vowed, mesmerized by the emotion he felt.

"Good night, Lane."

He leaned toward her, his hands gently on her arms, and closed his eyes, kissing her forehead. He straightened, and with his hands back at his sides, he looked at her. He uttered a simple, caring "Good night, Christian."

She opened the door for him and watched him walk slowly to his car. Her head rested on the hand that was holding the side of the door, his handkerchief still in it. He waved to her as he got into his car. The big Lincoln quietly left the side of the curb, as she continued with the good-bye motion of her other hand.

She shut the door behind her, leaning back against it. Closing her eyes, she lingered in the memory of the moment, with guarded feelings of caring.

Soon Christian George lay peacefully asleep in her room, Lane's handkerchief still in her hand, pressed to her breast.

Dennis Raskin and Ernest Hampton were at Ken's Steak House having lunch. They sat in a corner of the crowded room discussing the George case.

Ernest pushed a manila envelope toward Dennis, saying, "Here are the pictures of the people you wanted."

"Thanks, Ernest, I'll look them over later, then keep them in my file. There doesn't seem to be much point in pursuing further since we have Garcia made for it." He chewed his steak sandwich slowly, pausing several times to say something, but thinking better of it.

After a few moments of silence, Ernest figured he'd waited long enough. "You want to let me in on whatever's on your mind, or am I going to have to spend my lunch wishing I was reading through a dead-letter file?"

"Sorry, Ernest. I guess it's just the letdown of being taken off a case."

"Something tells me it's a little more than that, Dennis."

"Ernest, when I was with the bureau all those years, it was drilled into us to accept when a case was solved. 'Don't over-investigate.' No doubt you know the theory that if you press hard enough, you're bound to come up with something to complicate matters."

"Sure, but if there's something you can't let go of, you'd be better off airing it. It might just get it off your chest altogether

. . . and it sure as hell would make lunch more pleasant," he half joked proddingly.

Dennis didn't fully appreciate the way Ernest expressed his humor, but he respected the advice. "Take last night," he began, poking his fork at his salad. "I kept going over the car count in the hospital employees parking lot. I can't for the life of me figure where the extra car came from. It couldn't be a visitor's car. You have to have an ID card to get through the gate."

Ernest nodded and expected more. When it didn't come, he asked, "Anything else?"

"I got the report on Schneiderman. It seems he had been forced to give up a diminishing private practice owing to rapidly spreading rumors that he examined his female patients a good deal too thoroughly. Apparently he didn't decide to leave the Midwest any too soon—there was one woman, at the very least, considering bringing suit against him. There's more. . . ."

"Go ahead." Ernest took a swallow of his drink, the ice cubes clinking against the glass.

"One night I followed Schneiderman. He left his house like a man on his last leg, and when he got to the hospital he skipped across the parking lot like a twenty-year-old. The man has got to be on some kind of upper."

"Dennis, we did a missing drug case for a hospital, oh, eight, nine years ago. They had been missing a substantial amount of narcotics and felt someone had a nice little racket for themselves. It turned out that ninety percent of the missing stuff was being consumed by staff members. We found a lot of them were actually hooked. They start out just taking the goodies to give themselves a lift and then wind up behind the eight-ball."

"Schneiderman's been working two, three days straight," Dennis said. "I guess he's not doing it on Cheerios. It's a fairly small hospital; why would he work those kind of hours?"

"Guess he's rededicated himself." Ernest shrugged, tasting a piece of his roast beef. "Forget it for now. The only real problem we have is locating this Garcia guy. I hope your fed friends get his file in a hurry."

"How about his application from the hospital—past employment, prior address, references, next of kin? Maybe we can backtrack and come up with him."

"The man was hired as a cleaner, Dennis. I'm afraid personnel didn't really check him out. I've touched on a few of the areas of his questionnaire and came up empty. According to his application, he was supposed to have been born on October 12, 1947, in Boston. I checked the birth records at City Hall this morning. Nothing for that date and nothing up to four years prior or after —not even one Carlos Garcia."

"That's odd," Dennis said, puzzled.

"What's odd about it? Dennis, Boston isn't exactly your everyday Spanish Harlem," Ernest replied, smiling. "And these spics aren't exactly up for the Nobel Prize for telling the truth."

"All we know for sure," related Dennis, his forehead wrinkled up in a frown, "is where he's been, that he's probably with an accomplice, and what he looks and sounds like."

"We know two more things for sure. He's killed that woman in the park and raped Christian George."

"There's still one thing that really baffles me, Ernest."

"What's that?" He put his fork down and pushed his plate away, belching quietly.

"I just can't figure why a guy with Garcia's good looks would have to rape or kill a woman to get—"

"Laid?"

Dennis nodded affirmatively.

"If you'd seen those pictures in his pad you wouldn't wonder." Ernest glanced at the nearby tables to make sure no one could hear him and lowered his voice. "It's probably the only way the bastard can get it off."

Lane, seated behind his desk, reached for the phone and punched out a number with the eraser of his pencil.

"Hello," a gruff voice said, "Headquarters, Sergeant Finney speaking."

"I'd like to speak to Captain Tiernan."

"Just a moment, sir," he said in a low voice that sounded like a short-order cook calling out his order.

"Hello, Captain Tiernan here."

"Ray, Lane Garrett."

"Yes, Lane, what's up?"

"I have somethin' here that's gonna make you a deputy."

Ray Tiernan and Lane had been friends for many years. They often lent a helping hand to each other. On occasion, they would meet at Lane's home socially. Lane admired Tiernan for being a tough cop who came up through the ranks.

"If you have something there that's going to make me a deputy, I know what it is."

"Okay, you got one guess," Lane said.

"You got a check for ten grand that you're going to let me donate to the mayor's campaign."

"I got somethin' better than that."

"Better?" quizzed Tiernan.

"Yeah, better."

"Give me twenty minutes, and put the coffee on."

"You got it, pal, see you then."

Linda knocked at the door.

"Come in."

"Mr. Garrett, I thought you might like a cup of coffee."

He dialed Christian's number, watching Linda set the coffee on his desk and leave.

"Hello."

"Hello, is this my number-one agent?"

"Yes, it certainly is."

"What's cookin'?"

"Lane, Teddy hasn't stopped talking about the pool. He's driving me absolutely crazy. When my mother and I mentioned we might go out for lunch today, he asked if we could go for Chinese food."

"He didn't by any chance mention me?" Lane added with an indignant air.

"Yes, he did."

"What did he say?"

"He said when he grows up, he wants a car just like yours."

"Just for that, he can't use my pool again. He was supposed to say what a great guy I am, and all that other good stuff."

"Well, his mother said that . . . all that good stuff," Christian said softly.

"His mother's a very smart lady." Lane's voice became mellow. "It was a great day, wasn't it?"

"Yes it was."

"Is everythin' okay there?"

"We're fine, Lane."

"Okay, enough idle chatter. I gotta earn a livin'. I'll call you later."

"By, Lane."

"Aloha, number-one agent."

Linda had buzzed Lane on his intercom advising him that Captain Tiernan had arrived. Lane asked her to show him in.

"Hello, Ray, sit down. Linda, please get the captain a coffee."

"Lane, I hope this is worth the trip," barked Tiernan. "I had a date with a sergeant."

"Oh, you switched on me." Lane smiled.

"The sergeant is a she, and what a knockout."

Linda brought in the coffee for Captain Tiernan.

"Thanks, dear," he said.

"You're welcome, sir."

Tiernan tasted the coffee. "Well, Lane, what've you got?"

"Just one moment, my friend, we gotta clear up the ground rules first."

"Are you in some kind of jam?" Tiernan probed.

"Nope," Lane said smugly.

"All right, it's your ball and bat, shoot."

"Whatever rules I bent to give you this information remains a dead issue. It stays with you and me."

Tiernan studied Lane. "Did you have to kill anyone?"

"Christ, no."

"Beat them up?"

"Ray, you know that's not the way I work."

Tiernan smiled. "Considering the operation, anything else would be normal investigative procedure."

"Does that mean we got a deal?"

"Deal," confirmed Tiernan.

"I got the guy that raped and murdered the girl in the Commons."

"You have what!"

"You heard right, Ray. Here's his picture."

"A real pretty-boy face," he commented with surprise. "What's the backup, Lane? Before I put my ass out on a limb, I hafta have a way to get down the tree."

"You're not going to like it."

"I'll suffer through it," said Tiernan dryly.

"We bee and eed his apartment. Here are some photos of the pictures he had on his walls."

Tiernan sorted through the photographs that Ernest had taken. "Well, that proves one thing: He's a wacko, which qualifies him. But do you have anything that puts him there?"

"Yeah, I just happen to have a recordin' of him, puttin' himself there."

"You got someone undercover with him?"

"No."

"Lane, you didn't tap the man's phone?"

Deadpan, Lane blinked at him. "Yep."

"How were you on the guy in the first place?"

"Uh-uh, Ray, that's a no-no. I'm workin' for someone, and this creep fell into my lap during the course of the investigation. That's it."

Tiernan sighed as he said, "Okay, let's hear the recording."

Lane took the player from his desk drawer. They listened to it several times. Finally Tiernan motioned he'd heard enough.

Lane took an extra tape from the drawer and handed it to Tiernan, saying "Remember, I don't know where you got that."

Tiernan was thinking. "What was the thing at the hospital he was referring to? What thing, and what hospital?"

"You gotta take my word for it, Ray, nail him on the murder. The other situation wouldn't be of that much interest to you."

"You leveling, Lane?"

"Haven't I always?"

"Yeah. How about the other man—sounds black to me—you gotta make on him?"

"We don't have any idea who or where he is."

"Where is this Carlos Garcia living?"

"Ray, that's the sixty-four-thousand-dollar question. After the call on the tape, he skipped. His apartment's clean."

"You must have something, anything."

"Well, the guy's a porno freak. We know he plays the combat zone quite a bit and I have a list of past employment, et cetera, that I can give you, but we think they're all phony. We figured the best bets were the combat zone and the apartment he just moved out of. Someone must have known him, seen him moving out. You know, like that."

"I'll schedule a press conference for tomorrow and give them a composite drawing. The story will be that we have a witness who put this man in the Common the night of the murder. Our position will be that he is wanted for *questioning* in the rape-murder of the girl."

"You might want to add he had a *black* accomplice."

"No, Lane, I think I'll hold that back. Maybe the black guy will cop out to save his own ass."

"That could backfire," Lane cautioned.

"How?"

"Supposin' Garcia figures the black guy is the only one that knows about him. My hunch is that you'll find the spade in a trunk."

Captain Ray Tiernan had a sinister smile on his face. "Well, Lane, that's the chance we'll have to take."

"The way I see it, Ray, that's the chance the black guy will have to take."

chapter 13

The phone at Christian George's home was ringing. As she climbed the back stairs from the yard, she assumed it was Lane calling back.

"Hello," the muffled voice said.

Her heart skipped a beat. Terror swept through her at the sound of his voice. She didn't want to accept that it was him calling. Her throat began to quiver as she asked, "Who is this?"

"It's me . . . Carlos . . . Carlos Garcia."

She spoke to him, stammering as she fought to gain control of herself. "You told me your name. Aren't you afraid I'll . . . call the police?"

"It doesn't matter . . . your friend Lane knows about me."

My God! He knows about Lane.

"I saw you yesterday."

She was frightened as she asked, "Where?"

"In the swimming pool." At Lane's house!

She braced herself against the sink's edge before she regained some of her composure. Her mind raced. He was there at Lane's! He saw us. He's watching us.

"Christian . . . are you there?"

Why is he so calm today? It almost sounds like he's half asleep, on tranquilizers . . . something. Think . . . keep him talking. "Yes . . . yes, I'm here."

"That was quite a commotion you had . . . at your house last night."

"What commotion?"

His voice became icy. "Be nice, Christian. Be honest with Carlos. You know . . . when Lane drove off with that man in the car. Did you think that was me in the backyard?"

"Yes . . . we thought it was you."

"That wasn't very nice what you did. You might have hurt the poor man. What did Lane do with him?"

"He took him . . . to the police station."

"Then . . . what?"

"I don't know."

"You're lying again, bitch. Then he came back to your house. I was outside . . . I watched him . . . I was close enough to . . . kill him."

His voice didn't frighten her as much when he talked slow like that . . . so calm, like he was floating on a cloud.

"Why would you want to hurt him?"

"Because you went with him."

She took a deep breath before she spoke. "He's my brother-in-law."

"He's an investigator. He's trying to catch me . . . but he never will."

"I never said he wasn't an investigator. He is, and he is my brother-in-law. He's just trying to help me."

"He might get hurt . . . ha, ha, ha."

His laugh sent chills through her. "Carlos, listen to me."

"Yes . . . Christian."

"If Lane gets hurt, I'll never speak to you again."

"Don't worry, I won't hurt . . . your brother-in-law. Christian, tell me that you're mine. Tell me you want me to make love to you again."

She bit her lip; her insides were shaking. "I'm yours, Carlos. I want you to make . . . love to me again."

"I want you to go away with me . . . far away."

She took a deep breath. "When do you want me to go, Carlos? Where? Do you want me to meet you somewhere?"

"I'll let you know, Christian . . . I'll come for you."

The phone went dead. She sat like a rag doll at the kitchen table, dialing Lane's office.

"Hello, Garrett International."

Her speech was broken as her trembling hand held the phone. "H-hello, may I . . . speak to Mr. Garrett?"

"I'm sorry, he stepped out. May I ask who's calling?"

Oh, Lane, where are you? she thought. "Yes, Christian George. Please let him know I called. It's important."

Washington Street in downtown Boston during the afternoon rush hour was a mass of cars. Lane dodged between them, crossing to the corner of State Street.

Lane muttered to himself: Ya take your goddamn life in your hands crossin' that street.

As he entered his office, Linda informed him that Christian had called, saying it was important, and also that Gina was waiting for him in the conference room.

He stuck his head into the conference room, saying "Honey, gimme a minute, I'll be right with you."

Lane went into his private office and dialed Christian's number. No answer. They must have gone out to lunch, he thought. He walked out of the office to just inside the conference room door. "C'mon, hon, I'm ready for you."

"Are you sure?" Gina said, smiling.

They returned to his office, and Gina shut the door. Lane stood there not moving. She took that as a signal from him and wrapped her arms around him, kissing him.

He held her for a moment, then said, "It ain't the same, is it?"

"What ain't the same?" she asked, knowing full well what he meant.

"You and me, we ain't the same."

She searched nervously in her pocketbook. "Where the hell are those cigarettes?"

Lane lit one of his for her. "Here, take this."

"I wanted to talk to you about the George case." She fidgeted. "It's not gonna go away."

"What, Lane, what is it?"

"I'll tell you what it is. What it is, is what didn't happen when you just kissed me. There was no sirens, no bells. For Christ sakes, there wasn't even a little whistle."

"Lane, please don't."

His voice was soft. "Gina, we've known each other too long to con one another. When I talked about bells and sirens, it didn't happen to me . . . and I know it didn't happen for you. So big deal. Let's not go off the deep end because we don't turn each other on."

"You know, don't you, Lane?"

"Honey, I don't know the who, that's your business. I just don't want to pretend with you, or you with me, 'cause that makes everythin' we ever did together lousy!"

"Have you got a 'who'?" she asked.

"What the hell is this, true confession time?"

"Lane?"

"Yeah."

"Did you ever love me?"

He was serious as he spoke to her. "You know, I think I'll always have a special kinda love for you. Guess I always did. It just wasn't the kind that goes with washing machines, dirty dishes, and kids."

William Fulton had put into motion the intricate network of the FBI's investigative process. As a result, forty-one pages of research were tucked securely within the briefcase he firmly grasped in his hand. He had agreed to meet Dennis Raskin again on Commonwealth Avenue in Brighton. Upon spotting the parked car, he hurried over, opened the door, and shoved the briefcase at his friend.

"Dennis, here is the rest of the information you requested on what's left of that list of nineteen people you gave me."

"Did you find any more skeletons in the closet?"

"No, not really. Basically, it looks pretty much routine except for one or two probables."

"I thought as much," replied Dennis.

"Oh?"

"We have Carlos Garcia definitely pegged as our man. However, looks like the D.A. owns him for murder and rape."

"The Carron woman in the park?" Fulton studied Dennis and shifted in his seat.

Dennis smiled. "Yes, as a matter of fact. How'd you come up with that?"

"I recalled reading about it. It seemed to fit the profile of one of your probables."

"We got lucky, Bill. I only hope our luck holds out until he's apprehended. If it weren't for one key mistake on his part, it could have been months before we knew it was him."

"Oh, how's that?" Fulton asked curiously.

The corners of his mouth turned slightly upward as Dennis spoke. "Someone overheard a conversation with Garcia and another man—he put himself *right in* both cases."

By the look on Dennis Raskin's face, William Fulton decided not to pursue the subject too closely. "I have a feeling I shouldn't ask you how it was overheard."

Ernest had just reached a rented car parked exactly one block from Christian George's home. He took a set of keys from his pocket, opened the trunk, and removed a small tape recorder. Ernest parked the car there yesterday and returned today to change its location and to listen to the tape containing the telephone recordings of Christian George. The tape recorder at his side was voice activated and listened every time the phone in the George home was lifted. It then transmitted the sound to the tape recorder that Ernest had left in the trunk of the rented vehicle. Ernest would return daily to move the car within the four-block area of its signal range, so as not to alert the curiosity of the local residents.

He rewound the tape and listened. Noting the significance of the conversation between Garcia and Christian, he removed the tape, replacing it with a blank one from his pocket. He left the vehicle with the recorder back in the trunk and walked three blocks to his Ford Thunderbird. He stopped at the nearest phone booth and dialed Lane's private number. Lane answered.

"Lane, it's me, Ernest."

"What's up, pal?"

"Garcia. He called the George woman."

Lane became incensed. "That creep! Did he come on heavy with her . . . still layin' the same shit on her?"

"It's worse than that, Lane."

"Worse . . . whadda you mean, worse?"

"He was outside her house last night. He saw you take someone out to the car. He knows about the commotion in the backyard."

"God damn it! I tipped that neighborhood upside down, goin' and comin' . . . I didn't see 'im, Charlie didn't see 'im. Where the hell is this guy hidin'? That son of a bitch!"

"Lane, he's got you made. He followed you yesterday."

"I spotted the tail yesterday. I tried to get behind 'im, but he shook me."

"You might have thought you lost him, but somehow he kept on your ass. Lane"—Ernest hesitated—"the man loves your pool."

"Christ! What did he say?"

"He told her he was in the woods . . . watching you swimming."

"How? No way did he get back on my tail. It's impossible! I wouldda spotted him."

"I gotta agree. That must mean he already knew where you were heading," concurred Ernie.

Lane thought for a minute. "Ernie, that doesn't wash—wait, lemme give it some more thought."

"You want me to bring the tape over?"

"Keep it with you, Ernie, I'm gonna go collect a favor from an old 'friend,' then I better see Christian. I'll call you at your place later tonight."

In the course of his years as an investigator, Lane Garrett had been called on many times by Tony Bucelli. Bucelli was a well-known underworld personality who frequented the more posh places in the city of Boston. He always dressed fashionably, in the most expensive clothes. Neat silver-gray hair, a manicure, a sharp crease in his trousers, and not a speck on his clothes attested to Bucelli's fanaticism on cleanliness.

Rumors around Boston called him one of the leading forces in the world of organized crime. On more than one occasion, Bucelli's hired help would run afoul of the law, and Lane Garrett would be called in to join in the defense of the man. Lane would do all the investigative work, including background checks on the witnesses for the prosecution for any shred of evidence to shake their credibility. Bucelli himself had several years ago faced certain incarceration for a crime that carried up to twenty years in the state penitentiary. Lane Garrett, exercising all of his investigative ability, had, through his evidence, walked Bucelli out of the courtroom a free man, completely absolved of the crime. As a result, Bucelli owed Lane a big one. Today Garrett planned to call in his marker.

Lane was confident he needed no assistance finding Garcia. What worried him was how long it might take. When he learned that Garcia had him connected with Christian, he had decided to pull out all the stops. Garcia would be more careful than ever. Further, Lane felt indirectly responsible for this new feeling of hostility that Garcia had unleashed upon Christian George.

Lane took the elevator to the thirtieth floor of the luxurious Harbor Towers. The building faced the Charles River and the horde of sailboats that frequented its calm waters. Joggers sprinted on the wooded paths bordering the river and extending up to a major traffic artery that led to downtown Boston or the Mystic River Bridge.

As Lane approached Tony Bucelli's penthouse apartment, his steps fell hushed on the thick scrolled carpeting. He knocked. The door was opened.

"Lane, it's good to see you; come in." A gold smoking jacket clung to Bucelli's tall frame. The white-on-white brocade shirt accentuated the black trim of the jacket's lapel and cuffs. Not a strand was out of place in the silver-gray hair that rippled over his head. The warm smile showed his perfect capped teeth.

"Tony, it's real good to see you," Lane greeted, extending his hand.

They walked through the lavish Victorian living room and sat facing each other by the window that fronted the river.

"Can I get you something?" Tony asked.

"Yeah, Tony, some white wine, if you got any."

Tony Bucelli neither drank nor smoked and detested the latter. He was also a health addict. The almost sterile condition of his immaculate apartment confirmed the fact. He returned with a smile and a glass of Corpon Charlemagne, then observed, "Lane, my friend, you're the man who's in a mess. What can I do to help?"

"I need some help finding a man, Tony."

Bucelli sipped on a soft drink. "Lane, I told you any time you need something, ask. You never have, until now . . . so shoot, what is it?"

"The guy is leanin' on a special client of mine. This is strictly off the record now, Tony—he raped her while she was in the hospital. He's the same weirdo who raped and murdered that young Carron girl in Boston Common the other night."

Bucelli's jaw tightened, the muscles twitching. His voice was icy as he spoke. "Lane, a man like that is garbage. He's not worth talking about. I'll take care of it for you."

The words were indirect, but the meaning was there. Bucelli's solution to any problem like this was "put 'em in a trunk." Bucelli never said it quite that way of course, but the results were the same.

Lane smiled. "I gotta tell ya the truth. If you're gonna plant this guy, I pass."

Bucelli ignored Lane's statement. "Lane, I'll need a picture of 'im. Maybe a lead on some of his haunts."

"I can have it to you by tomorrow. As far as his haunts go, the guy's a porno freak. If there's a way to come up with this bum, it's gotta be somewhere in the combat zone." Lane paused, staring Tony in the eye. "Tony, what I said about you plantin' this guy . . . well, you know it's not my action."

Tony Bucelli took a long sip of a soft drink. His voice was without emotion as he spoke. "Lane, you know the rules—you knew 'em before you asked my help."

"Tony, if this is gonna come down heavy . . . then, well, I'll have to handle this myself."

A hard look crossed Tony Bucelli's face.

"Tony, I don't mean any disrespect. You know me a lotta years. Sometimes I say things . . . and maybe they don't set well with people. The one thing you know about me, Tony, is, I never conned ya. When I worked on the cases you gave me—sometimes you didn't like what I said, but I always gave it to you straight. I . . . well—"

Bucelli interrupted him. "Lane, men have died for the way you have talked to me. But you, my outspoken Irish friend . . . well, let's just say you're in another ball game—one I understand and respect you for. You walk into my house and you say, 'Tony, I want.' You don't kiss my ass—you're not afraid. You say, 'Tony, this is how it's gotta be.' I don't like that, but I respect you for it."

Bucelli was smiling at Lane. "You got a lotta balls. I always said you were the only mick I ever really trusted. I got this hunch that you got something goin' with this 'special client' of yours.

You go take care of her—she sounds special. I'll take care of this guy you're looking for." Bucelli paused as Lane cast a quizzical look. "No . . . no, Lane, I won't hurt the man. I'll find him, tie 'im up with a red ribbon—and drop him in your lap."

chapter 14

Lane had picked up Christian at her house. He had listened intently to her describe how Garcia sounded on the phone, as though he were hearing about the call for the first time.

"His voice, what did you say about his voice?"

They were in a small restaurant. Christian stirred cream into her strong coffee and answered Lane.

"It almost sounded as if he were on tranquilizers. He frightens me with some of the things he says. Toward the end of the conversation, he told me he'd come for me. It was just the way he said it—it sent cold chills through me."

Lane looked at her for a moment. "Christian, that's what this man is workin' on, your fear of him. When you were in the hospital, you were easily accessible. It's a different story now. There was a car followin' us on our way to my place on Sunday."

"You knew he followed us?"

"Remember when I pulled off the road to check my tires?"

"Yes."

"Well, there'd been a car followin' us at *that* point. He passed us while we were parked and took the next exit. I gotta bet any kind of money that we weren't followed from that point to my front door."

"Well, how did he know about us being at your house? Swimming in the pool? He said he was watching from the trees."

Lane took a long drag on his cigarette. "The only thing I can figure is, when we left your house, he saw us. Remember Teddy was carryin' his swim trunks in his hands. Maybe the guy took a shot in the dark and assumed that I had a pool and that's where we were headin'."

"He told me he watched us from the trees. How could he know about the trees, if he wasn't there?"

Lane felt certain that Garcia had been watching from the trees, even though he was just as certain he wasn't followed to his house. But he wanted to dispel the theory that Garcia had been there, to set Christian's mind at ease.

"I've thought about that, Christian. There's the possibility that Garcia somehow knew my address. Maybe from seein' my car parked out in front of your house. He could've taken the license plate number, gone to the Registry of Motor Vehicles, and run down the address. Any time after he had that information, he could've gone by my house, and bingo . . . he knows what the surroundin's look like." Lane paused, satisfied he had relieved some of Christian's tension. "Now, c'mon, let's get out of this joint and get some fresh air."

They drove toward the north shore. Lane was thinking how he would break the news that Garcia's face would be on the front page of tomorrow's evening papers. He reasoned that it would alarm Christian further when she read the story that he was wanted for the rape-murder of the girl in the Common.

The black Lincoln cruised down an almost barren street. The ocean was to their left. It was after eleven and the small shops, food stands, and amusement rides were closed at the outdoor entertainment center facing the ocean.

Lane turned the wheel, crossing the divided street. He pulled into an empty parking lot that jutted to a cliff's edge high above the ocean's crashing waves. His bumper gently touched the metal guardrail separating any cars from the drop to the rocks below. The motor was off when he reached in front of Christian's lap to open the glove compartment and take out a Sinatra tape. The windows were down and the fresh salty smell of the sea filled their nostrils. Sinatra was singing "All of Me" as they watched the planes in the distance. The approach pattern was over the water for landing at Boston's Logan International Airport. Tiny lights flickered in the black sky as several planes were in their guide path to the airport. The continuous pounding of the waves and the regression of the tide left the sand on the beach rippled, like the open pages of a book. The night was crisp, with the stars shining brightly.

Christian and Lane gazed across the waves breaking on the rocks and far out into the ocean where a lighthouse beacon blinked steadily in the darkness. She puffed lightly on a cigarette, laying her head back on the car's soft leather headrest—the first to break the silence.

"You like him, don't you?"

"Who?" he asked, his thoughts interrupted.

"Sinatra."

"Yeah, I really dig the man." He took a drag on his cigarette. "The guy's got style . . . real style."

Lane would like nothing better than to talk about Sinatra—or anyone or anything else at this point. He struggled with himself, and finally resigned, he decided to tell Christian about Garcia.

"Christian . . . it's about Garcia. They're gonna run his picture in tomorrow's paper."

"Will that mean . . . they're going to print the story . . . about me?" Christian tried, tried hard to speak calmly, but her sudden pallor and shaking voice betrayed her.

Lane turned to her as she faced him. "Didn't I give you my word that your story would never see print, that you would never see the inside of a courtroom on this?"

"Yes," she admitted nervously. "But how . . . what about Garcia, the picture?"

"I met with a pal of mine today, Captain Tiernan, with some of the material I developed. He's gonna hold a press conference in the morning, saying this guy is wanted for questionin' in the rape-murder of the girl they found in the Common."

"Did he do it? Did he rape another woman . . . and then murder her?"

"Christian, you see, it is like this—"

"Lane," she said, cutting him off, "don't lie to me. Please don't do that. Did he do it? Did he?"

"Yeah," he said, dropping his head. "Garcia raped and murdered that girl." Looking at her, he touched her cheek. "You gonna be okay?"

She reached the hand that was touching her cheek and gently squeezed it. "I'm just a little shaky now, but I'll be all right . . . as long as someone catches him . . . before he catches me."

Gina opened the trunk of her car and removed a manila envelope with information on the George case. She walked through the darkened street and into the building. She took the elevator to the fourth floor, turning left when the doors slid apart, and walked toward her apartment. As she passed the stairwell door, it opened ever so slightly. A man watched her put the key in the lock. He quietly opened the stairwell door, slipped into the hall, and scurried across to Gina. Her back was to him and, with knife in hand, he grabbed a fistful of her jet-black hair.

"You make one sound and I'll slit your fucking throat!"

He held the knife pressed to her throat and pushed her past the unlocked door, slamming it behind him.

Her heart raced. She was gripped with terror as she felt the knife's point against her throat. His arm was wrapped around her, holding her arm, pressing her to him. Her other hand tightly held the clutch purse. As he talked to her, his hot breath was on her neck and the foul smell of it repulsed her.

"I've been waitin' for hours, baby. We're gonna have a little party . . . just you and me."

She struggled to compose herself. "Hey, listen"—her voice was slightly quaking—"violence turns me off. You don't need that knife . . . I'll do what you want."

He reached around and pulled her purse from her, throwing it across the room. "Strip, baby . . . strip for me," he ordered.

Gina had her back to him as she began to take her clothes off. He released his arm from around her while she took off her blouse. She felt her bra being roughly unhooked. Spinning her all the way around, he ripped it off as she stifled a yelp of pain. The bra sailed through the air in front of her. The light-brown hand reached around, squeezing her breasts, the long fingernails cutting her skin.

She swallowed hard as she spoke. "Easy . . . that hurts."

He rubbed his calloused palm hard against her nipple. Spitefully, he pinched and yanked it hard. "The rest of them . . . take them all off."

Her skirt fell to the floor as she felt her panties being jerked down. She heard a zip and suddenly felt his hot erection jabbing at the crease between her buttocks. Without asking, she slowly dropped to her knees and rolled over on her back, facing him.

She opened her bent legs and tried to be convincing as she spoke seductively.

"C'mon . . . we might as well get comfortable."

She stared up at his bulging eyes and her mind screamed: *It's Garcia!*

He smiled sadistically at her, unbuckled his stylish pants, and let them drop to the floor. He pulled off his turtleneck shirt so quickly, his eyes hardly left her crotch.

"That's what I like, baby . . . a little cooperation." He knelt down between her legs and started to insert his throbbing erection.

Gina touched his hand, the one with the knife in it. "Why don't you warm me up a little and I'll show you a real good time . . . the works." She heard herself force the words.

A vulgar smile crossed his lips. Lying down beside her, he stabbed his finger into her vagina, ramming it in and out, cutting the soft flesh with his jagged fingernail. His vile-tasting mouth was crushed against hers, and she nearly gagged when he heaved his drooling tongue inside her. She forced herself to writhe, groaning sounds of pleasure instead of the repulsion she felt. Excited, he dug his teeth cruelly into her neck. She kissed his sweaty chest and stomach as Garcia lay backward onto the carpet, the knife still in his hand. She worked her way down his thigh, her hand resting on his folded knee. Her mouth neared his standing penis. The smell was putrid. She squeezed it with one hand, looking at his face.

His head was lifted, his eyes open wide in erotic anticipation. "Do me, do me, you bitch!" he ordered. "You bite me and I'll cut your tits off." He leaned over long enough to trail the knife sharply along her bosom. He plopped back again and began gyrating his hips, groaning, "Eat me, baby . . . eat me!"

She took a deep breath and, with all her strength, drove her hidden, clenched fist into the center of his testicles, driving them up and almost into his stomach. He yowled in pain, dropping the knife and reaching with both hands for the incredible agony between his legs. Gina scrambled to her feet and made for the door. Carlos sat hunched over on the floor holding his groin, cursing her.

She flung open the door, running down the hallway naked, screaming at the top of her lungs. *"Help! Help! Help me!"*

Garcia, still in immense pain, staggered to his feet. Scooping up his clothes, he limped toward the stairwell while struggling to get his pants on.

Upon hearing the commotion, a man in the apartment at the end of the corridor opened his door and saw a nude Gina running toward him hysterically. "What the hell!" He was riveted to the spot as Gina nearly knocked him over, charging through his open apartment door.

It was ten A.M. and the street was lined with police cars in the heavy traffic on Harrison Avenue in downtown Boston. Policemen milled about outside the huge cement structure with the words BOSTON POLICE HEADQUARTERS visible on the doors. Small clusters of men with cameras climbed the steps and entered the building.

Captain Ray Tiernan had called a news conference to announce the latest developments in the rape-murder of the young Carron girl found in the Boston Common.

The meeting room on the second floor of the old building was teeming with media people. A podium facing the room was cluttered with microphones clipped to the edge of the wooden top. The smoke-filled room was buzzing with speculation about the impeding announcement. Several reporters anticipated the context of the report that was about to be given by Captain Tiernan as he stepped to the podium. He looked at the eager faces that appeared before him like racehorses chomping at the bit.

"Gentlemen," he began, and then, as an afterthought, "and ladies. The composite drawing that is now being passed among you is that of Carlos Garcia, the man we seek for questioning in the rape-murder of Michelle Carron. Reliable witnesses have placed this man in Boston Common on or about the time Miss Carron was assaulted." Tiernan continued. "We ask that you not sensationalize the story in this case, as a medical profile on this man indicates him to be extremely unbalanced. Anything, and I don't use the term freely, *anything* could be the determining factor in causing this man to go over the edge. However, we hope that through your cooperation, we can enlist the public's aid in learning his whereabouts. Are there any questions?" The queries came in rapid succession as bulbs flashed and network cameras ground out their evening reels.

"Captain, how many witnesses?"

"Three."

"Who are they?"

"All I can say is that the composite is the result of the description given to our police artist by two men and a woman."

The questioning continued for another ten minutes before the first of the reporters left to write their stories for the evening edition.

The Boston papers all ran it as their lead story with headlines that read: CARRON KILLING WITNESSED . . . RAPIST-KILLER IDENTIFIED . . . PSYCHO IDENTIFIED AS RAPIST-KILLER.

At six P.M., the early news, presented by Norm Adler, flashed on the television screen in front of Carlos Garcia and his black companion.

"Good evening, this is Norm Adler with the news. Boston Police Captain Ray Tiernan announced today that several reliable witnesses have identified Carlos Garcia"—the sketch of Garcia appeared on the screen—"as being a prime suspect in the brutal rape-slaying of Michelle Carron."

The rest of the story went unheard as Garcia and his companion sat motionless, disbelieving. They had both read it in the late editions. However, seeing it on television had brought them both to the stark realization that they were indeed in trouble.

Garcia lifted his needle-tracked arm upward across his head, his hand wiping the sweat from his face. The other man had shut off the television.

"Hey, man . . . we got some heavy problems."

Garcia looked at his friend. "That lousy mother-fucker!"

"Who—who the hell you talkin' about?"

"Those private pigs! Garrett International, that's who put the badge on us."

"Fuck 'em, man, we gotta think of a way outta this shit. I say we split."

"We ain't splittin'," Garcia insisted.

"Hey, man, they ain't got my picture. I'm splittin'."

"We ain't goin' nowhere until I off one of them private pigs," hissed Garcia.

"Carlos, man, you're flippin' out. I just wanted to ball that chick in the park . . . you was the one decided to carve her up.

I'm tellin' ya, with or without ya, I'm makin' it . . . I'm hightailin' it the hell outta this crazy town."

"Ya gotta help me with the private fuzz first." Carlos glared at him.

The black man got the drift of Garcia's threatening look; it incensed him. "Hey, Carlos, don't you give me none of your jive shit. I'm not some little bitch in the park. I ain't helpin' you with nobody. And another thing, don't fuck around with me or I'll stick that shiv up your ass!"

Garcia studied him for a moment, then heaved an apologetic sigh, apparently relenting. "Sorry, man," he began, shaking his head slowly. "I'm just strung out, uptight."

"Now you're talkin' straight, Carlos," the man said with a trace of suspicion in his dark eyes.

"If we're goin' tonight," Garcia shot back urgently, "we gotta moooove, man—before we get nailed."

"Damn right!" The tall man spun toward the bedroom. "Grab some things an' let's split."

Garcia flew into the room where he'd been staying and packed his things, being careful not to leave a solitary item behind. He darted to the black man's bedroom.

Aware of Garcia's presence, he spoke as he hurriedly moved about collecting his things. "Carlos, I tell ya, this is the only smart thing to do."

"We better move ass, man. Lemme give ya a hand."

As Garcia fidgeted by the bed, his buddy recognized a growing case of the jitters.

"Cool it, Carlos, we'll make it," the man urged, dumping the last pile of his belongings onto the mountain already in the open suitcase.

"But where to?" Garcia brooded nervously. Now pacing up and down behind the man unable to close the suitcase on the bed, Garcia continued his agitated interrogation. "Think we got enough bread to hit L.A.?"

The black man impatiently pushed around the contents in his open two-suiter, hoping to distribute things more evenly. "No sweat, man, I got a stash." Grabbing the hard top of the suitcase, he took a deep breath, ready to exhale it while pressing down on the luggage with all his might. "Ahhh . . . eee . . ." He groaned through clenched teeth.

Garcia had plunged a long, sharp blade straight into his kidney. He pushed the man, forcing him forward over the suitcase, so as to be able to quickly withdraw the knife. To Garcia's displeased surprise, his victim had not collapsed as expected, but instead was beginning an attempt—faltering in pain—to stand and turn at the same time. Garcia clutched the knife handle in both hands, thrusting its blade forcefully into his target's back.

The black man slumped to the floor, face up, erratically gasping for breath. His speech was labored as Garcia stood above him, blood dripping from the knife.

"Carlos . . . you . . . you . . . Jap . . . mothah . . . fuckah."

Garcia straddled him, leaning down and plunging the knife again and again into his chest. He raved at the lifeless form. "You creep, you gonna stick the knife up my ass . . . you gonna leave Carlos . . . yeah, you gonna leave him . . . dead!"

The grin on Garcia's face suddenly and grimly changed. "Where's the fuckin' list?" he shouted to the stilled body beneath him. He ran to the kitchen and started to throw everything on the floor. He had to find that damn list. He recognized his scribbled handwriting on a short piece of paper, grabbed it and held it before his eyes. It had the names and addresses of Gina Cataldo, Lane Garrett, Dennis Raskin, and Ernest Hampton. Once he had gotten their license plate numbers, it had been easy getting their addresses from the Registry of Motor Vehicles.

He stared at the names, committing them to memory. As he repeated them without looking at the paper, his face filled with feelings of hate . . . and revenge.

Carlos Garcia walked to the door with suitcase in hand. He set it down there, took a can of lighter fluid from the cupboard, and doused the wooden furniture in the black man's bedroom. Smiling slightly, he lit a match. *Whoosh,* the room was in flames instantly. He casually opened the door, picked up his suitcase, and disappeared, taking the black man's money and the keys to his car with him.

Lane Garrett had received a call from Gina earlier in the day. He wasted no time reaching her apartment. She cautiously answered his knock. He closed the door softly behind him and reached out to hold her in his arms, neither saying a word for the moment.

"Are you okay?" His voice was concerned, tender.

"Sure, I'm fine," she answered quietly.

"Garcia, are you sure it was him?"

"It was him . . . I could describe him right down to his ding-dong."

Lane took a short step back, holding her by the shoulder, and smiled at her. "You know, you got a one-track mind."

"There's a good chance I put him out of commission for a while. It should be at least a month before those little aggies of his drop down from inside his stomach." She smiled. "Want some coffee?"

"Yeah, let's sit down."

Gina poured them both a cup as they sat in the small kitchen. She took a sip and spoke.

"Lane, he was really disgusting. Cruel, sadistic . . . smelly, his foul breath . . . and that face . . . that virgin face. It was unreal. He really blew my mind."

Lane took out a cigarette from his package, lit it, and handed it to Gina. He then lit one for himself, took a long drag, and slowly let the smoke out. He looked at her. "Your gun, sweetheart. Why didn't you blow the son of a bitch away?"

"I never got the chance. Besides," she stated with a straight face, "you know me, I love pain."

"For Christ sakes, be serious."

Her voice trembled as she spoke. "I'm too goddamn scared to be serious!"

Lane got up from the chair and walked over to her. He leaned down, kissing the top of her head and holding her.

She broke, crying and sobbing. "Lane . . . he's a madman. Filthy hands, he . . . touched me . . . all . . . over, hurting me. I was on . . . the floor . . . he almost . . . had . . . had me."

The two men stood facing each other. Elliot Rothman, backed against the wall in his apartment, the sweat dripping into his swollen eyes, pleaded with Garcia.

"You're blinding me, Carlos." He rubbed his eyes to try to erase the painful stinging within them.

Carlos laughed, then jabbed several shots with his already bruised fists into Rothman's unguarded stomach.

"God"—Rothman cringed—"that kills . . . I've got an . . . ulcer."

His hands fell to his beltline and he grabbed at his gut like a pregnant woman holding herself up. As he did so, Garcia lashed out again and again at Rothman's face until blood started to run from a cut above the man's eye.

"Christ, Carlos." Rothman moaned, as he started to slide downward along the wall to the floor. "You're killing me . . . please . . . enough . . . I've had enough."

"You don't look pretty enough for me." Garcia sneered, propping Rothman back up against the wall with one hand and smashing his other fist into the man's badly bruised and discolored cheekbone.

Dennis Raskin was seated at his kitchen table drinking the last of his coffee. His wife had gone out, commenting that while it was still light out, she'd better do the grocery shopping.

Dennis had the photos that Ernest Hampton had taken spread on the table before him. One by one, over and over, he carefully studied them. The pictures, something kept drawing him back to the pictures. Dr. Harrison, Dr. Spellie, Don Spencer, Dr. Schneiderman, nurses, orderlies, kitchen help—all there except the X-ray tech's. Over and over, Dennis scrutinized the photos.

The phone's ringing broke into Dennis's thoughts. Absentmindedly he groped for the phone, noting for the first time that it had become dark outside.

"Hello. Hello, Dennis?"

"Yes."

"It's me, Elliot, Elliot Rothman."

Elliot Rothman was an informer who had worked for Dennis in his FBI days. Since then Rothman would occasionally call him with a hot tip that Dennis would pass on to the proper sources. Rothman, as well as other informers, had Dennis's private number.

"Elliot, how are you?"

"I gotta see you."

"When?"

"In an hour," Rothman rasped, then urgently added, "It'll really make you flip."

"What is it?" asked Dennis.

"Uh-uh. All you get over the phone is, it's someone hot."

"Where do you want to meet, Elliot?"

"Pick me up on the corner of Dover and Washington streets."

"Will do, Elliot, see you then."

The phone went dead. When it came to Rothman, Dennis knew two things: that the information was usually accurate and that the man would want a small amount of money.

Half an hour later, Dennis was ready to leave. He walked quietly into the kitchen where his wife stood with her back to him putting away the groceries. As she reached into one of the brown paper bags on the counter, Dennis moved up behind her and, in a flash, his arms were around her middle-aged spread, squeezing her in a tight hug.

"Oh!" She yelped in startled surprise. "You'll be the death of me yet, Dennis Rascal," she scoldingly said, immediately clutching the hands clasped beneath her bosom. "You almost scared the life out of me." She patted his hands as if to say that it was all right but that she had things to do.

He understood her message but, rather than release her, he inched the back of her even closer to him, resting his chin in the scoop of her shoulder.

He hadn't fooled her for one second. Mary Raskin knew that an outward display of affection such as this from a man such as Dennis could only mean one thing—he had something to tell her that he knew she'd rather not hear. Pressing her folded arms against his in a long hug, she waited.

"Hon, I'm going out. I'll be back in an hour," he whispered in her ear.

"Oh, Dennis . . ." She moaned in disappointment, knowing that "an hour" of his was more like three or four hours her time. "Not tonight." As he relaxed his arms, she unfolded them with her hands and turned slowly toward him. "Must you go?" She knew the answer but continued her warm pleading. "We so rarely have a whole evening together . . . for just ourselves."

Dennis knew that she wasn't referring only to those nights he was gone, but also to those he spent at home working hours on end on some case. He knew she had to be lonely. He cupped her cheeks in his hands. "After I get this case wrapped up," he began with sincerity in his eyes, "we'll go on that long trip . . . just the two of us, I promise."

Mary Raskin had memorized those words long ago. "All right, dear," she responded compassionately, "I understand."

He leaned over and kissed the soft smile on her lips. "Oh, heck, I'll be late if I don't get a move on."

"Pick me up some cigarettes, dear, I forgot to get some." She turned her back, pretending to busy herself so he wouldn't see her face.

"You ought to quit smoking those things," he called, heading for the front door.

"Get me four packs; I'll quit right after that."

He smiled to himself as he got into his car: She's been quitting after four packs for the past twenty years.

As Dennis pulled up to the corner of Washington and Dover, he did not see Elliot Rothman. Elliot was hidden in the shadow of a building, and, spying Dennis, he hurried to his car and got in. Nervous, he immediately looked around to see if anyone had seen him enter Raskin's car.

"Easy, Elliot, take it easy, no one saw you."

As Dennis suddenly got a full look at Rothman, he did a double-take at the misshapen face—bruised, swollen, and cut with one eye nearly sealed shut.

"Elliot, are you okay?" he asked.

"Yeah, yeah, just drive, will ya, Dennis."

"Who did this?"

"It's the guy I gotta talk to you about." Rothman suddenly slid all the way down in his seat as the car approached three men standing on a corner. His fear distorted his face all the more.

"It's all right now, Elliot. You can sit up, we passed them," advised Dennis.

Cautiously peering around, Rothman eased back up in his seat. "I got somethin' big, really big. It's gonna cost you three hundred."

"Three hundred!"

"I'm tellin' you, Dennis, this information is heavy."

"All right, what is it?"

"How about the three hundred?"

"I have to know what I'm buying first. You know that."

"If you don't like what you hear, you let me out of this car and forget I ever said it. Deal?" He slid his pointed forefinger under his runny nose and waited anxiously for an answer.

"Deal," agreed Dennis.

"The guy whose picture's in the paper, the one who hit on the girl in the park, I got *him!*"

Dennis did not appear enthusiastic as he spoke. "Do you know where he is?"

"Who'd ya think did this number on me? I know where he is, but are you buyin'?"

"If you come up with the address, I'll buy," said Dennis.

"I got it . . . the address." Rothman fidgeted.

Dennis reached into his pocket, keeping one hand on the wheel. He had one hundred sixty dollars in cash. He gave Elliot one hundred fifty. "Where can I find him? I'll give you the rest tomorrow."

"For this I should get the whole bundle, but for what that prick did to me, I'll give you credit. He's at my place, stoned out of his skull, passed out on the bed. If he wasn't, I'd be on a slab in the morgue. He showed up at my door this A.M. . . . wanted to stay there . . . so he beat the shit out of me. He's been shot up all day—he's out of it."

"Show me, Elliot."

Rothman gave the directions. They entered into a predominantly black section of Boston. As Dennis passed a row of dilapidated tenement buildings, Rothman waved his finger wildly at where he was now living. Dennis parked the car and followed Rothman down a flight of steps to the basement apartment. As Rothman nervously indicated a splintered wooden door, Dennis automatically patted the gun he wore at his side. Rothman opened the door, pointing to a door at the far end of the room.

"That's the bedroom; he's in there." He whispered in a jittery voice, "Lemme check him out first."

With Rothman leading the way, the two quietly headed for the closed door. Just as Rothman's hand touched where the knob used to be, Dennis felt a sharp pain in the center of his back. Instinctively Dennis tried to pull the gun from its holster, but Rothman grabbed onto his wrist with both hands and held him. The big knife gleamed in the dim light as once again Garcia plunged it into his back. Dennis jerked straight up, stiffening, his eyes glazed. He only had time to think of his wife and the sad fact that Rothman talked too much.

"Damn you, you creep," Garcia shrieked at Rothman. "Cut him, cut him. You cut 'im or you gonna end up next to him."

Rothman, now shaking hysterically, suddenly pulled big Buck lockblade from his pocket and, joining Garcia, began stabbing Dennis in the midsection again and again. Dennis slumped to the floor, the air escaping from his lungs.

chapter 15

Lane Garrett had stopped at a small convenience store around the corner from his office. He had purchased the Boston *Globe* and the *Herald American,* the two Boston morning editions. He tucked them under his arm as he approached the front of his office building. He spotted Dennis Raskin's car parked there, a ticket on the windshield. Lane thought to himself: That Dennis, he's pushed his luck parkin' in the no parking zone. Lane took the ticket from the windshield, reading the time it was issued—nine-twenty A.M. He replaced the ticket and glanced at his gold watch. Nine forty-five. He was probably in a hurry, Lane thought. He entered the office expecting Dennis to be waiting for him. He paused before Linda's desk.

"Any calls, hon?"

"No, sir," she replied.

"Dennis waitin' for me?"

"No, sir."

"He isn't here and hasn't called?"

"No, sir. I haven't heard from Mr. Raskin."

Lane went into his office, turning on the lights. That's strange, he thought. Maybe he's havin' breakfast with someone. He dialed Christian's number.

"Hello."

"Hello, Christian?"

"No, Lane, it's me, the older version. Just a moment, I'll get her."

"Hi, Lane."

It was a happy "Hi, Lane" that he heard. He knew before he asked that she hadn't received another phone call last night.

"I take it our Spanish friend didn't call you last night."

"You take it right. Neither did my Irish friend."

"Whadda you want, two guys callin' you?"

"Yes, when the other one is you."

"Okay, uncle. You got me dead to rights. I was workin'."

"The old working trick," she said happily.

"Listen, I gotta problem."

"What is it, Lane?"

"That pool of mine is gettin' stale again . . . and I was wonderin', well, if you aren't doin' anythin'."

She interrupted him. "What time will you pick us up on—"

"Eleven sound okay?" He rushed his answer before she could say Sunday.

"Yes, that sounds fine."

"By thc way, don't let your mother make any plans. I'm dyin' to catch her in a bathin' suit."

"I'll be sure she comes with us. She's waited all year to wear her new bikini." She paused, her voice becoming serious. "Lane, I read about Garcia in the papers and watched the television accounts."

"That publicity will put a ton of heat on this guy. Someone will drop a dime on him; he's as good as gone. Hey . . . I don't want to, but I gotta go. I'll be in touch."

"By, Lane."

"Good-bye, number-one agent."

He hung up the phone and muttered to himself: Where the hell's Dennis? He's gonna have a conniption when he finds that fifteen-dollar ticket on his windshield.

Lane's intercom buzzed.

"Yeah, Linda, what is it?"

"Mr. Garrett, I have Mrs. Raskin on line one."

"Thanks, Linda, I'll take it."

"Hello, Mary," Lane answered, lighting up a cigarette.

"Lane, I'm worried sick."

"Mary, what is it?" The smoke puffed from his mouth with each word.

"I wanted to call you earlier but I thought I'd wait until ten.

It's Dennis. He left the house last night to meet someone and hasn't come home yet."

"Who did he go meet?"

"Lane, you know Dennis. He got a phone call and said he'd be gone about an hour. He never tells me who he's meeting."

"Mary, try not to be upset. I'm sure there's a reasonable explanation." Lane tried to calm her. "I know he can't be far; his car is parked right outside the building."

"Lane, please have him call as soon as you see him."

"Don't worry, I'll track him down and give 'im hell for stayin' out without callin' you."

"Thank you."

A cold chill came over Lane. He knew Dennis was not the type to stay out the whole night, not even if it meant capturing Al Capone. He thought about the ticket on the windshield: It had been ticketed at nine-twenty. But could have been there all night.

Lane slowly crushed out his cigarette in the desk ashtray, pushing aside the ashes with its stub. He couldn't get Dennis's car off his mind. He rushed from the office, calling back as he ran, "Linda, I shouldn't be gone too long."

"Yes, Mr. Garrett."

Lane walked briskly through the lobby and front doors to Dennis's car. He got in and looked around the interior. No note, nothing. He sat there thinking: Damn it, Dennis just wouldn't stay out like that . . . he'd call Mary or let her know that he was still on a case. Something, he'd tell her something. *Where the hell is he?* Reluctantly he got out the driver's side and walked slowly to the rear of the car. He stared at the trunk, hoping he wouldn't see any indication of—anything. There! On the lip, between the trunk and the bumper . . . dark-red spots stained the light-colored finish. Lane put his finger on one of them, rubbing it against his thumb. It was still moist, sticky. His heart skipped a beat as the realization struck him.

"No!"

He raced to his office, immediately calling his friend Captain Tiernan. "Ray, this is Lane. Meet me out in front of your office in ten minutes. Make sure you bring a set of General Motors master keys."

"What the hell's the problem, Lane, you lock yourself out of your car?"

Lane's breathless voice was urgent and alarming. "Ray, please, just be there!"

Not waiting for Captain Tiernan to ask questions, he banged the phone down, his thoughts already across the room. He dashed over to the wall, sliding back the glass cabinet doors as his eyes skimmed the gadgets and the electronic paraphernalia. Grabbing what he wanted, he flew out of the office past his startled secretary and down to Dennis's car. He almost hit a passerby as he swung open the door and jumped inside. He popped the ignition switch off with a slide-hammer and then, with two fingers, he pulled out the exposed wires. When he touched two exposed tips together, the car's engine groaned and started. He twisted the two wires together and slammed the car into drive.

Lane had no patience for the heavy morning traffic on Washington Street. He darted in and out between cars, oblivious to the curses of the drivers. More than once he sped through intersections, ignoring the red light.

Recognizing Tiernan's large form coming down the steps just up the block, he accelerated, blaring the horn until he slammed on the brakes in front of police headquarters. Tiernan recognized a man in a hurry and immediately jumped into the passenger side.

"Where's the police garage?" Lane demanded before Tiernan could speak.

"Just around the corner." He pointed, totally perplexed.

"Got the keys?"

"Yes . . . but . . ."

Before he could finish, Lane was turning the corner on two wheels.

"Lane, what the hell is going on? Whose car is this?"

"Dennis Raskin didn't get home last night. I think there's blood on the lip of the trunk."

Lane headed the car to the far corner of the huge underground parking area. Both he and the captain bounded from the car, rushing to the back.

Holding the keys, Tiernan asked, "Do you want me to open it?"

Lane just shook his head and took the keys, inserting one and tried turning the lock . . . nothing. The fourth key worked.

The trunk lid snapped open.

Lane and Tiernan were momentarily frozen to the cold cement floor. They gaped at the crumpled, lifeless corpse of Dennis Raskin—his eyes still open, the look of horror and shock still in them. His shirt was ripped to shreds and saturated with blood. Blood seeped from his stomach, forming a dark-red pool on the bottom of the trunk. Lane leaned over and gently closed the eyes and touched the cold face.

"Holy Christ . . . why? Why?" As if expecting an answer, Lane talked to Dennis. "How'd they get to you . . . who did this to you, pal?" He turned his head away, tears streaming from his eyes.

"I'll take care of it, Lane," declared Tiernan, placing a hand on his friend's shoulder.

"Yeah." Lane choked softly, crying. "You . . . take care . . . of him."

Lane walked off to the side of the garage. He was bitter and frustrated, hurt and angered. He would not, could not, stop the tears. He was unashamed as policemen filed past him making preparations to remove the body and dust the car for prints. He thought about his friend Dennis Raskin: He had faced a hundred criminals in his time, kidnappers, hijackers, bank robbers, murderers . . . and he took 'em all down. Twenty years, not a scratch. Now . . . now, he had to go like this. He thought about the way Dennis's body was mutilated. Garcia! The hate welled up in him. That little son of a bitch was gonna take a *hard* fall if I hafta track 'im to hell! he thought angrily.

Tiernan approached Lane. The tears had stopped, but he still shook inside as the captain spoke. "Lane, how do you want me to break this?"

Sniffling, Lane answered. "Better just say he was on vacation. If we crack that he was working on the Garcia thing, it wouldn't do us any good. I don't wanna scare that bastard off!"

"All right," Tiernan agreed slowly, "we might slant it toward an alleged old enemy that he had from his days as a federal agent."

"Yeah, that's as good a story as any. I don't want any more heat put on that spic, Garcia. Let's not make him run . . . not now."

"His wife, I'll tell her before we release it," Tiernan murmured sadly.

"No, Ray, no. You gotta let me take care of that."

Tiernan drove Lane back to his building. Without checking with his office, Lane proceeded to his car. It was a twenty-five-minute drive to Dennis's house, and Lane kept mulling over how he'd break the news to Mary.

The black Lincoln pulled up in front of Dennis Raskin's home. The grounds were beautifully kept, for it was Mary's hobby. Lane went somberly to the front door and rang the bell. He waited for a moment—no answer. He walked around to the side of the house, opened a small white picket gate, and entered the backyard. Mary was on her knees, her back to him, tending her flower bed.

"Mary," he called softly.

She turned and stood up. She saw Lane's reddened eyes, tear-stained face, and sober look. Panic rose in her as she spoke.

"Dennis . . . he's hurt, isn't he?"

Lane walked toward her without answering. She still had the gardening spade in her hand, her white gardening gloves on.

"Lane . . . is he badly hurt?"

Lane took her by the shoulders. Try as he might, he could not hold back the flood of tears. His voice cracked as he whispered, "Mary, he's gone."

The spade dropped from her hand, clanking against the cement walkway. "My God! Lane, he's not . . . dead?"

She began crying, sobbing. "Oh, Lane, not now. We had so many plans. What happened to him . . . what happened?"

"We think it's a result . . . of one of . . . his old arrests. When he was with the bureau."

"What . . . will I do . . . without him?" She sobbed.

Lane walked her into the house and remained until her sister and family arrived. He called his office and quietly instructed Linda to have Ernest, Gina, and Tom O'Brien waiting for him in the conference room within the hour. After consulting with Mary, he placed a call to Welling's Funeral Parlor in Framingham to arrange for the interment of her husband. He instructed the owner that he would "pick up the tab," and not to advise Mary Raskin until after the burial.

Lane walked into the conference room. They were waiting for him there. He instructed Linda to lock the door, inform the answering service to take all calls for the next hour, and to join them. The mood of the hour was written on his face.

Gina, not knowing about Dennis's death and sensing Lane's somber mood, attempted to cheer him up. "What's the matter, boss, you get your eviction notice?"

Lane did not acknowledge her. "I wanted you all here so I could tell you before you heard it through the media." With swollen red eyes, he looked directly at them. "It's Dennis. He was murdered last night. I think Garcia . . . somehow suckered him."

They sat there stunned. Silent.

"I found him . . . in his trunk. He was ripped apart. They stabbed him—"

Lane got up as his eyes overflowed and walked to the window. Gina had her hands cupped to her face as tears spilled between her fingers.

He turned back to them. "Listen," Lane said, his voice cracking, his throat parched from crying, "there had to be two of 'em. This kid Summers, maybe he's workin' with Garcia. Maybe it was the black guy . . . maybe . . . maybe."

"Jesus Christ," Ernest cursed. "Where the hell does that kid fit in?"

"We're gonna find out," seethed Lane. He took a handkerchief from his pocket, blew his nose, and lit up a cigarette. "I'll put out some feelers on my own. No one gets off Garcia! I want him to go down. And I want us to do it. You all understand that?"

He looked at each of his people in turn and they all nodded their heads in agreement.

"All right. Then what are we sittin' here for?"

Two hours later Lane was seated at his desk as his intercom buzzed. It was Linda informing him that Captain Tiernan was on the line.

"Yeah, Ray."

"Lane, the black man that Garcia was running with. We found him."

"Where?"

"He can't do us any good, Lane, he's dead."

"How do you know it's the guy we're looking for?"

"His apartment was set on fire. One of the neighbors called it in before it had a chance to do much damage. On a hunch, I had

Garcia's picture shown to the people in the building, and two of them made him. As for the black guy, all the stab wounds were unusually large—they match up with the same ones we found . . . in Dennis's back."

"I knew it. I knew that lousy bastard Garcia was behind it," Lane groaned out.

"Lane, there's a good possibility Garcia has another man working with him. The wounds in Dennis's abdomen were much smaller than those in his back. We figure it's Garcia and at least one other man."

"Ray, I got someone else workin' on this case too. If he comes up with anythin', I'll call you."

"If you find him first . . . don't do anything foolish."

Lane ignored the remark. "Thanks for callin', Ray."

Lane scanned the reports on his desk from his other operatives. He made notations on each of them but was finding it increasingly difficult to concentrate. The intercom buzzed and Linda advised him that Mrs. George was on line one.

"Hello, Christian, is anythin' wrong?" Lane was automatically apprehensive that she had received another phone call.

Her voice was soft, consoling. "No, Lane, we're all fine. I just wanted to call you. I just heard a radio bulletin about that man who worked for you. I'm sorry."

It touched Lane that she had called. "How's Teddy and your mother?"

She had already told him that they were all fine, so she sensed he didn't want to talk about Dennis any further.

"Teddy is in the backyard playing with one of his friends—I'm watching him out the window—and my mom's gone to the store. Lane, I have to be in town this afternoon; will you have time for lunch?" She lied about having to be in town. She felt he needed someone to be with.

"That's the best news I've gotten . . . well, in quite a while. Yeah, that would be great. What time?"

"How about if I meet you in front of Zito's at one-thirty?"

"That's fine with me; see you then."

"Good-bye, Lane," she said affectionately.

He felt a need to be with her as her voice warmed him. "Good-bye, number-one agent," he said, almost whispering.

As he hung up the phone, his mind's eye pictured her. Lost in thoughts, he was interrupted by the buzzing of the intercom—Linda advising him Dr. Spellie was there to see him.

Lane rose to greet Spellie as he walked in and over to the desk.

"Lane, I wanted to stop in and tell you how badly I felt about your man, Dennis Raskin."

"Thanks, Bob, I really appreciate it. You know in this business you learn to expect anythin'. But this, I dunno . . . I just can't get it through my head that the guy's gone, that I'm never gonna see him walk through that door again. I've handled hundreds of cases in my time, but this one, with Christian . . . the whole number is straight out of the horror show." He lit a cigarette from the one already burning. "The woman's husband is killed, she's raped in the hospital, and, if that ain't enough, this nut is loose killin' people . . . and Gina, before that he tried to rape Gina. I tell you, Bob, this guy's a one-man crime wave."

Robert Spellie repeated slowly, *"Killing* people?"

"Needless to say, Bob, that stays inside these walls. You might as well know. He's killed two people—besides that Carron girl—the black guy he was runnin' with and . . . Dennis. I'm only tellin' you this to impress on you how dangerous the guy is. I keep gettin' this feelin' that he's gonna show at that hospital. I don't know why . . . somethin's in my head that tells me he's got a reason to go back there."

Spellie was shocked. "Lane, three people, he's killed three people! Do you think there's any danger to the people at the hospital?"

"Bob, you're the shrink, you tell me. I only know that the guy's a lunatic . . . I wouldn't put anythin' past him."

"I feel responsible," Spellie confessed. "I brought you into this mess. Maybe if I hadn't, Dennis would be . . . alive."

"You're outta the ballpark with that kind of thinkin'. It's like me sayin' that if I'd caught the guy sooner, everythin' would be okay. Well, I gave it my best shot, and you gave it yours by callin' me. No, Bob, we're not responsible . . . it's the freako with the knife, he's the one responsible."

"Mrs. George, how is she? Does she know about Garcia doing the killings?"

"She had every right to know . . . I told her. Bob, she's okay. She's scared, but who the hell wouldn't be? She's some kinda lady."

"She must be going through hell, Lane."

"That reminds me, who's the head man in that hospital?"

"The chief administrator and chairman of the board is Jonathan Prendergast."

"Have you kept Prendergast posted on the George case?"

"Yes, I have Lane, and he's very grateful to her for not bringing it to the attention of the media."

"I'd like you to do somethin' for me, Bob."

"What?"

"I'd like you to arrange a meetin' between me and your Mr. Prendergast."

"Is there something I can help you with?"

"No, I think I'll have to take it up with Prendergast. I wanna find out just how *grateful* he is."

"Lane, could I ask you what you have in mind?"

"Bob, the lady was raped in that hospital. That nut is still callin' her, puttin' her through hell. She's afraid to go to the store; she carries a *gun.* The guy has told her he'll hurt her son if she doesn't play with him. Why, her and her mother're so damned scared they nearly killed one of my agents who was in their backyard tryin' to protect 'em. What I have in mind is compensation, money, bread." Lane's voice quieted. "Besides, she needs it. I checked her out; she's in bad financial shape."

"I agree with you, but Prendergast is a very tough customer. The man has ice water in his veins."

"Bob, you set up the meetin'; I think maybe I can warm 'im up."

Gina sat with Don Spencer in a lounge that was off the beaten path. She had called him at his apartment and said that she had the day off from the insurance company. As they sat there sipping their drinks, she could not hide the hurt she felt from the death of Dennis Raskin.

"Gina, what is it, what's wrong?"

She fidgeted nervously with her cigarettes. "Did you read about the ex-FBI agent, Dennis Raskin?"

"Yes, I remember hearing about it on the news."

"He was a friend of my father's. Don . . . I miss him so, he was like a second father." She lied about the fact that he was a friend of her father's but not about her missing him.

Don reached across the table and placed his hand on hers. "Gina, the man was in a business that has no guarantees. He could go out every day for a hundred years and never have a problem . . . or get hurt. It happens to some. Maybe they get careless for just a second—maybe it's just bad luck or fate. Whatever the reason, it goes with the territory. Some men get killed."

Her eyes had filled up. "It stinks, Don . . . the whole world stinks."

He smiled at her. "I hope you don't include me in that."

She squeezed his hand. "I'm sorry, Don . . . I just keep looking for a reason why a man like Dennis Raskin should get killed, and I can't find one. It doesn't seem right. Why Dennis . . . why?"

"Why anybody? Why cancer, why . . . why . . . why, Gina? I don't know the answers. I only know one thing for sure." His look was warm and caring as his eyes met hers.

"What—what do you know for sure?"

His hand was warm on hers. "The only thing I know for sure is that I love you."

It took her completely by surprise. She felt herself weaken. Her throat went dry. It seemed like an eternity before she could speak. "Don, you don't know anything about me."

The love flowed from him as he spoke. "Yes, yes, I do. I know from the time I get up in the morning until I close my eyes at night, I think of you. I know when I see something beautiful, or soft, or warm . . . I think of you. I know that when I leave you at night I can't wait until the next day . . . to see you. Gina, I don't know the reasons, and I'm not pushing you to say you feel the same, I just know I love you very much."

Her hands trembled as she picked up her drink, nearly finishing it in one swallow. "I'll say one thing for you," she quipped nervously, "you certainly know how to brighten a girl's day."

"Is that all you want to say?" he asked.

"Don . . . don't . . . not now."

He leaned across the table. "All right. I'll find out what I can at headquarters about your friend Dennis Raskin."

He kissed her gently on the lips, as she thought: My beautiful, beautiful liar. She knew he lied about his job, but not about loving her. Nothing else mattered.

Unaware of the Garrett operative following her, Christian met Lane in front of Zito's at one-thirty. Rather than dine there, they walked six blocks to the Quincy Market. Lane wanted to avoid all the well-meaning people at Zito's who he knew would extend their condolences. They walked at a leisurely pace with Lane steering Christian toward a vendor selling hot dogs.

He looked at her, a childish smile upon his lips. "I gotta tell you somethin'. I can't pass one of these carts without buying one. It's been that way ever since I was a kid. I dunno what it is, but their franks always seem to taste better. Maybe these guys got a secret recipe. Want one?"

"Yes, love one. Onions, relish, mustard, the works."

"You're a lady after my own heart." He turned to the vendor. "Give us two dogs with the works, and gimme a couple of them sodas."

They sat on an empty bench, eating and watching the throngs of people passing through the marketplace.

"Christian, about Sunday, well, with Dennis . . . it's probably bad timing."

"I understand," she answered warmly. As he had done so many times with her, she now tried to cheer him. "Lane Garrett, you're a crafty, devious person. Yes, that's what you are, crafty and devious."

"What! Smile when you say them words. Just what do you mean by that?"

"I mean, you have filled me up on these cheap hot dogs and that's a very sly way out of buying a girl a decent meal."

"I had no such thing in mind. Why, if you want, we'll go right from here to the swankiest joint in this broken-down town." He smiled as he said it.

"Listen, as long as I'm full, can I have the money instead?"

"Hey," retorted Lane, "that's a hell of a line. I'm gonna steal it from you. After all, you're always usin' my stuff."

"Be my guest." She tried her Bogart imitation on him again. "Sweeeetheart."

They walked slowly back toward the office, Lane automatically hooking his arm under hers. As they stopped in the parking lot beside her small car, Lane saw his operative get into a car, ready to follow her back home.

"I'd like to take you into Zito's for our after-dinner drink"—

Lane smiled—"but there's a lot I gotta take care of. I'm probably gonna be busy for the next few days."

"Lane, will you do something for me?"

"I don't think you could ask me anythin' I'd say no to."

"There doesn't have to be a reason, but if you just feel like talking, will you call me?"

Lane Garrett was not aware of the people passing, nor the cars that entered and left the parking lot. For the moment he only saw Christian and felt her warmth. "Yeah." He spoke softly. "I'll call, and if I can't think of a reason . . . I'll make one up."

She kissed him on the cheek. "Take care. I'm with you, Lane." She turned to leave.

"Christian."

"Yes?"

"You're stealin' my lines again." He grinned.

A hazy sun broke through the morning sky, shining down on the funeral procession in Saint Michael's Cemetery. The hushed closing of the car doors and the quiet shuffling of mourners replaced the morning stillness. Mary Raskin, her grown son, and her family were at the graveside of Dennis Raskin. Slowly the rest of the procession joined them. Directly behind Mary Raskin was Lane Garrett, Gina, Linda, Ernest, and Tom O'Brien. William Fulton of the FBI was there with a number of his colleagues. There were scores of friends and relatives along with Captain Ray Tiernan and a contingent of Boston Police that knew Dennis Raskin. They were all there in one common bond—to pay homage to Dennis Raskin.

The priest, who looked older than Methuselah, was a master with the words of his faith. As it ended, Lane leaned forward, holding Mary Raskin by the arm, and kissed her on the cheek.

"Mary, I'll be in touch."

She nodded her thanks.

Leaving their cars at the church, Gina, Linda, Ernest, and Tom O'Brien had all ridden with Lane to the cemetery. They headed toward his car as Lane felt someone tapping him on the shoulder. He turned. It was William Fulton.

Lane held his hand out. "Bill."

"Lane, do you have a minute?"

"Sure." Lane motioned the rest of his people to his car, calling "I'll be right with you."

William Fulton and Lane walked out of the path of people leaving the graveside.

"Any leads on Garcia?" asked Fulton.

"Bill, we seem to be one step behind him . . . close, just close."

"Dennis was one of my closest friends, Lane."

"I know, Bill . . . I loved the man."

"Are you sure it was Garcia?" Fulton frowned.

"All the facts point to him and, one other thing that never failed me, my gut tells me it's him."

"Lane, it had to be someone he knew, to call him at his house, to get him out."

"I thought about that. The way I see it, maybe a stoolie he used to work with. If he's tied in with Garcia, the guy's probably a junkie."

"We had the same idea and we're checking out everyone who ever gave him information."

"Will you keep me posted, Bill?"

"Lane, let's keep each other posted."

"I won't argue with you on that, Bill. I'll stay in touch."

He started to walk away as Fulton called to him. "Lane."

Lane turned. "Yeah?"

"Until we find Garcia, you own my office. *Anything* you want, call me."

Lane was driving back to the church. Gina, who sat next to him, and the others in the back were all silent, filled with their own thoughts. They had driven several miles without a word being spoken before Lane broke the silence.

"This is no good."

"What is it, Lane?" inquired Ernest.

"The guy was our pal. Yeah, we all loved him, but this mopin' around ain't gonna do any of us any good. There's no place in the book that says we shouldn't talk about him or shouldn't reminisce about some of the good times we had together." A smile crossed Lane's face. "Remember last year on his birthday, we called 'im into the conference room and I sent that young thing into the room in her birthday suit?" Lane laughed. "Why, for Christ sakes, he came runnin' outta that room like it was on fire."

Smiles began to cross their faces.

"And the time we sent dirty books to his house. Why, the guy almost had a hemorrhage."

"Lane, remember the time you had that friend of yours put on a habit and pose as a nun?" reminded Ernie.

"Yeah, yeah, I remember. I introduced her to Dennis as Sister Marie. Then I left the room sayin' I had to go to the john—I still got the taped conversation. Dennis was making a lot of small talk about the Catholic Church and this chick is goin' along with 'im. And then she says, 'I think the church should relax its posture as far as the good sisters are concerned.' And Dennis asks, 'How so?' The girl"—Lane was gasping for air, he was laughing so hard—"looks right at him, speaking naivelike and pure, sayin', 'Well, I think they ought to let us get fucked if we want to.' "

Lane was pounding the steering wheel with his fist and the others were roaring as he continued. "Dennis nearly dropped dead, as he came up with 'I beg your pardon, sister,' and she says, 'You know, sonny—do the dirty thing . . . get laid.' And then Dennis is like paralyzed, as she lifts her skirt, showin' him the works and sayin', 'Why don't you and I get it on?' " Lane was killing himself laughing. "Well, Dennis came tearassin' outta my office and I, with a straight face, said, 'Well, what's wrong?' He turns to me stutterin', 'Lane . . . Lane . . .' he says, 'the nun, she's gone crazy . . .' And I say, 'What did she do?' Before he can answer, the nun comes out of the office and walks up to us and very politely says, 'Mr. Raskin, it was very nice meeting you. Mr. Garrett, I have to run along.' She leaves and I say to Dennis, 'She seemed okay to me; what was wrong?' Well, Dennis just stares at me. Now I can't hold it back any longer and I double over, breaking up. Now, you know Dennis, he thought pooh-pooh was a bad word for him to say. He looks up at me and says, 'Lane . . . Lane, you're a prick!' "

They were all in hysterics, laughing with tears rolling down their cheeks, as Lane let each of them off at their cars. He pulled out of the parking lot and headed for Easton and home. He took a deep breath and spoke aloud.

"Dennis, I'm gonna miss you, pal . . . I'm really gonna miss you. Don't go gettin' mad at me for tellin' those stories. You know why I told them, 'cause if I didn't . . . well, it's hard to drive when your eyes are full of water."

chapter 16

It was the Monday following Dennis Raskin's funeral. The place was FBI Headquarters in Boston, Massachusetts. William Fulton had called a meeting of twelve key agents. These were all seasoned veterans—friends of Dennis Raskin.

"Gentlemen," Fulton began, "I'm making this top priority. But as far as the news media is concerned, we have only a passing interest in this case, in that Dennis Raskin was a former agent. I'm making this top priority for two reasons: first, because we strongly suspect that it was an informant who was responsible for his death, and second, but no less important, Dennis was once one of ours. I have passed among you a picture of Carlos Garcia, the man we believe to be responsible for the death of Dennis Raskin. Along with that picture, you will note a list of some one hundred and fifty names. Those are the names of informants that Dennis worked with in his years with the bureau. We believe that one of them lured Dennis to a meeting place where Garcia waited and killed him. I want every man on that list checked out. If they remain local residents, it is essential that their every movement be monitored. Check for a witness who may have seen them leaving the area after the murder. Remember these two men may be users, or pushers, or both. But more important, be aware at all times that they're vicious killers, so work in pairs."

Tony Bucelli stood by the picture window in his luxurious apartment overlooking the Charles River. He wiped a slight smudge off the windowpane with an edge of a tissue, which he quickly tossed into a wastebasket. Four well-dressed men sat forward in their deeply cushioned chairs, waiting for their Don to speak. They wished he would hurry it up instead of continuing the house-cleaning ritual he was going through. They each had their hierarchy of organized crime to attend to.

Finally he stopped his white-glove inspection and confronted them.

"We've been looking for this . . . this maggot Carlos Garcia under every rock in this town, yet no one comes up with him." He glanced around the table, his eyes cold, his manner chilling. "Every guy with a badge in this city is lookin' to grab this man. Now the feds have even got into the act. We can't operate with these people crawling all over our operations—it's costing us a ton of money. This kid has become a real pain in the ass. We gotta find him. We're all gonna put up five grand each for the guy that takes him down. It's the only way to stop all this heat." They all nodded in unison. "That's twenty-five grand. A lotta money, but I want this kid found and the matter taken care of."

The huge room was filled with policemen sitting in chairs, drinking coffee from thick paper containers, smoking and talking among themselves. Sergeant Sean Fitzhenery was a veteran of some nineteen years on the force. Although somewhat pugnacious, he was a savvy, intelligent cop. The chatter in the room was loud and boisterous as Fitzhenery shuffled his papers on the wooden table that faced the group of officers. He stood and hiked up his pants, his voice booming above the noise in the room.

"All right, knock it off." The room was quieted as he cleared his throat. "The hot-car sheet this morning looks like the entire production line of General Motors. Pick it up on the way out." He checked his papers and continued. "Last night was unusually quiet: four armed robberies—nothing big; three stabbings; seven breaking and enterings; two pages here of misdemeanors; and yeah, we caught a guy running down the street in his wife's bloomers. Gentlemen, that does it for the small potatoes. Now let's get to the main event—our murdering junkie friend, Carlos Garcia. Every one of our asses are on the line until we catch this yo-yo. If any of you see somethin' comin' down on the streets, I don't care if it's pot, pills, heroin, coke . . . if you catch a kid takin' a goddamn aspirin, you show him that composite of Garcia. If this guy decides to take out someone else or rapes another kid in the park, we'll have to run around this city in disguises to avoid getting lynched! This guy is makin' us look like a bunch of assholes. The vacation is over. Now hit the streets and bring his mangey ass back to this station!"

Linda had instructions that they were not to be disturbed. Steam rose swirling from the coffee in front of Lane as he took a long pull on the cigarette in his mouth. He, Gina, and Ernest sat listening to the Garcia tapes. They strained for a telltale hint that might help lead to his capture.

"I have the tape for Saturday and Sunday on the George phone. Do you want to hear it now?" ventured Ernest.

Lane flushed a bit, remembering a conversation he'd had with Christian. Not that it had been that private, but it showed a more subdued side of him that Gina and Ernest had never seen. He stalled in answering, tasting his coffee and pretending to burn his lips. Ernest, grasping what was on Lane's mine, continued.

"Lane, I didn't see any sense in listening to anything but what is pertinent to us—the only conversation I kept was Garcia's. He called her again."

Lane nodded in unspoken approval. Each man knew what the other was thinking. Gina sat passively drinking her coffee.

Ernest switched on the recorder.

"Hello," Christian had answered the phone.

"Hello, pretty baby . . . it's me, Carlos." His spaced-out voice came floating out of the tape recorder. "Did you have a nice lunch with brother-in-law Lane?"

"Yes, we had a nice lunch," Christian answered hesitantly.

Damn it! Where was he? Lane wondered.

"I saw you at Zito's," Garcia slurred.

"Carlos, you sound tired. Are you all right?"

That's it, Christian, pump him, thought Lane.

"I'm . . . as right . . . as could be. Christian . . . I want you. I want to make love . . . to you again. Tell me again . . . tell me you're all mine."

"I'm all yours . . . Carlos. Why don't I ever see you when you're around me? Don't you want me to see you?"

"You'll see me . . . Christian. When . . . I come . . . for you."

"Did you like the dress I wore the other day?"

Lane could detect the tenseness in her voice.

"I like . . . anything you wear. I watched . . . you and Lane when . . . you were . . . eating . . . at Zito's."

Lane caught it right away; so had Christian.

"Carlos, did you think it was funny when the waiter spilled the drink on Lane?"

For a moment there was silence. "I was glad . . . when the . . . waiter . . . spilled the drink . . . on him."

There was a muffled voice in the background.

"Christian . . . I have to leave," he wheezed. "I'll call you . . . again. I'll come for . . . you."

"Carlos, wait, don't hang up," Christian urged as the phone went dead.

Ernest looked at Lane, baffled. "What the hell was that all about? 'Carlos, don't hang up.' "

Lane was smiling as Gina remarked, "Is this a private joke?"

"Boys and girls," he boasted, "you just heard the first interrogation by our number-one agent. The lady, for your information, was tryin' to keep him talkin'. You see, *we never* had lunch at Zito's that day. We *met* at Zito's, didn't *lunch* there."

Gina was puzzled. "The part about the waiter spilling the drink on you . . ."

"Never happened. We've finally caught Mr. Garcia tellin' a little white lie. Now all we gotta figure out is how this creep is keepin' the peek on Christian without us spottin' 'im. He could've followed her to Zito's and disappeared when he saw me meetin' her. Could be he didn't wait around long enough—just took it for granted we ate there."

Ernest looked troubled. "Lane, he tells her his name and still uses something over the mouthpiece . . . why?"

"Very simple, Ernie. This is one smart, sick spic. He knows no one has any solid evidence on the murders and figures someone is probably tapin' his calls. He assumes if he ever gets nailed, we still can't prove it's his voice."

Gina's mind flashed back to the night when Garcia attempted to rape her. "The only way he could get away with following her after that is by wearing some sort of makeup or facial disguise."

Ernest smiled. As Lane caught the look, he held up his hand, saying, "Ernie, that's not so far-fetched after all. This bum could be runnin' around like a little old lady. It sure wouldn't be the first time we ran up against a guy that is cute enough to pull somethin' like that."

The FBI, Boston Police, Lane Garrett, and Tony Bucelli were all searching for Carlos Garcia. All had their own personal reasons for wanting to see him apprehended. An awesome representation of mind and manpower bonded together with the singleness of purpose—to find Garcia.

Garcia was in Elliot Rothman's apartment. They were alone, going over the final details of a drug deal.

"How much? How much do we hafta come up with?"

"Five thousand should do it. I did a couple of other numbers with this guy—I know the stuff is good," added Rothman.

"Five grand? Might as well be five million," Garcia said disgustedly.

"If we can somehow dig up the bread, we can triple it when we move the stuff to the streets."

Garcia looked questioningly at Rothman. "How long you know this cat?"

"Three, maybe four years. Why?"

"How bad would you feel if somethin' happens to him after we gets the stuff?"

Rothman smiled. "*After* we got the stuff?"

"Yeah, after."

"Carlos, I never dug the guy that much anyway."

A sinister grin crossed Garcia's face. "Why don't you bring your friend here so's we can set up some kind of a deal?"

"This seller is real careful, Carlos."

"Have you ever burned the dude before?"

"Ya mean not pay 'im?"

"Yeah, exactly."

"No, no, I always paid him . . . had no choice."

"Well, then, the man ain't got no reason to feel uneasy. You bring him here and lemme do the rest."

"Carlos."

"What?"

"I'm—I'm a little shaky. I need a lift . . . a shot."

"Elliot, you go out and find the dude. Then ya bring 'im back here. *Then* I give you some stuff."

chapter 17

Don Spencer and Gina were leaning back on a bench in Boston Common, watching a jogger, some children playing ball, and people on their lunch break. It was Spencer's day off from the hospital. He had taken her to lunch at the fashionable Ritz Carlton directly across the street from the Common.

Gina smiled at him as a light breeze ruffled his hair. "That's the first time I've been in the Ritz. It's lovely but awfully expensive."

He chucked her under the chin, saying, "Don't get used to it . . . unless they make me a captain."

It no longer bothered her that he insisted he was the law. She was resigned to the fact that in his own good time he would tell her he worked in a hospital.

An accordion player was close by and began singing "An Italian Ballad." Don and Gina heard the melody as they gazed lovingly at each other. Very gently, he leaned over to kiss her. She rested her head on his shoulder, her hand lost in his. They sat close, inhaling the fresh air and the smell of the newly cut grass, watching the swanboats lazily drifting around the pond.

It started slowly at first, then Don's wheezing graduated to the point where he was gasping for air. Gina bolted into an upright position. She stared at him. With his eyes running and chest gasping for air, he reached into his shirt pocket and took a tiny pill, popping it into his mouth. For a moment she was seized with fear as she recalled Lane's words: "They don't have a stamp on their forehead marked rapist . . . maybe he's normal with some other women and then maybe he gets bad with others to get his jollies off."

She quieted somewhat, remembering that they had the goods on Garcia. "Don, Don, are you all right?"

After several minutes his labored breathing returned to normal, his eyes ceasing to tear.

"What is it, Don?"

He had his handkerchief in his hand, drying his eyes and face. "It's this damn allergy. It has something to do with the pollen in the air. When the pollen count is high, it comes on me all of a sudden. Maybe it's the just-mowed grass that triggered it."

Gina was worried. "Don, you nearly scared me to death."

He smiled.

She was patting his face and leaned to him, kissing his lips. "Are you sure you're okay?"

The warm smile was still there as he spoke. "If I thought I was going to get all this attention, I wouldn't have taken my pill."

Her arms sliding around his neck, she nipped his ear and whispered, "I'll make you a deal. You take your pills . . . and I'll take mine . . . and I'll give you all the attention you can handle."

Elliot Rothman was speaking to a man on a street in the combat zone. The man, Big Byron Fenton, a black belt in karate and an ex-marine, was one of the top drug dealers in the city.

Fenton stood listening to Rothman's plan to purchase his drugs. He was unimpressed. "You know the way I do business, Elliot. The money has to be up front . . . or we don't deal."

"I tell you, Byron, I got the bread. My money man is back at my place. C'mon, meet him. The man will take some serious weight."

It was greed as much as Elliot Rothman that finally talked Fenton into going to Rothman's shabby apartment. Rothman opened the squeaky door to his apartment to find Garcia in front of the television set. Upon hearing them, Garcia turned and got up.

"Carlos, this is Byron." Rothman stood there rubbing his sweaty palms together.

Fenton studied Garcia, saying, "Elliot here tells me that you can use some big quantities."

"Yeah, I can. I got a lot of people on the street . . . a lot of people that's dryin' out waitin' for me to come up with some stuff," declared Garcia.

"Why don't you get it from your usual source?" Fenton asked.

"He got picked up by the heat. I can't wait no longer," he explained.

"I understand you want to start with five thousand."

"I made some calls when Elliot split to get you. I'm gonna need at least twenty grand's worth—can you handle it?"

Fenton surveyed Garcia. "Carlos, I can handle ten times that, if you can handle the money end."

"No sweat—when can ya have the stuff?"

"Less 'an a hour."

"All right, let's make it exactly one hour. You have the goods here and I'll have the money."

Garcia stuck his thumb in the air and Fenton nodded while he departed.

They waited until they were sure Fenton was gone before Rothman nervously addressed Garcia. "I hope you didn't spook him, asking for twenty thousand worth."

"Spook him! You musta saw that greedy look in that sucker's eyes." He laughed.

"Carlos, this guy is tough. He's got a black belt in karate. He ain't gonna be easy to take out."

"You gotta hammer in this damn place?" Garcia asked and angrily spat on the filthy bare floor.

"Sure." Rothman was jittery, in need of a fix.

"Well, you get it—now, man, and shove it under them there papers on the table. Then, he comes in and I makes sure he has got the stuff on him . . . I got my shiv, see, and move on the turkey . . . you nail him on the head with the hammer. Ha! Then we takes that *black belt* offa him and tie it in a pretty bow around his neck." He was seized by a fit of hysterical laughter.

Byron Fenton had been gone a bit longer than the hour agreed upon for the meeting.

"I told you, Carlos," sputtered Rothman, sweating, quivering with his need. "I told ya, ya musta spooked him."

Garcia was about to swear at him when the knock came at the door. He winked at Rothman and motioned to let him in. As Rothman turned the knob, the door flew open—knocking him backward onto the floor. Byron Fenton and two other men burst into the room, slamming the door behind them. Garcia stood petrified as he stared at the men with the guns, silencers attached to them.

Garcia's voice was quivering as he spoke. "Hey . . . hey, man, that won't do you no good. I didn't get the bread yet."

The steely-eyed man stepped forward. "We're not interested in your bread, kid."

Elliot Rothman, whimpering and still on the floor, crawled toward the man. Getting to his knees, he looked up at him and pleaded. "Please . . . please don't hurt me . . . don't hurt me." *Phittt, phittt, phittt*—the noiseless gun fired three times, tearing into Rothman's face.

Garcia, seeing the blood gush from Rothman's disfigured face, began to beg for his life. "Hey . . . why you comin' down on us like this? I'll do a hit for you guys. Please . . . please, man . . . don't kill me. I ain't done nothin' to you guys."

One of the men shot him in the stomach. Clutching at the gaping hole as he fell to the floor, blood spilled through his fingers. He lay there moaning, writhing in pain as the men approached him. Still alive, he held up his hand in their direction, gasping . . . begging . . . pleading. They reached down, stuffing a handkerchief into his mouth, causing him to gag. Two of the men held him in place while a third pulled his pants down. Garcia saw the switchblade come out of the man's pocket. The cloth in his mouth choked him and muffled his cries as the man grabbed his penis.

William Fulton was sitting on the corner of his desk in his FBI office, being briefed by Special Agent Carl Walton. Walton was among the twelve men assigned to the Garcia case. After having worked around the clock, checking out informants who'd worked for Raskin, they'd finally gotten a break.

"Bill, of the entire list of Dennis's informants, only twenty-three of them still live in the Boston area. On a long shot, we obtained a record of phone calls made from those residences. The night Dennis was killed, a call was made from the residence of Elliot Rothman to Dennis's home phone. We have a team of men on surveillance outside his apartment at this very moment."

Fulton began shaking his head. "It's amazing, Carl. The man

could have gone to a pay phone and it could have taken us months to find them. Maybe we never would have."

"Rothman probably figured that he would never be thought of in connection with the case. It's lucky for us he was careless."

"When you have Rothman in custody, no matter what time of night or day it is, call me."

"I'll call you the minute we make the arrest, Bill."

Later in the day, the surveillance team, staked out at the tenement where Elliot Rothman lived, had made a decision to enter his apartment. They alerted William Fulton, who instructed them to wait for his arrival.

A backup team surrounded the building as Fulton and five other agents approached Rothman's apartment. Fulton rapped loudly on the wooden door. No answer. He knocked again, announcing himself.

"This is the FBI, Rothman. We have a warrant for your arrest. Open the door."

Still no answer. Fulton gave a nod to the two burly agents next to him. They crashed against the wooden door; it splintered and flew open.

Carlos Garcia and Elliot Rothman lay in the middle of the floor. Garcia had blood drooling from his mouth; the severed penis could be seen jammed between his teeth.

Fulton looked at his men. They had seen this kind of hit before. Rothman and Garcia had been executed in gangland fashion, and William Fulton hadn't the vaguest idea why.

Fulton put through a call to Captain Tiernan of the Boston police. He would turn the case over to the local police, since the federal agency lacked jurisdiction. The Boston police would receive credit for finding the bodies.

More than twenty detectives converged on the neighborhood. They knocked on every door looking for a single witness who had seen someone or heard something. They left as they had come, empty-handed and without a single clue.

Ray Tiernan called Lane's office with instructions for Lane to meet him at the station. Lane, upon returning from lunch with Christian, immediately proceeded there. The two men sat in the privacy of Tiernan's glass-caged office.

"Lane"—Tiernan smiled—"I have something that's going to brighten your day."

"The way things have been goin', it's not likely, pal."

"We found Garcia dead."

"What! Where? How?"

"He and a junkie named Elliot Rothman were discovered in Rothman's apartment. Fulton found 'em. They both had three bullets in them. Garcia's joint was cut off—stuffed in his mouth."

Lane felt relief in knowing the nightmare was over for Christian George. But he felt frustration when thinking of the way the men had been killed. He knew full well it was a gangland killing, and his friend Tony Bucelli dominated his thoughts as he heard Ray Tiernan speak.

"Lane, both of these guys were nothing but a couple of punks. The stoolie, Rothman, was a junkie, yes, but nothing big. Garcia, yeah, he killed some people, but he didn't fit into the organized crime picture. Why the hell did the 'boys' take a part in this thing?"

Lane's thoughts would never cross his lips. "You got me, Ray. Maybe one of them was connected and you just haven't come up with it yet."

"C'mon, Lane, for Christ sakes, the big boys in this town wouldn't touch those two freaks with a ten-foot pole."

Lane's voice was cold. "They touched 'em with thirty-eights and they whacked them out for a reason. Maybe they welched on some deal. I gotta tell you, it wouldn't surprise me if you never find out who it was. Another thing, who's gonna look that hard for the people who snuffed 'em?"

Christian was in the living room as Lane drove up. She saw the Lincoln through her picture window and hurried out to meet him. Lane got out of his car and strode toward her as she spoke to him.

"C'mon, let's go in the house; I got a little news for you."

She tried to pry it out of him as she tugged him into the kitchen. Teddy and Mrs. Day were at the kitchen table and excused themselves, going into the backyard.

"Now, Mr. Garrett, what news do you have for me?"

"Christian, you don't have to worry about Carlos Garcia any more."

"Lane, they caught him!"

"Not quite, but just as good. He was found dead with a junkie friend of his. They'd both been shot in the head."

"Oh, Lane, how terrible." Christian had mixed emotions. She was greatly relieved that Garcia was out of her life, but shocked by his death.

"The man was a very violent guy, Christian. He lived in a violent world. Don't waste your time thinkin' about him. He's gone and no one is gonna miss him."

She stared at Lane, saying, "It's over . . . it's finally over." Her eyes filled as she cupped her hands to her face, repeating it. "It's over . . . over."

Lane moved to where she was sitting. He crouched before her, touching her hands. "Hey, what are you cryin' for?"

She took her hands from her eyes, sniffling but still weeping. "I don't . . . know . . . I just am."

He took his handkerchief from his pocket and handed it to her. "You know, you still got the last one I gave you. You gotta be sellin' these things."

"Lane, you're crazy."

"Did I ever tell you otherwise?"

She shook her head no.

"I want you to do somethin' for me."

"What . . . is it?"

"Before the week is out, I want you to celebrate with me. I'm a helluva cook. I'll get some lobsters and clams and you and I will go to my place. I'll treat you to the best meal you've ever eaten."

Her tears had stopped as she smiled and asked, "Who's buying the lobsters?"

"You capitalists are all alike. You really know how to hold on to a buck. I'll buy."

She held his face between her two hands and kissed him on the forehead, saying, "I'll do the dishes."

A warm glow came over Lane as she kissed him. She had a settling effect on him. He spoke softly as he stood up, looking down at her sitting there.

"You got a deal, you crafty lady. Let's make it the night after tomorrow. It'll give me a chance to put out the word I'm looking for the biggest lobsters in town."

Christian walked Lane to his car and lingeringly watched him drive away.

It was after midnight. All the lights were out in Lane Garrett's home and his bed was empty. He was sitting alone by the darkened pool, listening to the ever-flowing water drowning out the sounds of the crickets. He looked up toward the sky, as the smoke rose from his mouth, glowing in the soft moonlight. A crisp, clear, lonely, and troubled night for Lane. His thoughts were about Christian. His feelings for her confused him. He'd known many women intimately during the course of his life. But Christian was so unlikely an attraction for him—she was so unusual. Sure she was a beautiful and sensitive person, but he'd always been used to a more down-to-earth woman, except . . . except for his Lisa. He paced up and down by the side of the pool and wondered about their relationship. In his work he often had dealings with women, many of whom became attached to him. Their confidence in him and the sense of security he gave them oftentimes transferred into deeper feelings for him. He understood that it was much like a woman falling in love with her doctor. This situation, however, was quite the reverse. He never felt any deep emotion for a client, if indeed that was what he now felt.

He finally surrendered to the lateness of the hour and headed back to the house, his bedroom—and sleep.

It was the next day when a tired Lane entered his office and saw a very distinguished man waiting for him. Lane cast a questioning look at Linda.

She whispered, "His name is Jonathan Prendergast, the head of Wilmington General Hospital. He said he had an appointment with you."

Lane nodded and walked over to Mr. Prendergast.

"Mr. Prendergast, my name is Lane Garrett."

Prendergast rose like a tree from the ground. He looked down at Lane as he returned the greeting. "Ah, Mr. Garrett, my pleasure." He followed Lane into his office. When Lane offered him a coffee, which he declined, he sat in a blue chair, saying, "Mr. Garrett, I neither drink coffee nor smoke. They're both, if I may use the old cliché, hazardous to one's health."

Lane lit up a cigarette. "Well, Mr. Prendergast, I hope you don't mind if I smoke?"

"Not at all, Mr. Garrett. I had talked with Dr. Spellie and he related your desire to speak with me about Mrs. George. I hope you will forgive me, but I was in the neighborhood and took the liberty of telling your secretary that I had an appointment.

Lane had been studying Prendergast as he spoke. His air, the way he presented himself, reeked of confidence. He knew that Prendergast came from old Yankee blood. Lane was assured of two things about his character: one, that he would be extremely tight-fisted, and two, that the thought of a scandal connected with the hospital would send him into apoplexy.

Prendergast continued. "Mr. Garrett, shall we get right down to business? We're both busy men and I see no point in wasting time. What do you have in mind?"

"Certainly, Mr. Prendergast. As you know from Dr. Spellie, I represent Christian George, the woman *raped* in your hospital. Since that time the man that raped her, who incidentally was in your employ, has nearly driven her crazy—until his recent murder. What I have in mind is some type of compensation for the mental and physical anguish she suffered."

Prendergast smiled. "Mr. Garrett, you'll be happy to learn that I have taken the liberty to see to it that Mrs. George is not sent a bill for our services."

"Mr. Prendergast, I'm sure she'll appreciate that. However, what I have in mind is more compensation than the amount of the hospital bill."

"And what might that be, Mr. Garrett?"

"Considering that so far she has kept the hospital's good name out of the news, I don't think three hundred thousand dollars would be too much to ask."

"That is ridiculous. There isn't any reason why I would authorize such a preposterous sum. Five . . . ten thousand dollars would, I'm sure, suffice any trauma that Mrs. George has endured. Incidentally, I don't believe you have any proof of her allegations."

Lane smiled coolly. "Mr. Prendergast, I'm sure neither of us want to see this become a court case. Mrs. George has taken a test—sodium pentothal. It leaves no doubt . . . the lady *was raped—in your hospital.*"

"I see. Mr. Garrett, I and the board might be able to go as high as twenty-five thousand." A slow smile crossed Prendergast's lips. "By the way, Mr. Garrett, I feel confident Mrs. George would be more than reluctant about going to court. The publicity . . . everything exposed in the press, a very distasteful business. Mr. Garrett, twenty-five thousand. Take it or leave it."

Lane took a long pull on his cigarette. "Yeah, you're right, she would find it very distasteful. But I gotta tell ya somethin'. For the kinda money we're talkin' about, she'd do it."

Prendergast smiled. "I'm willing to take the gamble she won't."

Lane leaned back in his chair, his hands clasped behind his head. "You know, Mr. Prendergast, I just had a thought."

"And, what might that be, Mr. Garrett?"

"Your whole purpose in bein' here is to protect the good name of the hospital, isn't that so?"

"Quite frankly, that obviously is the main reason for my being here."

Lane leaned across his desk, his hands folded in front of him. "Did you report the incident?"

Prendergast appeared flustered. "What—what do you mean?"

A hard smile crossed Lane's face. "What do I mean? Let's cut out the unnecessary bullshit—you know exactly what I mean. By *law* you are required to report any incident . . . or *suspected* act of this nature. Now I'm gonna ask you again: Did you report this to the police and the state board licensing hospitals?"

Prendergast grew pale. "No—no, I didn't; I thought this could be settled amicably."

Lane drew a deep breath. "Well, my friend, to put it bluntly . . . Your ass is in a sling; you're in direct violation of the law. Now let's get to number two—that new Certificate of Need you filed. You sure as hell can kiss that off. By the way, I got a pal that works for the Boston *Globe.* They love stuff like this. By the time that article hits the street, that hospital of yours will become a parkin' lot." Don't get cute with me, *Mr. Prendergast,* you're playin' in my ballpark now."

Prendergast was visibly shaken. "All right, Mr. Garrett. But three hundred thousand . . . it's simply out of the question. The burden . . . the hospital simply cannot afford that sum of money."

"A hundred thousand, Mr. Prendergast. You pay the lady a hundred thousand. And, as you put it to me, take it or leave it."

Prendergast studied Lane and knew he wasn't bluffing. "I'll authorize payment. Mrs. George will have to sign a release."

chapter 18

The evening visiting hours past, all the patients at Wilmington General Hospital had been checked and tucked in for the night. At the end of the quiet corridor, Virginia Merguson was sitting at her desk busily going over the patient medication charts.

A man's form appeared silently before her.

"Mrs. Merguson."

She looked up. It was Don Spencer. Her response was warm, friendly. "Yes, Don."

"Mrs. Merguson, I'm afraid this is going to be my last night working here."

"Don, is it a question of money?"

"No, it's a personal matter."

"You know, I've been happy with you here. Must you leave?"

"I'd like to give you notice, but I'm afraid I simply can't."

She stood up from her chair. "If you should change your mind, you know your job is waiting for you."

"There are other matters I have to attend to. I don't think I'll be coming back."

"Do you want us to send your last check?"

"I'll call and let you know."

"Don, it would be no trouble at all to send it to your home."

"That's all right, Mrs. Merguson, I'm moving. I'd just as soon either pick it up or call you with my new address."

"If you are ever in need of a reference, I'd be happy to furnish you with a rather complimentary one."

"Thank you. I'll be leaving now."

"Good luck, Don."

Lane had busied himself the entire day gathering the necessary ingredients for the celebration that he and Christian would share that night. He stopped at a liquor store and carefully selected one of the finest years of Château Lafite Rothschild along with several types of liqueurs. A friend who owned a well-known lobster restaurant met Lane at his seaside fish supply house soon after closing time. Lane left with two huge lobsters, a large container of steamers, and three pounds of shrimp. They were sealed in a Styrofoam container packed with dry ice.

He arrived at Christian's house as the first signs of evening appeared and, after a brief conversation with Mrs. Day and Teddy, they proceeded to Lane's home. As they whisked along the highway, Lane casually lifted an envelope from his pocket and handed it to Christian.

"You're big on surprises," he murmured, his eyes to the road. "Here's one for you."

"Well, it can't be Zits cream," she conjectured, smiling. "The envelope isn't thick enough."

She carefully opened it and took out the slip of paper. She stared in disbelief at the check from Wilmington General Hospital. She read it again to be sure. There was no doubt about it. The check was made out in her name in the amount of one hundred thousand dollars.

"Lane . . . this check . . . what is it for?"

"It will never make up for what you went through, Christian, but the people at the hospital wanted you to have some type of compensation for everythin' that happened to you."

"But, Lane . . . a hundred thousand . . ."

"Christian," he said softly, "if I asked you to go through the same thing for ten times that, would you?"

"I would rather die."

"You see, they should've given you more."

"Lane, you're making me a wealthy woman," she breathed.

"Believe me, it wasn't intentional. Now you won't need this broken-down detective."

He could feel her eyes staring at him and he glanced at her serious face as a passing car overtook them.

"That's not true, Lane." The words bathed his body with goose bumps.

She continued to watch him, waiting for a response. He was at a loss for words, but finally he broke the silence.

"I cook the best lobsters on the East Coast, ya know. I hope you like lobster."

"I love them. What else are we having?"

"Clams, shrimp, wine, the works."

"It looks like I'll be washing dishes till dawn," she said with a laugh.

It was dark by the time they pulled into Lane's driveway. After switching off the house alarm, he opened the door. He flicked on a small light in the foyer and walked, with Christian trailing close behind, down the short passageway to the kitchen, where he turned on the lights.

"Now, Christian," he stated, rubbing his hands together, "I'm gonna see how good you are in the kitchen. In that cabinet"—he pointed—"you'll find all the pots and pans. Take two of the largest pots, fill 'em with water, and put 'em on to boil."

"I think I can handle that," she said, smiling, her hands on her hips.

"While you're doin' that, I'll go out to the car and bring in the goodies."

By the time Lane returned with the first armload of supplies, Christian had quickly accomplished her task and waited nonchalantly with her hand on the stove.

"How's that, boss?" she exclaimed, tipping her head toward the water-filled pots.

"Not bad, not bad." He nodded. "Lemme go out and get the rest of the stuff."

Lane had been gone a minute or two when she decided to go out and help him. She'd just gotten to the front door when she saw the dark outline of a man. He was creeping up behind Lane as he carried the chest of lobsters. The man, partially hidden by Lane's shadow, was raising his hand. Christian could see he had something in it. She screamed out a warning.

"Lane!"

It was too late! The hand and the instrument came crashing down on Lane's head. The Styrofoam box fell, tumbling to the ground as Lane dropped to his knees, falling forward on his face. Watching in horror, Christian slammed the door, bolting it, and flicked off the foyer light. She hesitantly looked through a glass pane on the door. She saw the man leaning over, putting Lane's hands behind his back. Christian strained her eyes but all she could see was a shadowed figure. Racing to the phone, she picked it up, dialing the operator. She listened. The phone was dead! Suddenly she spied the form coming toward the front door. Tearing into the kitchen, she yanked open several drawers, frantically searching. After what seemed an eternity, she found the cutlery drawer and grabbed inside. She stood by the foyer entrance to the kitchen, carving knife in hand, trembling, waiting. She heard the breaking of glass and saw a hand come through the smashed pane, reaching for the lock. She hesitated, then broke and ran out the back door into the woods. Her heart was pounding as she tripped and fell over the roots of trees. She heard the man cursing.

"Where are you, you bitch . . . you whore? I'll find you."

She lay cringing flat on her stomach under a bush, afraid he could hear her every heartbeat. Although he was very close by, he seemed to be veering off in another direction. She shuddered and held her breath, listening to his rantings as he wheezed and snorted grotesquely.

"Where are you? . . . I want to make love to you. . . . You're mine . . . slut. I want to fuck you again. . . . Where are you? . . . You won't get away!"

Oh, no, God! It can't be! It can't be him! Christian's mind was in a frenzy. Petrified, her body was shaking violently. Please don't let him find me . . . don't let him find me! Her knuckles were white from her steellike grip on the knife handle.

"You whore! You lousy whore! You're mine!" His choking and gasping for air increased. "I'll . . . come . . . for . . . you." His struggling, wheezing voice seemed to be fading farther away. "When . . . I do . . . you'll never . . . never leave me . . . again."

She lay there trembling uncontrollably, trying not to make a movement that would attract his attention. She heard a rustling in the distance and raised her head slightly to see the tree-filtered moonlight touching his dark form disappearing like a shadow into the night.

Christian stayed there five, ten minutes, listening, afraid he was still out there somewhere, lurking, waiting. She thought about Lane. Oh, God, let him be all right. Ever so quietly, she made her way through the trees, circling the house, until she could see Lane's prone figure. She crouched down and moved carefully to the edge of the grass, looking around once more. Slowly, on her hands and knees, she crawled across the lawn to where Lane was lying. His hands and feet were tied and he was gagged. Thank God. She sighed gratefully, seeing he was still alive. She winced, noticing the large lump that appeared on the back of his head. Quickly she untied the gag and took the cloth from his mouth. He was conscious.

"Christian . . . Christian . . . are you okay?" His voice was weak.

"Lane, I'm all right," she answered, cutting the twine from his feet and hands. "It was him . . . he's alive, it was him!" There was a frightening urgency in her hushed, shaky voice.

Lane reached for his gun. It was still there. He drew it as he attempted to stand. He got halfway up and fell back to his knees. Christian grabbed him and helped him up again, his arm and weight resting on her shoulder. They stumbled up the front stairs and through the open door, closing it behind them. Lane hit the switch by the door to activate the alarm. Its shrill ring blared and he immediately shut it off.

"The back door—it must be open."

Christian left Lane propped against the door and, running into the kitchen, shut the back door, bolting it.

"Lane, it's closed," she called.

He threw the switch again, reactivating the alarm. He staggered into the living room, stumbling just short of the long couch. He rested his back against it. Christian entered the dark room as the foyer light behind her filtered through her silklike skirt.

"Lane, the phone is dead. Maybe I'd better take the car and go for a doctor," she ventured, still trembling.

"No . . . there's some brandy in one of the . . . cartons . . . I brought in. Get me some."

Christian shakily filled two water glasses with brandy and quickly returned to Lane. Handing him one, she took a long swallow from the other. She returned to the kitchen, shutting off the stove as she passed it, and got some ice cubes out of the freezer, packing them within a clean dish towel.

Lane was sipping on the brandy as she knelt by him holding the ice pack to his head. He winced.

"Does it hurt?" she asked.

"A little. That bum musta . . . hit me . . . with a hammer."

The brandy seemed to clear Lane's head and settle Christian down. Their glasses empty, she went to the kitchen again to refill them. Then she sat down beside him on the carpeted floor, holding the ice pack to his head. They continued drinking the brandy as she spoke.

"Lane, how . . . it was him. How?"

"Christian," he said, holding her hand, "we made a mistake. We had Garcia figured because we knew he raped the girl in the park . . . and he killed Dennis." He smiled at her. "You better take that ice off my head. I think I'm gettin' frostbit."

She laid her head on his shoulder. Tears came to her eyes. "Lane . . . oh, Lane, what . . . what are we going to do?"

He gently patted her face. "It's gonna be okay."

The tears streamed from her eyes, wetting the fingers that were on her cheek.

"I won't let anythin' happen to you," he said very softly. She turned her face to him, gazing through watery eyes.

They sat in the almost darkened room, the dim light from the foyer upon them. He looked at her and kissed her on the eyelids. "I promise it will be all right."

Opening her tearful eyes, she lifted her face to him, kissing his mouth with moist, parted lips. He enfolded her in his arms, gently kissing her back. It was a long, tender kiss. She pressed her hands against the back of his neck, her sorrow turning to desire as her tongue slid softly into his mouth. Her lips still on his, breathless, she murmured, "Oh . . . Lane."

She slid one hand to his shoulder, her fingers clutching at the muscular roundness of it. In an unspoken, mutual consent, they both eased slowly backward onto the plush carpet. He leaned over her, kissing her, his tongue in her yielding mouth. Her hand, now under his shirt, sent a thrill along his back with its feather touch. He trembled as his mouth left hers and he kissed the softness of her breast through the blouse. Her body quivered and she clasped his head in her hands, holding him to her. His hand shaking, he gently unbuttoned her blouse. She raised herself a bit as he sought the clasp on her bra. He unhooked it, slowing lifting the bra from her as she held her arms outward to help him undress.

He was bent over her, his mouth sucking longingly at her breast, while thrusting inside her. Sounds of pleasure tumbled from her lips.

"Lane . . . Lane." She groaned. "It's been so long . . . please, I need you . . . I need you so."

Passionately, he drove within her, his stroke quickening, plunging deeper . . . deeper as she cried out, "Oh, yes . . . oh, yes . . . ohhh . . ."

He exploded in her with a torrent of hot liquid gushing from him. He kept pumping, pushing into her, their bodies compelled by desire as they came again.

He fell beside her, holding her gently, kissing her tenderly. Christian's hands were all over him, lightly rubbing his back and sliding down over his bottom. They were close together, still trembling, breathlessly kissing each other.

Hoarsely, weakly, he spoke in a whispered tone. "I . . . don't know what came . . . over us."

She kissed him softly. "You . . . made me . . . feel alive again. You taught me something. It was Ben who died . . . not me."

They lay on their sides, pressed tightly together, their bodies entwined, braided in a loving embrace.

He drove her home, kissed her good night, and watched her go into the house. As he headed back to his own home, his mind flowed with thoughts of Christian. He could still feel her next to him; her perfume filled the air inside the car, her sweet fragrance lingering in his nostrils. Over and over in his mind's eye, he held her in his arms, picturing her beautiful naked body next to his.

He parked in his driveway, walked to the door, turned the alarm off, and went upstairs to his bedroom. He lay on the bed, restless, feeling her presence and being warmed by it. He turned, his head on his arm, and thought of her lips upon his own. He went to sleep dreaming of her in his arms.

Lane awoke the next morning as the early sunlight filtered through the verandah doors. He lay there thinking about Christian. It engulfed him with a peaceful warm feeling. He got out of bed and went into the bathroom to take a shower.

The full force of the pulsating water sharpened his senses,

bringing back into focus the stark reality that the rapist was still free and was getting bolder. He thought over every minute detail of the night before. Try as he might, he could not figure out who it could be who continued to plague Christian—how whoever it was seemed to know their every move. A thought crossed his mind: Why not? Could be. He decided to call Ernest Hampton as soon as he got to his office.

Christian was up at her normal time, fed Teddy breakfast, and chatted briefly with her mother. She poured herself a cup of coffee, taking it out into the backyard, to be alone with her thoughts.

There was a chill in the morning air. She sat at the picnic table in her long-sleeved sweater, the hot cup warming her hands. Her thoughts were of Lane and a night of fulfillment. Her breasts tingled at the memory of his gentle hands caressing her body and his warm lips kissing her ever so softly.

Suddenly the realization struck her that she was no longer frightened of the man who stalked her. Her strength came from the knowledge that Lane somehow would stop him.

chapter 19

As Lane entered his office, he was greeted by Ernest Hampton.

"Morning, Lane."

"Good mornin', Ernie." He turned to Linda. "Any calls?"

"No, Mr. Garrett."

"Then give Gina a call. Ask her to come directly into the office before she goes out on assignment."

"Yes, sir, Mr. Garrett."

"And oh, yes, ring the phone company and find out how soon they can get a guy to my house for repairs." Without hesitating, Lane motioned to Ernest. "C'mon, pal, we got business."

As Ernest closed the door to Lane's office he asked, "What's up?"

Lane sat down and lit up a cigarette. "I'll tell you what's up. You and I and everyone that works for this outfit is up—up the creek. Garcia might have been the one that murdered the Carron dame and Dennis, but he was not, I repeat, Ernie, *was not* the man that raped Christian!"

Ernest Hampton's mouth dropped open, his eyes widening. "Lane, there's got to be some mistake."

"There is, Ernie, and we made it. Our 'friend' paid me a visit last night and damn near cracked my skull open and almost got to Christian again. This creep seems to know every fuckin' move I make. First of all, I want you to go over these phones in this office with a magnifyin' glass."

"Isn't that a little farfetched?"

"Ernie, you're not the only guy in this city that can open a locked door. This office isn't exactly a bank vault. Now, I know this guy keeps showin' up where I am. Somehow he's gettin' that information, 'cause I can tell you he sure as hell isn't followin' me . . . unless his car's invisible."

"He could have a beeper planted in your car. You know, with a transmitter in his vehicle, he could follow you from six blocks, listening to the tone signals. You'd never spot him that way."

"You got a point there, Ernie. When you're finished checkin' the office phones, take that overgrown living room on wheels apart and check it out. Remember, I want you to check for bugs everywhere else too—my private office would be the likely spot. Do we have any new operatives that might be passin' along information?"

Ernest thought for a moment. "Lane, for Christ sakes, *I* don't even know where or when you're going someplace."

"Yeah, you're right. Guess I'm reachin'. By the way, I suppose you took the tap off Christian's phone."

"Yes, that's the first thing I did after Garcia turned up dead."

"Retap it!"

"I'll get right on it, Lane."

"This guy's makin' us look like bums, Ernie. Let's get our act together and nail 'im. I think our problem is that we've been underestimatin' the creep. Let's take it for granted that the guy knows all the moves, like we were workin' against someone like ourselves."

"I know you want me to put the surveillance team back on the George woman's house."

"Yeah, right away. Also, I want you to retap Spencer's and Schneiderman's phones. And I want you to pull all the stops and find that Summers kid. He looks real good to me right now." He paused. "Ernie . . ." Lane said, troubled.

"What is it, Lane? What's bothering you?"

"Ernie, sometimes in this business you do things that go against what you believe in. There are two people that are very close to me and I'm gonna hate myself for what I'm about to do. I know I don't have to say this . . . but what I say now gotta stay with you and me."

"Lane, I've been with you a long time. I never told stories out of school. If you have something that we have to do that doesn't set well with you . . . well, then I have to figure there must be a good reason."

"Bob Spellie has been a friend of mine for a good many years. I gotta tell you, I dig the guy, but he's one of the few people that knows every aspect of the case. He's the one that gave me the list of people that worked at the hospital the night Christian was raped. I've known for some time now that he excluded one name. His own! I had to assume that he didn't feel it necessary to tell me that because of our friendship. Maybe that's the reason he didn't tell me; I hope it is. From the beginning, Bob told me we have to prove she's being untruthful. I don't have another choice —I gotta check him out for sure. Ernie, put a tap on his phone."

"You're not saying it's Spellie?"

"No, I don't think it is . . . but after what's happened, I can't rule him out."

"Bob Spellie's your friend. If you find out that it was him, what will you do?"

"I'm in a box, pal. You see it's more than a case of helpin' Christian. For the first time in twenty years, I've let my business become a personal matter. Christian is not just another client; the lady means somethin' to me, Ernie. Spellie is my friend. If it turns out bad and he's our man . . . I don't know, I just don't know."

Ernest started to leave. "All right, Lane, let me take care of the George woman's tap and get that surveillance team reassigned to her house."

"Hold it, Ernie, I'm not finished yet. We got one other lousy item to take care of. I might as well tie up all the loose ends. It's Gina."

"Gina? What about Gina?"

"We both know Don Spencer has called at her apartment and she's called him at his. I've got a feelin' from somethin' she said that she digs the guy. Well, that was her own business until now. You know, Ernie, when you start thinkin' with your heart in this business, things could go bad . . . really bad. Normally Gina'd make damn sure of herself before she ruled anybody out. I think the broad is leadin' with her heart this time. I guess today's my day to be a rat—tap her phone."

"Lane, are you having someone tap mine?"

"Ernie, you know me. If I thought you were in it . . . well, I guess I'd do what I had to do. You'd expect that. No, no one's tapping your phone."

Ernest was grinning. "I'd find it anyway."

"Yeah, I guess you would. There's one other item before we finish. Take one of them young trainees we have and stick him in the woods at my house—the side that faces the street. Tell him to take every license plate on every damn car that passes the joint."

"Is that it?"

Lane took a long drag on his cigarette. "Ain't that enough?"

A large moving van was in front of Don Spencer's apartment. Spencer was in the middle of the living room supervising the men as they steadily moved out all of his belongings. He made one final check of the apartment, making sure that nothing was left behind.

That morning he had been to all the utility companies requesting final bills on his telephone, electric, and gas. He paid all the current charges with the promise that when a final bill was ready, he would return and pay them. He left no forwarding address with the local post office.

With the van fully loaded, as instructed, the moving men proceeded to a storage warehouse where Spencer's possessions would be held, pending further notice. With that, Don Spencer left and drove off in his car.

Gina had detoured to the office when learning of Lane's request that she report in before going out on her assignment. When Gina arrived, Linda instructed her to go right in, that Lane was expecting her.

Lane spent the better part of the first half hour bringing Gina up to date on the Christian George case. "Gina, as for Spencer, I want you to check out his work history from the list Tiernan gave us. Check out the last three places of employment he had, nearest relative, you know, the works."

"All right, Lane, but I don't think Don Spencer is our man."

"It's someone from that hospital, Gina, and Spencer is still a candidate until we can show why he shouldn't be."

The incident in the park, when Don's allergy had flared making strange sounds, flashed across Gina's mind. She felt sure Don was not the rapist and would not reveal to Lane what she had witnessed in the park.

"Lane, I'll check it out."

"I gotta ask you somethin', Gina."

She smiled. "I hope the question isn't too difficult. I'm not that alert in the morning."

"Are you seein' this Spencer guy?"

Gina became irritated. "Wouldn't you say that question comes under the heading of personal business?"

"Gina, you've known me too long to take the heat like that. I would never pry into your personal business. This guy just became number one on the suspect list in this case. Now, if you're seein' him, that ain't your personal business . . . it's *our* business!"

Gina was silent.

Lane uncrossed his legs to lean forward on his desk and continued. "Honey, listen to me. Please believe me, I'm not interested in the personal side of your relationship with this guy. I'm not sayin' he's the guy . . . but do you realize if he was and somethin' happened to you, I could never forgive myself? For Christ sakes, gimme a break. You know you own a piece of this black heart of mine."

"Lane, I've said it before and I'll say it again. You're a prick!"

He smiled at her.

"All right . . . all right!" Gina said.

"You wanna coffee?"

"No!" Her voice softened. "And yes, I still see him."

"Did you see 'im last night?"

"No, but that doesn't mean he was the one out at your place."

"I'm not sayin' that, Gina. C'mon, take off the boxin' gloves. When's the last time you saw him?"

"Three nights ago. We took a ride to a little place in York Beach, Maine—the Cob 'n Kettle Restaurant. It was late when we got back. He . . . well, he went home after he dropped me off."

Lane knew she had started to say "he stayed over" but pretended it had passed by him as he spoke again. "Gina, I swear to God, I hope he's not the guy. Can you tell me anythin' . . . anythin' that could make us both buy that we shouldn't look any further at him?"

"Lane, I've worked for you for six years. That has to count for something. I'll admit, I feel something for him, but it's not that reason that keeps telling me he's not our man. I'll check out every lead I get on him, for your sake as well as my own. I just want one favor from you and I think I rate it."

"Ask."

"Until we find out for sure, don't interfere in my relationship with him. Don't spoil it for us."

"What do you mean 'interfere'?"

"You know, Lane, don't have us followed or have that electronic genius of yours, Ernie, go tapping our phones."

"Hey—hey, that's hittin' below the belt. What kinda crumb do you think I am?"

She studied him for a moment. "Lane . . . I'm sorry, I guess I was out of line."

"Forget it, hon, that's love for you."

She smiled at him. "Does it show that much?"

"Like a nude broad at Sunday mass."

At the very moment that Lane and Gina were talking, a telephone truck was parked in front of Gina's apartment. It was not a truck owned any longer by the telephone company. It was one of the surplus vehicles owned by Lane Garrett and kept undercover by Ernest. None of the other investigators had ever seen it. Above the parked truck, Ernest Hampton, dressed as a telephone linesman, was climbing up a pole. He could just as easily have entered Gina's apartment, but he knew better. Gina, he had assessed, would be apt to stumble on the drop placed in her phone.

Complete with tools hanging on his side, he quickly spliced the line leading to her apartment and clipped on a small transmitter. He went directly from there to Dr. Robert Spellie's house. As he started up the pole, Spellie's wife appeared out the door and yelled to him.

"Is anything wrong?"

Ernest called down to her. "No, ma'am, just checking the lines. We're putting in more services in this area."

She waved at him and walked back into the house. Ernest then proceeded to Donald Spencer's corner apartment, employing the same route he had with the previous taps.

He then set about the task of placing his receiving recorders throughout the neighborhood. With one of his young assistants, he rented a total of four cars. Each time he'd drive to within the transmitters' signal, park the car, and place the receiving recorder in the trunk. They'd leave the command posts, his own "on-the-job" trainee picking him up in Ernest's car and driving him back to the rental agency to sign out the next rental.

The entire process lasted but a few hours and Ernest headed back to the office with his case of electronic equipment. He waited until Linda had left for lunch before he began checking the phones and thoroughly searching the offices for any type of transmitting devices.

When he was finished, he marched into Lane's office and plopped into a chair.

"Ernie, how'd you make out?" inquired Lane.

"Lane, I reassigned the surveillance team and hit all the phones except the Georges'. I'll get that one tonight." A picture of the Georges' phone line running along the far side of the house and into a clump of bushes flashed through his mind.

"Be careful around her house, Ernie. Remember what happened to our other man. Christian and her mother damn near killed the poor bastard."

"I won't let them get that close."

"You be sure, Ernie, the lady's got a gun. I dunno about Christian, but you can bet your big ass the old woman would blow you away. Now, how'd you make out here in the office?"

"There's not a damn bug on the premises, Lane. You can take my word for it . . . and your car is clean."

"Too bad," said Lane. "If there had been, then we'd know the bastard would hafta be close by."

Later, in the early evening, Lane called Christian, talking for more than twenty minutes. For the life of him, after he hung up, he couldn't remember what they had talked about for so long. He told her that he would be tied up for the evening and would call her in the morning. He advised her to stay close to the house and she cheerfully replied, "I'm staying right here until you pick me up."

As soon as he replaced the receiver, he picked it up and waited for the dial tone. He dialed Spellie for the fifth time that evening and, finally getting an answer, advised Spellie that Garcia was not the rapist.

"You sure!" exclaimed Spellie.

"Wish I wasn't," declared Lane.

"If there's anything, anything at all I can do, Lane, just ask."

"Thanks, Bob, I knew I could count on you," said Lane, "but

if I was you, I'd have Prendergast tighten up his security at the hospital."

"I'll certainly advise him to do so at once," assured Spellie.

Early the next morning, Gina was waiting in one of the private offices of Garrett International. She had Don Spencer's employment listings in front of her. Next to them was an application Don had filled out at the job just prior to Wilmington General. On a separate piece of paper, she had carefully written out the last three places that Don had given as work references. She placed the first of three phone calls.

"Good morning, Allied Laboratories."

"Good morning," said Gina. "May I have Personnel?"

"Just a moment, please."

"Hello. Personnel, Miss Goddard speaking."

"Miss Goddard, my name is Paula Roman from Wilmington General Hospital. A Mr. Donald Spencer has applied for employment here and has given your firm as a working reference from June of 1978 to February of 1980. I wonder if you might give us a recommendation?"

After several minutes, Miss Goddard returned. "I'm sorry, Miss Roman, the gentleman you mentioned never worked for us."

"Perhaps I've given you the wrong dates," Gina suggested.

"We file our past employees alphabetically, Miss Roman, not by the year. I assure you, the man was definitely never in our employ."

"Thank you . . . thank you very much."

Three employers, three alleged next of kin—the reaction was identical: Mr. Spencer has never been in our employ; Don Spencer, a relative . . . sorry, we never heard of him. The only accurate information on the application was his present address and telephone number, she thought.

Ernest Hampton had checked the recording on Spencer's phone. He had listened to the ringing of the phone as the operator cut in saying, "I'm sorry, that number is no longer in service." Being less than a block from the apartment, he decided to investigate further.

Ernest knocked loudly several times at Spencer's door. There was no answer. He glanced up and down the hallway and inserted a piece of plastic between the door and the jamb. Feeling the spring lock beginning to give, he pushed against the plastic strip. The lock snapped back, and Ernest entered the apartment. He looked around. The place was completely empty. He thought: What the hell is this, every time I show up, someone moves. I must be keeping the goddamn moving companies in business.

He heard voices right outside Spencer's door. He quickly turned the lock to open and pushed the button up. He opened the door to find a surprised couple standing with a puzzled man.

The man looked at Ernest and said, "May I help you? I'm the rental agent."

Ernest smiled casually. "Well, the door was open when I got here, so I came in to take a look around. It's very nice, but not what I'm looking for."

The man was a little suspicious. "We're the exclusive agents. How did you happen to know about the availability of the apartment?"

"My friend Don Spencer lived here, and he advised me it would be available."

The man took a card from his wallet, saying, "If we can be of service to you, please feel free to call us."

He nodded. "Thank you, I might just do that."

Ernest went to the nearest phone and called Lane.

"Yeah."

"Lane, I got bad news."

"Ernie, you shoulda been an undertaker. What is it now?"

"One of our ace suspects has flown the coop."

"Damn! Who is it, Ernie?"

"Don Spencer. His phone was disconnected so I paid a little visit to his apartment. It was cleaner than a pig's trough after feeding time."

"What the hell are you doin', Ernie, sendin' these guys telegrams? Every time you show up . . . they're gone."

"My feelings exactly."

"All right, pal, I'll catch you later."

Lane buzzed Gina, asking her to come into his office.

"How you makin' out with Spencer?"

She sat down dejectedly. "I checked out a previous job application. It's a dead end . . . everything on it, phony."

"When's the last time you heard from 'im?"

"The night we came back from Maine. He told me not to call his apartment, that he'd be gone about ten days."

"Sweetheart, I don't know how to tell you this 'cause I know you dig the guy, but your friend Don has split . . . blown town."

"Lane, you're wrong. I'm sure there's an explanation for all this."

"Honey, I just got information that tells me his phone is disconnected and his apartment has nothin' in it but four bare walls."

"Lane, are you sure?"

"Would I say it if I wasn't?"

Gina was silent.

"Gina, if you got somethin' on your mind, I'm a good listener."

"You're going to blow your top," Gina stated.

"If it's important, spit it out . . . I'll get over it."

"We had lunch at the Ritz last week. After, we took a walk through the Common. We were sitting on a park bench when suddenly he began to gasp for air . . . wheezing and making strange hoarse sounds."

Lane slammed his fist on the desk. "Damn it! What? Why didn't you tell me that before?" Lane got up and paced back and forth. "Christ almighty, we had him . . . you had him right in the palm of your hands. Instead of you settin' him up, he sets you up!"

"Lane, I'm sorry . . . I—"

"Gina, sorry ain't good enough. You're supposed to be a pro. I told you a million times, when you think with your heart in this business, you get burned."

"What do you want for me?" she blurted angrily. "You want me to quit? You want to throw me out the window? For Christ sakes, Lane, I made a mistake . . . so shoot me. Do anything you want. I feel bad enough about it without listening to your 'I told you so' routine."

Lane glared at her, snatching up his cigarettes.

"Lane"—Gina lowered her voice—"it's not that I made a mistake that you're upset about, what's upsetting you is what it's doing to Christian George, isn't it?"

"Are you on that mind-readin' kick again?"

"Answer me . . . isn't it?"

"Lay off, will you, Gina?" he snapped. Abruptly rising, he walked to the window, his back to her.

"Lane, for once will you drop the tough-guy number? You're the one who told me we could talk to each other," Gina urged. "Answer me . . . you bum," she added affectionately.

Calmer now, he faced her. "Yeah . . . yeah, I suppose you're right. I'm the guy that's supposed to watch over her—I'm the guy that keeps tellin' her not to worry, and bingo, right in my own backyard this guy knocks me out, ties me up like a rag doll, and chases her into the woods. If it wasn't for her, I'd probably still be tied up in my own goddamn driveway!"

It was midafternoon when Christian began preparing the evening meal. Teddy and Mrs. Day had taken a walk to the corner store, yet Christian's mind was at ease. Unknown to her mother, they had an unseen escort, an agent from Garrett International. Lane had advised Christian to try to maintain a normal profile. He confided to her that whenever she or her family left the house, they would be well looked after. She had been furnished with photos of Lane's men, so she would be alerted if someone else had followed her.

She had just mixed the giblets into the stuffing as the phone rang. She answered it, expecting it to be Lane. "Hello, this is your number-one agent speaking."

"I should say you are." The muffled voice laughed snidely. "Did you ever get to eat your lobster?"

As an automatic reaction to his voice, Christian began to tremble.

"Christian, are you there, my Christian?"

"Yes . . . yes, I'm here."

"I should have killed him . . . I should have killed Lane."

"You promised me . . . you wouldn't hurt . . . him," she said.

"I should've split his skull. Christian . . . I wanted you . . . but you hid from me. Why? You don't have to be frightened of me. I won't hurt you. I never hurt anything . . . that's mine. Next time you run away . . . from me . . . I'll kill him."

She tried to keep him talking. "But . . . he means nothing . . . to me."

"He's trying to keep me from you. Nobody can stand between us . . . nobody!" He wheezed, heaving a series of disgusting grunting, snorting noises. "No . . . I won't kill him . . . just yet! I'll get around him . . . you'll see what a fool . . . he is." His evil laugh mixed with his choking and snorting. "He thinks I'm like that imbecile bank robber you caught. Yes . . . that's what I'll do . . . first."

"How—how are things at the hospital?"

"Shame on you, Christian. Are you trying to trap me?"

"No—no, I just couldn't think of anything else to say."

"Tell me what I want to hear." His gargling voice grew demanding. "Tell me . . . say it . . . say it!"

She nearly gagged on the words. "I'm all yours . . . I want you to make love to me again. Your name isn't Carlos; what is it?"

"Christian . . . I'm coming for you . . . I'll tell you then."

The phone went dead. Christian immediately called Lane.

"Good afternoon, Garrett International."

"This is Christian George. May I speak to Mr. Garrett?"

"Certainly, Mrs. George, just a moment, please."

"Hello, is this my number-one agent?" inquired Lane.

"Lane, he just called me!"

"Relax. Just take your time and try to tell me everything he said."

"He said he should have killed you the other night. He told me he's coming for me. He asked me if we had a chance to eat the lobsters."

"Christian, did he say why he didn't kill me?"

"Yes, he said he wanted to prove you were a fool first and that he's no imbecile like that bank robber we caught in the backyard. Lane, I'm frightened . . . he keeps saying he's coming for me."

Lane was calm as he spoke to her. "Why don't you put the coffee on; I'll be there in less than an hour."

Lane made a rushed phone call. He stopped to pick Ernest up and sped toward Christian's house. He wheeled the Lincoln up in front of her walkway, his tires rubbing against the curb. Leaving Ernest in the car, he stepped out and looked all around as he shut the door. Across the street at the Dawson home, he spotted a man washing a car. It was Charlie. Lane did not acknowledge him but dashed into the house.

Mrs. Day showed him to the kitchen and poured him a coffee.

"Christian, why don't you join me in the backyard," pressed Lane.

"It's a little chilly out there," she answered.

He picked up his coffee, coaxing, "C'mon, don't be a sissy."

They sat down at the picnic table as Lane spoke to her. "Christian, can you get rid of your son and mother for a little while?"

She smiled uncertainly. "Wouldn't it be a lot easier to go to your place?"

Making sure no one was watching, he leaned over, kissing her on the lips. "There's nothin' I'd like better. But, er, I guess there's only one way to tell you—I think your house has a bug in it."

"A what?"

"I think somehow that someone planted a monitoring device in your house. I got my electronics man in the car. If it's there, and I'm sure it is, he'll find it in no time."

"Lane, how do you know?"

"You said he mentioned your havin' caught that bank robber. That was never publicized in the news anywhere. The only place we talked about that was in your kitchen."

"Maybe one of the policemen you turned the man over to told someone."

"Christian, believe me, you got a bug in that house, and it's gotta be in the kitchen."

"I'll ask mother to take Teddy to the store again and take her time."

"When we go back into the kitchen, watch what you say, and pull your mother aside to tell her about takin' Teddy to the store."

They returned to the house. Taking her mother into the den, Christian advised her of the situation. As Mrs. Day left with Teddy, Lane motioned Ernest into the house.

Ernest brought with him a walkie-talkie–type instrument and fully extended the aerial. Christian and Lane were forcing small talk and watching as Ernest started his search. He began over by the sink, working his way slowly around the room, in cabinets, drawers, behind shades, and up and down the walls. As he neared the wall phone, the needle suddenly zoomed to "transmitting signal" and the antenna pointed right at the statue of the Virgin

Mary with the roll of white paper held between its hands. Ernest nodded his head at them, pointing to the statue.

He carefully lifted the statue, laying it facedown, and, with a penknife, scraped the soft plaster of Paris at the back of the head. He had just begun when a round hole appeared where it had been filled. He laid the statue back in his hand as the bug fell into it. He put the statue up to his eye, looking through the mouth that served as a funnel for picking up sound. Ernest took out a glass jar from the case he carried and placed the bug into it, screwing on the lid again. He put his finger to his lips and returned to search the rest of the kitchen while Christian and Lane continued with their superficial conversation. He scanned all the rooms in the house, finding nothing.

He walked back into the kitchen, saying, "All right, we're alone."

"Ernie, you sure that ain't pickin' us up through the jar?"

"I disarmed it. I took out the battery."

"Thanks, pal. See if you can find the other end of that thing."

"We'll have to get lucky, Lane. This will carry for at least six blocks. It could be in a car, house, hidden in a bush . . . anyplace."

"Just do the best you can, Ernie."

"Aren't you the man who watched me one day?" Christian asked.

"I'm sorry. Christian, this is Ernest Hampton."

"My pleasure, Mrs. George. Yes, I was the culprit. You've got a great memory."

"Would you like some coffee, Ernest? And please call me Christian."

"I have to be on my way, Christian. I work for a real slave driver."

As Ernest left, Lane immediately asked, "Christian, who gave you the statue?"

"I don't know, Lane; it was sent through the mail. The note said they were sorry to hear about Ben."

"Do you still have the card?"

"It wasn't signed, so I threw it away."

"Now it all makes sense to me. The way the guy knew Garcia's name before the media announced it. Him knowin' about our meetin' at Zito's. No wonder he thought we ate there. That's how this bum knew about our day at the pool—that's how he knew where we'd be the other night . . . everythin'. He's been listenin' all the time. Well, that's one for him . . . but now we even it up."

chapter 20

It was seven-thirty P.M. Dr. Robert Spellie was speaking with Virginia Merguson at Wilmington General Hospital. They sat alone in the quiet confines of the small coffee room. Spellie had a paper cup of hot soup that singed his hand while Merguson was drinking some apple juice.

"This is my favorite time of day, Doctor. The patients are all fed and busy with their visitors. They won't be bothering a nurse for the next hour. It makes it so peaceful—heavenly, if I may say so."

Spellie looked quietly into her eyes. "Tell me, Virginia, has Lane Garrett ever visited you again?"

"You know my feelings about him. He's a despicable, uncouth man. He has not visited me again . . . and if he does, he shall never again gain entrance to my home."

"I'm sorry he upset you."

"I knew you would understand."

Spellie hesitated. "We've been together for quite some time and we've always gotten along well. Since it's your home, if you don't want him there, you have a perfect right to object."

"I understand you, Doctor." Merguson smiled. "We are indeed fortunate to have men like you at this hospital."

Ernest Hampton had received an early-morning call from Lane inviting him to his house for breakfast. Ernest sat by the pool as Lane trudged across the lawn with a tray—a pot of coffee, cups, milk, sugar, and toast. Lane set the tray on the table next to Ernest.

"Help yourself, pal," offered Lane.

"Just coffee," declared Ernest, controlling the temptation to ask Lane where the rest of his breakfast was.

Lane poured himself and Ernest a cup of coffee and, while munching on a slice of toast, he looked out over the pool to the trees that were just beginning to loose their leaves.

"Ernie, where did the summer go?"

Ernest smiled. "I never saw it. You've had me in buildings, bars, trucks, on top of telephone poles—bugging and breaking into half the city of Boston."

"Yeah, I guess you've been busy. Pal, it looks like we're both gonna get a lot busier." Lane lit a cigarette. "That bug we found at Christian's yesterday—you don't exactly find them in your corner drugstore. The way he sent the bug in . . . making sure it would be by the phone. This guy's cute, Ernie . . . real cute. It puts this bum into a whole new category."

"The man has to have more than an average amount of working knowledge in electronics," Ernest said. "His ingenuity, the way he operates—besides being a sickie—you would have to say that he's a bright boy."

"Ernie, there's a million broads runnin' around the city, not to mention a couple thousand hookers, yet it seems that none of them interest him. It's Christian—with all the risk, and knowin' the consequences if we nail 'im—he keeps comin' for. Why? That's the key to this thing. Why Christian?"

"Like you said one time, Lane, maybe the guy sees other women and is perfectly normal. This guy's a nut. If we start trying to read his mind, we'll wind up in straitjackets."

"I've been givin' Bob Spellie, that Spencer guy, and that Summers kid a lot of thought. I don't know about Spencer's or Summers' backgrounds, but I know Spellie's one of them ham radio freaks."

"Lane, being a ham operator is a long way from having knowledge about bugging equipment. And if he did, where the hell would he get his hands on it?"

"You didn't let me finish, Ernie. He's told me many times how he builds ham radio sets. It's like a hobby for him, you know, a way to relax. I still doubt that Bob is our man. But you know, Ernie, with Bob's background, how easy would it be to fake some sort of symptoms to throw people off the track. I tell myself it can't be my pal Bob. Then I tell myself he has the knowledge to put a bug together. He has the knowledge to have people believe that whoever's behind that voice has some sort of sickness. You know what, Ernie? It comes back to the bottom line: I gotta find out for sure."

"Lane, I would have to put Spencer right up there as number one. He has a relationship going on with Gina, conned her to the ears, and that was no easy task; Gina's been around a long time. The man completely falsified his applications. He picked up, lock, stock, and barrel, and disappears. That's the guy who fits the part for me. Spellie is stationary, reliable. He's a respected man in the community and by his peers. Spellie has everything to lose. Spencer, he's another case entirely—he's got nothing to lose."

"Yeah, Ernie, I agree with everythin' you said about Spellie, with one exception. When a guy has a screw loose, all those things go down the drain—they don't mean nothin'. If Spellie is our man, because of his background it's gonna be a lot tougher to bring him down. Remember, he called me in on this case, and, if he's the guy, it was a clever ruse to hide his guilt. Any cop in the city would buy that Spencer did it. But you take a popular guy like Spellie, a doctor no less—why, for Christ sakes, they'd rather lock you and me up before they put someone like that away. And another thing, Ernie, the guy's brilliant. If it is him, we're gonna have one bitch of a time hangin' it on 'im."

"How about Summers?" queried Ernest.

"Yeah, how's about him?" retorted Lane.

"There's the long shot he might be some kind of electronics genius. He's certainly got an old man with dough. He probably could afford to buy a whole Radio Shack store."

"There's that possibility," argued Lane. "Maybe New York's come up with a full background check on him. I'll give them a buzz later. But even if he is the bastard we're after, where the hell is he?"

"And then we have Schneiderman," deliberated Ernie, "who thought he was a free-lance gynecologist with his unsuspecting female patients in the Midwest. And to top it off, we know he's popping pills. Maybe the good doctor has become a Dr. Jekyll and Mr. Hyde from all those pills."

Several days had passed. The personnel at Garrett International had worked around the clock. Gina had contacted almost every "Spencer" in the Boston area, looking for anyone who might have known Don. It was fruitless. The others had checked out countless license plate numbers to determine the owners of vehicles. The license number of any car that passed Christian's house or the home of Lane Garrett was also noted and added to the list. Most of them were repeats, people who lived in or visited the area of the two locations. One by one they were methodically checked.

Lane had almost the entire staff working on the case. The first step was to obtain the names and addresses of the automobile owners from the Registry of Motor Vehicles. Operatives who worked for Lane went daily to the respective town halls. There they would look at the census list and determine what means the owner of the vehicle had for employment. Once the list of men was compiled, the names were placed in a "probably suspect" category, rating them from one to ten. The rating was determined by age, background, probable opportunity, and general analysis of the individual. It was, to say the least, a tedious task, but one that the agency members handled with intense tenacity. The list, once compiled, rated, and analyzed, showed little promise. There were but two men on the entire list who rated as high as four—a drug salesman and a hospital equipment representative.

Exhausted, Gina plopped in front of her television to watch the ten P.M. news. A Scotch and water was in her hand. As she brought the glass to her mouth, there was a knock at the door. She glanced automatically at the watch on her slim wrist and wondered who it could be at that hour. She edged the door open to the latch chain and peered out. It was Don Spencer! He was standing there smiling at her, a dozen roses in his hand.

"Well, aren't you going to let me in?"

"Don!"

"Well, who did you expect this time of night?"

"I—I—"

"The door," he coaxed, smiling.

As Gina closed the door, enabling her to slide the chain off, she had mixed emotions. She was ecstatic at seeing him and troubled about the manner in which he'd left his apartment. She opened the door, allowing him in, and he closed it behind him. He handed Gina the long-stemmed roses, holding her and kissing her.

"I missed you . . . I love you." He kissed her again. "I never want to leave you."

With the bouquet in her hand, Gina wrapped her arms around his neck, drawing him close to her. She kissed him tenderly, excited by the nearness of him. She touched his face. "Don, I've missed you. Where have you been?"

"I had some things to attend to. I promise I'll never leave you again."

"Drink?" she asked, trying to be casual.

"Yes," he answered, his eyes gleaming.

She was at the kitchen counter fixing them both a drink.

"I called your apartment. The phone was disconnected."

"I know," he responded, taking the drink from her. Changing the subject, he toasted her. "Here's to you. Wait, here's to us." Their glasses met and clinked as they smiled at each other.

"I left my undercover assignment. They transferred me to a permanent position. I knew about this two weeks ago, but I wanted everything to be just right before I told you."

Her words were empty as she raised her glass to him. "Congratulations, Don, I'm very happy for you."

He sensed the lack of enthusiasm in her voice. "Gina, what's wrong? It's not for me I'm happy, it's for us."

She forced herself to ask him, "Don . . . are you still living in your apartment?"

"No."

"Why didn't you tell me you were moving?"

"Please, Gina, trust me." He kissed her. She tried to let herself respond, but couldn't. Her mind was filled with Lane's words: "When you think with your heart in this business, you get burned."

"I'm trying to trust you, Don, but you're making it very difficult."

He looked at her, pausing for a moment. "Gina, I have to know one thing. Do you love me?"

"Don, I'm confused."

"Forget for the moment whatever else is in your mind. Do you love me, do you, Gina?"

Quietly, she spoke. "Don, there's just so much I don't know about you."

"Do you love me?"

She pushed all the suspicions from her mind and murmured, "Yes."

"I have a surprise for you," he whispered, tickling her ear with his breath.

She flicked her warm tongue on his lips. "What is it?"

"Put your coat on, we're going for a ride."

She snuggled to him. "It can't be that good. Let's stay here."

"We can come back . . . you won't be disappointed. C'mon, we won't be that long."

"Don . . . let's go tomorrow," she pleaded.

"Please . . . it's important. It will help you understand a lot you don't know about me."

They went out into the chilled night air. They got into his car and she cuddled to him, the warm glow showing in her face. He headed onto the interstate highway to Malden, a quaint suburban town north of Boston. Her head rested on his shoulder, with one arm spanning the length of his back and the other holding her close to him.

"Where are we going?" she asked him drowsily.

"It's a surprise. It won't be much longer."

They pulled off the main street into a quiet, older neighborhood. Huge maple trees lined both sides of the street, coming together in midair, causing a tunnellike appearance from the street below.

Don stopped the car in front of a modest Cape Cod–styled home, saying, "We're here."

"Who lives here?" asked Gina.

"C'mon, I want you to meet them."

They walked to the door. Don had a set of keys and opened it, turning on the lights. As he closed the door, Gina panicked for she saw the place was completely empty.

"Don," she said nervously, "there's no one here. It's empty."

She didn't know what to expect when he took her by the shoulders and faced her.

"Gina, I bought it for us. I want you to marry me!"

"Marry you . . . marry you? Oh, Don, marry you." She broke into tears as he held her.

"Does that mean yes?" he asked hopefully, kissing the tears on her cheek.

"Of course that means yes," she cried. "You big . . . dummy."

His hand came under her chin, raising her head, kissing her. She wrapped her arms around him, saying, "I love you . . . I do love you."

Room by room they went through the small, modest house.

"I wanted to wait until it was furnished before I showed you," he admitted.

"Oh, Don, it's like a doll house, it's beautiful. Besides, if you didn't let me help pick out the furniture, I'd have murdered you. Your taste in furniture . . . well, it's terrible."

"Sure, now that I popped the question and you have me hooked, now you tell me how you really feel. Is there anything else you want to get off your chest?"

Don had presented the perfect opportunity for Gina to ask him what was gnawing at her.

Half teasing, she asked, "Are you going to introduce me to your friends . . . at the station?"

"You bet I am. I'm dying to show you off."

Gina was taken aback. "You are?"

"If I hadn't been on that undercover thing for so long, I would have done it almost the day I met you."

"Undercover for whom?" she inquired.

"The CIB," he flatly stated.

"What CIB?"

"The Criminal Investigation Bureau of the State Police," he explained. "I've worked the division for the past seven years."

"Is that all over with now?"

"What?"

"Your undercover assignment."

"Sure, it's all wrapped up."

"Now that it's over, can you tell me about it?"

"I can see you're going to be one of those questioning wives. Yes, it's over. I suppose I can tell you about it. I worked undercover as an orderly at Wilmington General Hospital."

Gina was absolutely flabbergasted. "At the hospital?"

"Yes, we had a tip that large amounts of drugs were missing. I was planted there to see if there was any connection with the syndicate."

Gina was nearly in a daze. "Was there?"

"Not in this one. I had one person pegged for it, a man by the name of Carlos Garcia, who was found shot to death. I stayed on a couple more weeks just to make sure. There wasn't any other problem outside of maybe staff personnel popping it for personal use, so we're sure it was him stealing dope from the hospital."

Gina began crying again. "Oh, Don . . . you're a cop . . . a real cop."

He was dumbfounded. "Gina, what's the matter? I told you that almost the first time we met."

She began laughing and crying at the same time. "I—I was assigned to follow you! I'm a private investigator! A woman was raped in that hospital and you were one of our key suspects." She was laughing uncontrollably.

"You, a private investigator! You!"

"Yes, and you're a cop . . . a cop." Tears of laughter were squeezed from her eyes.

She playfully attempted to poke him on the nose. He caught her hand and pulled her toward him. Then he took off his jacket and her coat, letting them drop to the floor. He reached over her shoulder, shutting off the lights. They slipped to the floor, using their clothing to lie on. They made love in that empty house on the bare floor. It would be sunrise before they awoke in each other's arms, naked, covered by their coats.

Lane Garrett was at Dennis Raskin's home. He sat at the kitchen table as Mary hung up a dish towel and joined him.

"Even now, Lane, it's just so difficult for me to believe he's gone."

"I don't have to tell you how I felt about him, Mary. A hundred times a week I expect him to come through my office door. Are you okay? I mean, do you need anythin'? Can I do anythin' for you?"

"Lane, you're a lovely man. I'm fine. It's just going to take some getting used to, being here without Dennis."

"Mary, just before Dennis died, he asked Ernest to have a picture blown up for him. I think it could help us on this case we're workin' on. You don't know what picture he was talkin' about?"

"Why don't I show you into his study. Everything is exactly

the way he left it. I really haven't been able to bring myself to straighten it up."

Lane followed Mary into the small study. A black leather couch lined a walnut-paneled wall. Its matching chair was pushed under a large colonial wooden desk. On top of the desk and on the walls were scores of framed items, memorabilia Dennis had collected during his years with the FBI.

"Lane, please help yourself. I'll wait in the kitchen."

"All right, Mary, it shouldn't take me long."

Lane looked at the top of the desk—not a photograph or file. Two filing cabinets against the wall were his next objective. He went to the *G* section and pulled from it a rather large file marked "Christian George." It contained daily reports, information he had received from William Fulton, and a large assortment of pictures. The photos were some of those Ernest had taken, while others Dennis had undoubtedly obtained from private sources. Lane walked back to the kitchen with the entire folder.

"Mary, would it be all right if I borrowed this folder?"

"Lane, I'm sure I won't have any need for it. Why don't you just keep it?"

"Thanks, Mary, I appreciate it." He placed the folder on the table and took her by the shoulders. "I want you to make me one promise," he declared.

"What is it, Lane?"

"If you need anythin', I don't care what it is, I want you to call me."

She smiled gratefully. "Thank you, Lane, I know you mean it. I'll call if there is anything I need."

"Remember, you call, any time, anyplace."

"Lane."

"Yeah?"

"Thank you."

"Thank me, for what?"

"I was married to a federal agent for over twenty years. Do you think for one minute I believed that story from the funeral parlor: 'We don't need any money because your husband had a policy with Garrett International'?"

Lane flushed. "Now, Mary, that's old business; let's not get on that number."

She leaned over, kissing him on the cheek. "Take care of yourself, Lane."

He smiled. "They'll never catch up to a buzzard like me."

There was a touch of anguish in Mary Raskin's face. "You know, Lane, Dennis used to say much the same thing."

As Gina sat herself upon the edge of Lane's desk, Linda interrupted, bringing Lane his messages.

"Here's your list, sir," stated Linda.

"Thank you." He waited for her to leave before he glanced up at Gina. "All right, let's have it. You're bubblin' enough inside of you to explode."

"I'm fine, but you're going to need someone to be kind to you today."

"Why?"

"Because, Mr. Garrett, I have eliminated your number-one suspect from the George case."

"You found him?"

"He found me."

"You mean you were with him and you didn't call me?"

"The answer is yes, absolutely, positively . . . I was with him."

"Gina, I'm tellin' you this better be good, like the guy's a Fed or somethin'."

"You're close."

"Close, how close?"

"Cop!"

"Cop! You said the guy's a cop?"

She smiled broadly. "What am I speaking, Spanish? Like a police officer, you know, cop."

"Gina, if this is your idea of a gag, it ain't funny." Lane frowned.

"Lane, Don Spencer was working undercover for the CIB. He was assigned to Wilmington General Hospital because of the large amount of drug losses. He had Carlos Garcia figured for it. Lane, that's what Garcia meant when he said on the tape 'that thing at the hospital'—not the rape."

"Did you check it out—did you check the story out?"

"Here's his number at the state police in Framingham. He's a narc."

"Damn it, why didn't Spellie know he was undercover?"

"Don told me this morning the only one that knew was the head of the hospital, Jonathan Prendergast. Lane, there's one small matter."

"Is this gonna hurt?"

"Just a little."

"Is it gonna hurt enough for me to have a drink?"

"Yes—yes, I would say you'll need at least one."

Lane poured himself a straight shot of Chivas Regal. "Go ahead, I'm ready."

"Don bought us a house. We're going to be married! And he'd like me to quit this job!"

Lane stared at her, drank the Scotch, and poured himself another, gulping it down. He smiled at her, pleased. "So you found yourself a guy that thought of you like with washing machines, dirty dishes, and babies." He poured them both a drink. "Here, have one with me."

"Lane, I love him."

"I know you do. Here's to all the happiness in the world and a houseful of kids."

"Lane, I'd like to stay and see the George case through with you."

"You're thinkin' with your heart again."

"I'd still like to stay."

"Gina . . . I need you on this one; I'm glad you're stayin'."

chapter 21

Christian was curled up on the couch in the den watching television with her mother. They were watching *All in the Family* with the sound turned low so as not to disturb Teddy, who was asleep in his bed. Mrs. Day sat in her favorite chair, knitting, her attention on the screen.

"You know who that Archie reminds me of?"

"Who, Mom?"

"He reminds me of Lane."

Christian smiled. "I'm sure Lane would love to hear that."

"No, you know what I mean—Archie trying to act so hard and tough when he's really a pussycat. Lane's like that."

"I never quite thought of him as a pussycat. Although I'll agree he isn't as gruff as he would like people to think."

"You like him, don't you, Christian?"

"Sure, don't you, Mom?"

The old woman had a sly expression on her face. "Yes, I like him, but I think you like him more."

"Mom, I'm surprised at you."

"For heaven's sake, why?"

"If I didn't know better, I'd swear you were grilling me."

"Ah, Christian, you know your mother wouldn't think of doing that."

"Did you let Teddy go to the store today?"

"Yes, but I absolutely don't like the idea of his going alone."

"Mom, I want him to be a little independent."

"You know that's not what I mean. I don't worry about his

being on his own a little, it's that character that's still calling you."

"Mom, it's me he wants. Besides, you know Lane has men outside this house twenty-four hours a day."

"Well, I still don't like the idea."

The phone began ringing. Christian started to get up but her mother, being closer, said, "I'll get it." She placed her knitting in the basket by her feet and stretched her arm over to the desk, answering the ring. "Hello."

"Is Christian there?"

Mrs. Day recognized the muffled voice; she put her hand over the phone, saying, "It's him."

Christian jumped up to answer it and her mother handed her the phone.

"Hello," Christian answered.

"Hello, Christian . . . how are you?" His words were slurred and strange.

She was upset but not trembling. "Fine . . . I'm fine."

"Christian . . . you don't sound happy . . . to hear from me." There was a childish, pouting tone to his voice.

"I'm a little . . . tired . . . just tired," she lied.

"You know, Christian . . . someone has forbidden me to call you. I don't like that . . . that makes me want you all the more. I called you anyway."

"Who—who doesn't want you to call me?" She listened for several moments to the deep, pensive breathing.

"She told me . . . if I keep calling you . . . I'm going to get in trouble. That makes me angry . . . very angry."

"Who told you that?" Christian queried bravely.

"That doesn't matter. I told her you were all mine . . . why shouldn't I call you? Isn't that right, Christian? Aren't you all mine?"

"Yes, of course I'm all yours."

"I'm making plans for . . . us, Christian . . . I'll be coming for you soon . . . real soon."

Christian heard some type of music in the background. "The music is pretty. I didn't know you liked music too. Are you listening to the radio?"

"No . . . no, I'm not. Christian . . . are you ready to . . . come with me?" His voice was becoming urgent.

"Records, that's nice-sounding; do you have your special records on?"

"It's not important. Are you ready to come with . . . me?"

"Yes . . . let me know where."

"I'll let you know . . . soon." The phone's connection was broken.

Her mother anxiously stood by. "Christian, what did he say?"

"Mom, let me call Lane first." Christian dialed Lane's home number as she prayed: Be home, Lane, please be home.

His phone was ringing. "Yeah."

"Lane, he just called again."

They spent at least thirty minutes on the line as she reconstructed the words and emotions of the conversation. He told her he would see her sometime before noon the following day.

Lane placed a call to Ernest Hampton.

"Hello."

"Ernie, it's me; I hope I didn't wake you."

"No, it's okay. Just watching the news."

"Ernie, our friend has just called Christian. She said somethin' about music in the background. Pick up that tape first thing in the mornin' and meet me in the office by nine. Can you make it, pal?"

"I'll be there, Lane."

"Thanks, see you then."

When Ernest arrived the next morning, Linda waved him right into Lane's private office. Ernest simply nodded his greeting to Lane as he shoved the George tape into the recorder and clicked it on. They listened to it several times before Lane signaled Ernest to shut it off.

"Let's start from the top, Ernie. This guy runs hot and cold. One day he's like a ravin' maniac and the next, the guy sounds mostly like he just woke up. He's gotta be on somethin'—pills, coke, grass . . . somethin'. Do you go along with that, Ernie?"

"I agree, with one variation. There could be a possibility that he takes some sort of medication for his condition and is taking it to excess. Maybe it's some sort of relaxant."

"All right, I'll buy that. We know one other thing about this guy since he called her. *Somebody* is keepin' tabs on 'im. He kept referrin' to a *she* in his conversation. '*She* doesn't want me to call you'—*'she* told him he'd get in trouble.' Now, who the hell could *she* be?"

Ernest was contemplating the question. "Lane, it's a good chance it's not his wife, if he's even married. Wives simply can't take a joke like knowing their man is running around chasing other women. So I think we can rule that out. So who else is left? My guess, starting at the top of the order, is his mother, a sister, close relative, or, perhaps a little far-fetched, some female friend he feels a strong kinship to."

"I gotta go with the first two," declared Lane. "It's gotta be a mother or sister. The bond has to be a lot stronger than a friend. Yeah, Ernie, it's his mother or sister. Where do they draw the line and admit to themselves this duck is sick . . . and needs help?"

"An educated guess, Lane, if they haven't convinced him to seek help at this point, and they haven't taken the initiative to commit him . . . then I don't think they'll turn him in for anything short of murder . . . maybe not even then."

Lane tapped a cigarette on the desk. "Ernie, let's take step number three. The music, I couldn't make it out. Do you think you can amplify it so we can find out what it is? He said it wasn't the radio. If it's records or somethin' like that, it could give us another piece of the puzzle as to what makes this joker tick."

"That's no problem, Lane. I can have that done by late today."

Lane had promised Christian that he would take her, Teddy, and Mrs. Day out for lunch. He picked them up at their home. They drove less than a mile to a restaurant called Artie's Fireside, where they were enthusiastically greeted by the owner, Artie, an ex-fighter.

He personally escorted Lane and his companions to their choice of booths and handed them menus, saying, "Give ya a hot tip, the London broil, it's good today. I doctored it up while the chef wasn't lookin'." He waited for their nods of approval, then departed.

They had finished their dessert when Artie reappeared to advise Lane that he had an important phone call. Lane had left word with Linda where he would be.

Artie, knowing the sensitive nature of Lane's business, led his friend through the hustling kitchen to a phone in the rear.

Waitresses were calling out their orders to chefs who were

blurs of motion as they chopped, mixed, prepared, and rushed the orders out to the waiting girls. Lane walked to the phone adjacent to the back door and picked it up, glancing out the screen door into the parking lot.

"Yeah."

"Lane, it's me, Ernest."

"What is it, Ernie?"

"Lane, I got it, the recording."

"Ernie, don't say any more over the phone; they got extensions all over this joint. Meet me at the office in an hour."

Lane returned to their table and paid the check. He left Christian, Teddy, and her mother off in front of their house, putting the Lincoln into park as he waited for Mrs. Day and the boy to disappear behind the front door.

Christian poked her head into the passenger window. "We truly enjoyed it, Lane."

"So did I; I'll call you later on."

"Come here." Her eyes and tone were suggestive as she crooked her little finger, egging him over.

"They might see us."

"Don't underestimate my mother. By now she has Teddy busy in the backyard."

Lane slid over, held her smooth face between his hands, and kissed her.

As they drew apart, she asked, "Are you going to call me later?"

"You just convinced me,"

"You're easy," she responded.

"You're bad; I'll call you later."

Ernest and Lane began listening intently to the music coming from the recorder. Ernest, using a complex array of electrical equipment, had filtered out the voices and amplified the background sound ten times. Hymns flowed from the recorder.

"For Christ sakes, Ernie, that's church music." Lane's eyes became opened wide. A sharp look of realization swept over his face. "Merguson! Ernie, it's that wacky Merguson!"

"The night nurse at Wilmington General?"

"Yeah."

"Lane, Christian was raped; she ain't got the right equipment."

"Damn, Ernie! I don't mean she raped Christian. The music—the music, it came from her house. She's got a room fixed up like a chapel. That music was always playin' in the background. The whole setup—includin' her—is real screwy. The broad looks like she just crawled outa the ground and she's got a goddamn dog I swear is a werewolf. A break, Ernie, do you realize we finally got a break? A real lead."

"I'll get a team right on the house and have them stick to it night and day."

"No, Ernie, wait. She's as cagey as the guy that called from her house; she'd spot 'em in a minute. I'll give you an hour's head start, tap her phone from the pole. It's two o'clock now. She doesn't go to work until around six or seven. I'll give her a tumble about three-thirty, rattle her cage a little, and then leave. If he's in there, he'll scram right after I do. If he isn't, the first thing Merguson'll do is head for the phone to let him know I was there."

"All right, Lane, but what if we don't come up with him that way?"

"Well, then, we'll stick to her like flypaper," Lane declared, "and if that don't work, we'll go back and strangle the old bitch until she coughs him up."

Ernest Hampton left and went about his mission. He tapped Virginia Merguson's phone and waited.

Lane pulled up in front of Merguson's house. As he closed the door to his car and looked toward the house, he noticed her car in the driveway. That's the car! That's the car that followed me and Christian that Sunday, Lane thought. The dog wasn't tied to his usual place alongside the driveway. Lane thought about it. Fang must be in the house. He had carefully planned out the questions he would ask Merguson. They had to be not enough to frighten her off, but just enough to give her and whoever she was in cahoots with something to think about.

He knocked on the front door and waited. He knocked again, this time louder, as he thought: Maybe the old witch is meditating.

After several attempts to gain admittance, he called out to her.

"Mrs. Merguson, I know you're in there. I'll only take a moment of your time."

Still there was no response. Lane walked around to the rear of the house, his eyes searching for the dog. Where the hell is that fleabag? He hasn't made a sound. Maybe she sent him to the vet's to get his teeth sharpened.

As Lane approached the back door, he noticed it was slightly ajar. Expecting the dog to spring at him any moment, he held the door open a crack and called out.

"Mrs. Merguson, your door is open; may I come in?"

Lane was positive that she was waiting for him to enter, holding the snarling beast by his chain, ready to let him pounce. He wrapped his coat around his arm and stepped through the door. He inched his way into the house, calling her. "Mrs. Merguson . . . Mrs. Merguson . . ."

Lane stopped dead in his tracks. He saw the dog! His chain was strung over the top of a closet. One end was tied to the doorknob; the other, around the dog's neck, was holding the huge animal in midair, like a side of slaughtered beef. His throat was slit. Blood was still dripping from his black carcass, forming a huge red puddle on the floor. Like a statue, Lane jolted to a stop, horrified, watching the blood seep from the dog's severed throat and drip, splashing into the puddle below. He drew his .38, walking carefully past the hanging dog, silently, down a cluttered hallway to where the solemn music led him.

He reached the religious room and carefully peered in. Merguson was there all right. She seemed to stare at him. Her glassy eyes held the last view of life and the first glimpse of death. His stomach churned. The steel-shafted crucifix, plunged into her chest, stood straight up, mounted in her body. The music had stopped. Another record dropped and Ave Maria began to play. Lane crossed the room to the record player, his gaze following the record's spin, and shut off the machine. He stooped down, noting the pills that were scattered on the floor. Sedatives or tranquilizers, he thought.

Looks like Junior didn't want to take his pills. With the .38 poised in front of him, Lane searched the rest of the small house. No one was there but Lane, Merguson, and the dead dog.

He went back into her bedroom, slowly looking around. His blood drained as he spotted it. It was a picture of a woman on Merguson's bureau. It looked enough like Christian to be her twin. Lane walked over to it. There was a hand-painted sign by the candle in front of the picture: Lord forgive this woman for the terrible wrongs she has committed.

He took the eight-by-ten framed photograph and held it in his hand, studying it. The eyes, mouth, face . . . hairstyle—Christian to the smallest detail. He turned the glass-enclosed picture over, taking off the back and sliding the picture out. On the reverse side of it was stamped Deanna's Photomart, Dissinger Avenue, San Diego, California. Lane rolled up the picture and put it inside his suit jacket pocket. He wiped off the frame and placed it in one of the bureau drawers.

Slowly, methodically, he searched the rest of the house, looking for another clue that would bring him closer to this madman. Meticulously he searched, leaving no trace of his having been there. Finally satisfied that he missed nothing, he left with only the picture.

He had been in the house for over an hour. On an outside chance that someone might have seen his car, he decided to call his friend, Captain Ray Tiernan.

"Headquarters."

"Captain Tiernan, please."

"Just a moment, sir."

"Hello, Captain Tiernan speaking."

"Ray, it's me, Lane."

"Who do you want arrested, Lane? What's up?"

"Do you know the chief of police in Wilmington?"

"No, but I could call him. What's on your mind?"

"Well, whoever he is, he's got two dead bodies on his hands."

"Two bodies!"

"Yeah, one's a dog and the other is a wacky old broad who finally got her wish—to go see God."

"Lane, are you involved?"

"Only to the extent that I stumbled into the house and found them."

"For Christ sakes, Lane, you call me up and tell me you found a stiff! What's it about?"

"Not now, Ray. I'll catch up with you sometime today and fill you in."

"All right . . . all right. Give me the address."

Lane passed on the information to Tiernan, left the phone booth he was in, and went to where Ernest was parked.

Approaching the car and leaning into the driver's window, Lane barked, "Ernie, move it . . . back to the office."

"Why, what happened?"

"She's dead."

"Dead!"

"You know, like departed, gone . . . dead. Let's get the hell outta this area. It's gonna be swarmin' with cops anytime now."

"What about the phone tap?"

"Ernie, there's a *stiff* less than a block from here. Forget the tap!"

They were both just under way when the first of the screaming police cars passed them, whisking toward the Merguson residence.

chapter 22

Lane and Ernest had just returned from the Merguson house; Gina had been waiting for them. Ernest passed Gina the picture that Lane had taken from the top of Virginia Merguson's dresser.

Her eyes were riveted on the eight-by-ten glossy. "Christ! If I didn't know better, I'd swear this was Christian George."

Lane sighed deeply and wiped his hand down over his face thoughtfully. "We couldn't have missed him by more than a half hour."

"How do you know?" Gina asked.

"There were six records on her player and the last one dropped while I was in the room. He sure as hell didn't put those records on after he killed the dog and her."

"The only logical thing," stated Ernest, "is that it had to be someone she was very close to. And we gotta assume that whoever it is, is from the hospital."

"Ernie, it's gotta be someone closer than just from the hospital. That girl's picture says so, and the dead dog says so. There's no way that dog would let a virtual stranger into that house. Whoever it is walked right past that dog . . . and lemme tell you somethin', that's doin' some."

"You know, Lane," Gina mulled pensively, "if that's a recent picture, she's got to be around thirty-two, thirty-three. Is it possible that the girl is the woman's daughter?"

"C'mon, hon, you're not thinkin'. First of all, a woman with a kisser like that old witch, Merguson, could never have a kid that beautiful. And secondly, remember the words on the picture: 'Forgive this woman for the terrible wrongs she has committed.'

The words 'forgive this woman'—they're much too impersonal to be about a daughter. If that were her kid, it would've read, 'forgive my child, daughter, or baby.' You know, somethin' like that. Besides, if it were her daughter, it would knock the old lady out to think her likeness had been raped and was being tormented by a guy *she* covered for."

Ernest waited for Lane to finish and then spoke enthusiastically. "We got two strong possibilities of finally nailing this guy. Merguson's employment application from the hospital has got to give us something—past positions, marriage, children, next of kin. And the picture—we have to run down the studio and hope they still have the order form. If they do, it could tell us a helluva lot."

"I'll handle the photo," declared Lane. "And speakin' of photos"—he lifted one from his desk—"Jordan finally sent up one of the Summers kid."

"I don't think the kid killed her," offered Ernest.

"I agree," added Gina. "He was only at the hospital a short time. It wouldn't fit for that close a relationship between him and the Merguson woman . . . unless he knew her prior to working there."

"You both get a ten on the scale. But where the hell is the kid? Where *does* he fit in?"

"Maybe he saw whoever raped Christian," volunteered Gina, "and is holing up somewhere."

"Ernie," Lane continued, reaching for the thick folder he had taken from Dennis Raskin's home, "before Dennis died, he wanted you to blow up one of the pictures in this folder. There are forty-seven of them, some of which you took. The rest, well, I dunno how he came by 'em. But you blow 'em all up and see what we come up with. Gina, I want you to take the rest of the file—employment applications, reports, the works. There must be better than a hundred pieces of literature in there. I want you to sift through 'em with a fine-tooth comb and see what we got."

Gina and Ernest left while Lane called long-distance information. After several clicks, the San Diego operator answered through the static interference.

Lane obtained the number of Deanna's Professional Photo Service. In speaking to Deanna, he learned that the name, Deanna's Photomart, had not been used for seven years. He was advised that she had the files that dated back that far, but it would take the better part of a month to trace the picture. Lane thanked her and hung up, disgusted.

A month . . . no way, Lane thought. We can't leave this mental case on the streets for another month.

Lane Garrett walked down the stilled corridors at Wilmington General Hospital. He proceeded directly to Dr. Spellie's office, where, without knocking, he entered. Spellie was just rising from his knees as Father Travers blessed him, making the sign of a cross.

"Sorry . . . I didn't mean to interrupt; I guess I shoulda knocked," Lane said, somewhat embarrassed.

Spellie, a bit flushed at Lane's appearance, swallowed nervously as he answered. "That's all right, Lane, Father Travers was just leaving."

The priest, upon leaving the room, smiled at both men, shutting the door.

"Bob, don't tell me you're one of them born-again Christians."

Spellie looked a bit wan as he responded. "Lane, it's the first time in ten years I've been to confession and I must tell you it feels rather good."

"Bob, I'm here about Merguson," declared Lane, changing the subject.

"Lane, it's still difficult to believe that awful thing about Mrs. Merguson. Virginia and I came here about the same time nine years ago. I'll readily admit that she wasn't the outgoing, friendly type; however, she more than lived up to her responsibilities here."

"Was she friendly with anyone, Bob?"

"The police were here this morning and couldn't find a single person who knew her on the social level."

"How about her employment application? Do you suppose I could get a copy of it?"

"Lane, I'm afraid that's going to be a problem."

"How so, Bob?"

"The chief of police requested the same thing this morning. When I went to the files . . . her application was missing."

Lane studied Spellie. "This joint seems to have an epidemic of missin' files and people turning up dead. Where was she before she came here?"

"If memory serves me right, I think she was out west somewhere. I really don't remember the hospital as she didn't talk about her past experience. But she was a dedicated nurse and a competent administrator."

"Bob, you gotta know more than that."

"I wish I did, Lane."

"Was she instrumental in helping any male gain employment here?"

"Not to my knowledge."

"Damn it, Bob, the woman worked here nine years. You mean to tell me nobody knew anythin' about her?"

"Sorry, Lane . . . there just isn't anything."

"There's gotta be somethin' here that can help us, Bob, and I intend to find it."

"I sincerely hope you do. As I said before, she wasn't especially friendly, but I can't imagine why anyone would want to kill her. What a grotesque way to die."

"How was that, Bob?"

"Skewered by a steel crucifix."

The clutch of apprehension grasped Lane. "How do you know that?"

"The paper. It was in one of the morning papers."

"Oh, I hadn't read it." Lane started to walk away when a different thought crossed his mind. He turned back to Spellie and asked, "By the way, Bob, who was workin' the day shift when she was killed?"

"I don't know offhand, Lane, it was my day off. I can check into it if you'd like me to."

"Yeah, do that, Bob, I'd appreciate it."

Don Spencer had long ago moved into Gina's apartment as they awaited the completion of their honeymoon home. They were both just waking up as the first part of daylight sifted through the window. She touched his lips with her finger.

"I love waking up beside you in the morning." She sighed.

He was still sleepy as he responded. "You know, I've been late three times this week."

"Don't worry"—she laughed—"this is one day you won't be late." She teasingly twisted the curls of hair on his chest.

"We'd better go."

"Complaining?" she queried, reaching down and gently holding his testicles.

"No . . . love it. Love you." His palm was on her breast, slowly circling the nipple as it grew taut. "How long are you going to keep working?"

She put her warm tongue in his ear while talking to him. "Just until we wind up the George . . . case."

They couldn't have picked a better day for the wedding. A bright sun lit up a clear blue sky. Huge willow trees graced the sloping green lawns at the fashionable Montego Country Club.

The entire staff of Garrett International was there—along with scores of others, state police, relatives, and a handful of uninvited freeloaders.

After the wedding, Christian and Lane arrived at Lane's house, turned off the alarm, and went in. He switched on the stereo in the plush living room, saying, "Wanna fix us a drink?"

She kicked off her shoes and went barefoot to the kitchen. Dimming the lights, he could hear her humming softly as she poured the cognac into the glasses. She returned with two large snifters.

"What did you fix us?"

"Courvoisier." She smiled. "I thought instead of having it in glasses, I'd add a touch of class and use your brandy snifters."

"You could drink that stuff out of a Dixie cup and look classy."

"Lane"—she raised an eyebrow—"has anyone ever told you that you have a way with words?"

"Yeah."

"Who?" she asked, a little surprised.

"My English teacher, that's who. She told me, 'Lane, you have a way with words, a way that positively destroys them.' "

He sat in the couch and she curled up beside him. He had a stack of Sinatra's records on. They listened to the soft melodic lyrics.

"Did you ever meet him?" she breathed.

"Who?"

"Sinatra."

"Honey, that's like meetin' God. Very few people do it while they're alive. If it came down to havin' him here or you here, I gotta tell you it'd be a toss-up."

She kissed him. "Who do you think would win?"

"Well, lemme see . . . if it really came down to the wire, I guess I'd hafta choose you. You're a helluva lot prettier."

She glanced at his glass. It was nearly empty. "You want me to freshen that up for you?"

"Yeah. I'll tell you, you really spoil a guy."

Christian went into the kitchen and fixed them both another drink. "Lane, I hope you bought more Courvoisier." She walked into his living room with the cognac.

He stood up and held her carefully, kissing her. "You're beautiful. You're really somethin'." She handed him the drink and he lifted his snifter. "Here's to you and a million tomorrows."

She toasted with him as he reached into his jacket pocket, taking from it a small package. The gift wrapping was discolored with age. He set it in her hand, saying, "It's for you."

By the way he said it, by the way he looked, she knew it was something special. "Lane," she whispered, "what is it?"

He took a large swallow of his cognac. "It—it was a present for my wife's birthday. She died before I could give it to her. I never unwrapped it."

She touched his face. "Oh, Lane . . . I can't take this."

He gazed at her, his eyes saying what his lips found difficult. "Christian, you're the only woman I've met since she died that I wanted to give that to. I want you to have it. Take it . . . for me."

Her hands trembled as she opened it. She raised the lid of the dainty blue box. It was a gold heart, ringed in diamonds, and hanging on a gold chain.

"Lane . . . it's beautiful," she murmured. "Will you put it on me?"

He took the heart from the box and unhooked the safety snap, facing her while he placed it around her neck. As he hooked the clasp and released the heart, it fell into the cleavage between her breasts. He gazed at it resting serenely on the whiteness of her skin. He looked back to her eyes as tears spilled onto her cheeks. He reached up, wiping her eyes with his hand.

"Don't you like it?"

She did not answer but silently took him by the hand and led him up the stairs into his darkened bedroom.

Lane's thoughts were filled with Christian as he entered his office building the next morning. His eyes showed the telltale signs of little sleep—he hadn't gotten back until four A.M. after dropping Christian off.

His memories were cut short as he bumped into Gina standing in front of the conference room door.

"You didn't have much of a honeymoon," he declared.

Gina glanced coyly at him. "Oh, I wouldn't say that."

"Do you plan on getting away?" Ernest asked her as he entered the room.

"Don gets his vacation in a few weeks. We're planning on going to Vegas."

"My, my"—Lane grinned—"you musta raked in a fistful yesterday."

"Well, we certainly couldn't go there on what you've paid me the last few years," countered Gina.

"Let's get on with the program. Ernie, how'd you make out with the blowups?" inquired Lane, with an edge of impatience.

"Lane, I blew up every picture. I went through them until I thought my eyes would drop out of my head. I don't know what the hell Dennis had in mind."

"Gina," Lane said, "I know you've been busy with the gala festivities, but did you get a chance to go over those papers in Dennis's file?"

"Lane, I took each piece and really worked it over. It's pretty much run of the mill . . . his reports, employment applications I have a few outside possibilities, but they don't look very promising."

Lane was shaking his head. "You two are gonna make me hafta do it."

"Have to do what, Lane?" asked Ernest.

"You know do what! You know I hate flyin', and you two are gonna make me hafta fly to San Diego and tip that studio upside down until I find out who the girl in the picture is!"

Gina smiled at him. "Lane, don't give us that 'you're afraid to fly' routine. You're just trying to con one of us into going."

"This case," interjected Ernest, "is running into real heavy expenses, Lane . . . but I guess that's the hospital's problem."

"Ernie, we got no choice." Lane paused, then took a deep breath. "I gotta go to California. Damn it, Ernie, I don't wanna leave here. You can bet your ass that if we can put a name on that picture I found at Merguson's, it'll lead us to our creep friend."

"When are you leaving for California, Lane?"

It was precisely at that moment that Tom O'Brien knocked on the door and walked in hesitantly.

Lane looked at Gina and Ernest, then back at Tom. "Tom, you look a little pale. I think you need some sun."

"Pale . . . sun?" asked a puzzled O'Brien.

"Yeah, sun," answered Lane.

For two hours Lane and Ernest drilled O'Brien on what he was to look for and do at Deanna's in San Diego.

"How long do you think I'll be gone?" asked O'Brien.

"Tom, this Deanna told me it would take the better part of a month to locate the duplicate of the picture—no way. I figure if you're out there—with her helpin' and spreadin' some bread around—three, maybe four days."

chapter 23

The slumped figure was sitting on the edge of the rumpled sofa, glassy-eyed, staring at his picture of Christian George. He was in the dingy room on the fourth floor of an ancient tenement. There were several opened suitcases on the floor. Clothes were flung carelessly about the room and an assortment of his other belongings cluttered the splintered table. An empty, unmarked prescription bottle rolled back and forth by his foot.

He sat motionless, silent and alone. He was rocking from side to side as he cradled the photo in his hands. His face was expressionless, lifeless. Slowly and incoherently words began to slip from his mouth into the musty air. Gradually they became connected with a semblance of thought.

"Christian . . . she . . . tried to force me . . . to give you up. She . . . I couldn't . . . trust her anymore. I killed her . . . for us . . . for . . . for when I come . . . for you. You'll . . . never leave me . . . again." Tears magnified the glazed eyes and slid into the dark well beneath them and on down his face. "I . . . forgive you, Christian. I'll be coming for you . . . soon."

He listlessly raised himself up and walked over to a clouded mirror hanging from a piece of string wrapped around a nail that jutted from the soiled wall. He looked at his blurred image in the mirror, thinking: Almost ten years. I've waited almost ten years . . . and now, now I have found her.

He moved to the door, stopped, then retraced his steps to the closet. Opening it, he peered in to be sure everything was secure. Satisfied, he relocked the enclosure and left the dingy apartment.

Slowly he walked through the corridors at Wilmington General Hospital. He entered the door marked STAFF, went over to the pot of hot water and poured himself a cup, adding a bouillon cube. As the nurses and doctors filtered through the room, they acknowledged him as he sat with his broth, glancing at the newspaper.

Throwing his empty cup into the disposal bin, he began to make his rounds. Walking into a patient's room, he asked, "And how are you feeling today?"

Tom O'Brien had checked into the swank El Cortez in San Diego's Harbor Island—nothing was too good for Lane's money. He then placed a call to Lane's private number.

"Yeah."

"Lane, it's me, Tom, I'm here."

"Okay, call me the minute you have somethin'. Now unpack and get movin' on this thing."

"Got it, Lane."

With the change in time from East to West, it was still early afternoon as O'Brien entered Deanna's Professional Photo Service. And it was late evening when he left empty-handed, though not before he had requested Deanna to hire extra girls to help them find the photo proofs.

Christian was retrieving the morning mail. There was a thick business-size envelope addressed to her. She opened it, taking out the pictures. They were of her and Lane, taken in front of her house. Over each picture of Christian were three words: "Christian, you're mine." Each enlarged snapshot of Lane had a bullet hole painted in the middle of his forehead. Judging from the position of the subjects, Christian had concluded they were taken from the field across the street. She immediately called Lane.

Gina was at the office repeating over and over to herself, "Dennis, what were you looking for . . . what . . . what?" Again and again she leafed through the pictures.

Lane was seated in the den of Christian's home. A glass of wine was at his side. Mrs. Day and Christian were drinking coffee. Lane was slowly going through the pictures. He had taken one of the photos and handed it to Christian.

"Christian, do you see the dark spot in the upper right-hand corner of that picture?"

She glanced at the picture in her hand. "Yes."

"The guy took those pictures from the field across the street with a telephoto lens. He was lyin' down, hidin' in the field. Those blurred streaks are growth in front of his lens."

"Lane, the bullet holes drawn on your forehead. He's saying he's going to shoot you," Mrs. Day uttered apprehensively.

Lane did not want to alarm them further.

"I'll level with you," he lied. "If the guy wanted to shoot me, he coulda nailed me right there and then."

Tom O'Brien stared at the scores of cartons that remained to be processed and thought he'd be in San Diego forever.

Deanna's father, a man in his early seventies, walked into the shop and sauntered over to where the girls were working. He began to study the face of the girl in the photo that was tacked to the wall. Taking the picture down, he looked at it intently. He walked over to where Deanna and Tom were standing.

"Is this the girl you're looking for?" he asked O'Brien.

"Yes . . . yes, sir."

"I know the face," the old man said. "She was on the front page of every paper in California nearly ten years ago. The police theory was that her husband came in and surprised her and her lover. I remember it well."

"Sir, what happened to them . . . to the husband?"

"As I recall it, the wife's lover was found in the bedroom shot several times with a shotgun. The woman here," he said, indicating the picture, "was found in a trash bag. There was also a meat cleaver in the bag. Her husband had chopped her up with it."

"It was definitely the husband?"

"Oh, there was no doubt that he did it. The police found his fingerprints on the meat cleaver and all through the house on the bloodstained walls. They never found him."

Tom grasped the old man's hand. "Thank you . . . thank you so much."

"Don't you want us to keep looking for the name?" quizzed Deanna.

"What's the name of the newspaper in this town?" Tom blurted out.

"The San Diego *Union.*"

"They'll have all the information I'll need."

It was late afternoon in Boston. Gina sat hunched over the pictures from Dennis Raskin's files. She looked at a picture of Dr. Spellie and a group of people leaving the front entrance of the hospital. She had looked at it many times before. Suddenly she heard herself saying aloud, "My God! It can't be."

Her heart pounded as she flew from the office and raced toward the hospital. She parked her car inconspicuously in an area where she could watch the employees' parking lot. She had been there two hours before he came out. He slowly left the parking lot. Gina gave him an opportunity to get several car lengths ahead of her as she eased her car out of the parking space.

He turned right at the corner. She accelerated through the stop sign, swung right, and kept several car lengths behind him. He parked in front of a dilapidated old rooming house and went in. Giving him a few minutes, she followed. She could hear him on the stairs above her. She climbed them a flight at a time, each time waiting to hear his footsteps on the floor above her. She scampered up the third flight on tiptoe until she heard the steps creaking down the hall above. Slowly she took the steps to the fourth floor. Reaching the top of the landing, she cautiously peered around the corner. Empty. The dingy, dirty corridor was empty. She walked softly down the hall, watching the cracks at the bottom of the doors for light. She passed the first two doors, one on each side of the hallway. Nothing. The next set of doors she came to had a light showing under one of them. Ever so quietly she crept up to the door, easing her ear against it, listening intently.

Her head exploded! She slumped unconscious to the floor. A man behind her held a small but lethal hammer in his hand. His eyes narrowed, a sneering grin spread across his mouth, as he quickly opened the door, dragging her into the room.

He had seen her following him in his rearview mirror. Upon reaching the fourth floor, he had raced to his room and, snatching up the hammer, run barefoot down the hall, breathlessly watching her from behind as she approached his doorway.

He tied and gagged her. She was groggy but now conscious. Her head was pounding.

He stood over her glaring down into her eyes. "You never should have followed me. Never . . . never."

She watched him walk over to the drawer under the peeling cabinets. As he turned around, she saw it. He came stalking toward her with a butcher knife that gleamed in the dull light. She was filled with terror, her body convulsing in horror as he neared.

chapter 24

It was eleven P.M. in California and eight P.M. in Boston when Tom called Lane at his home. He let the phone ring endlessly, then hung up and dialed Lane's office. Again there was no answer. He placed a hurried call to Zito's without results. A longer delay would mean missing the connection to Los Angeles for his morning flight back to Boston.

It was after one A.M. Don Spencer had nervously paced the floor for hours, as Gina hadn't come home yet. Becoming very concerned and positive she didn't have a late assignment, he decided he'd waited long enough. He went to her telephone book and looked up Lane Garrett's private number. After several rings, a sleepy Lane answered his phone.

"Lane, this is Don Spencer. Gina hasn't come home yet, and what really worries me . . . she hasn't called."

Lane answered apprehensively. "Don, she left the office late this afternoon. Linda said she sounded excited and told her she wouldn't be back for the rest of the day."

"Did she say where she was going?"

"Linda said she flew out of the office without sayin' anythin' else."

"Lane, do you have any idea where she might be?"

"Don, I don't know where the hell she can be."

"I'm sorry if I disturbed you."

"Don, when she gets home, call me, no matter what time it is," he uttered, fighting thoughts of impending doom.

"I will; good night, Lane."

Tom O'Brien was at the airport in San Diego, California. He paced across the terminal waiting area nervously awaiting the boarding call. In his briefcase he had photostats of all the newspaper accounts outlining the double murder. Pictures of the woman and her husband were included in the stories.

It was two A.M. and, like a distant echo, came the incessant ringing of the phone. In the hope that it might be Don calling about Gina, Lane pulled the receiver to his ear and quickly talked into the mouthpiece.

"Hello, is that you—"

"Friend . . . detective," cut the muffled tones over Lane's voice, "or is it *lover?"* he added snidely.

It's our creep friend. Lane grimaced.

"Aren't you surprised?" the voice continued.

Lane lit up a cigarette and, taking a long pull, spoke. "I was wonderin' when you'd get around to me." Lane's mind raced; he didn't want to frighten him off. "Listen to me. You need help . . . no one is gonna hurt you . . ."

The muffled voice cut in again. "I'm willing to surrender myself," he suddenly declared.

"That's easy . . . walk into any police station," replied Lane.

"Only to you," protested the still-masked voice.

"Why me?" pressed Lane.

"I know the police . . . they . . ." the high, rasping snorting filtered through the phone. "They . . . shoot first. They'll hurt me. I want to live."

This bum is settin' me up, thought Lane. "First I gotta know who you are."

There was a long pause. "Brian . . . Brian Summers."

"Why'd you kill Merguson?"

"She saw me in Christian's room . . . steal the hospital files." His sinister laughter turned into a series of coughing and deep, hurried gasps for air. "Do you . . . do you want . . . to . . . meet me . . . or not?"

"Where?" Lane asked quickly.

"The parking lot across from the exhibition hall down by the pier. No . . . no police. No one . . . or I leave."

"I'll be alone," Lane assured him.

"An hour."

"An hour," confirmed Lane.

The long, darkened docks were desolate. Below the ocean lapped against the pilings, while above stood deserted wooden buildings dimly outlined by a cloud-covered moon. Lane Garrett and Ernest Hampton stood huddled together, hidden in the shadows a short block from the place where Lane had agreed to meet Brian Summers.

"Ernie, the guy said he was Summers. No matter who he is, I figure he's up to no good. If you see a car come tearin' outta there before mine, blow the son of a bitch away!"

"Let me go with you, Lane. You know the man is going to try to sucker you."

"This creep is holdin' all the cards. I haven't heard from Tom yet and if he comes up empty, we're back to where we started. You gotta just lay back until we see what's comin' down."

Ernest watched as Lane slowly drove away. The tail lights on the big Lincoln disappeared as the car turned into the parking lot.

It was well after three A.M. as Lane edged his car into the eerie surroundings. The parking lot was divided by a tall fence that kept the patrons of the nearby restaurant from taking spaces that belonged to the exhibition hall. A lone car was parked on the other side of the fence—the restaurant side. Lane parked his car, shut off his motor, and pulled a snub-nose .38 from his ankle holster.

He climbed out of his car, walking deliberately, hands at his sides, toward an opening in the chain-link fence. Slowly he strode toward the building that was on the opposite end of the lot. A chill was in the air and Lane could hear the soft lapping of the waves against the pilings that surrounded the dock.

He was perhaps twenty feet from the dwelling, his back toward the restaurant. With every step, his wary senses were more acutely alert. His eyes had to strain to see as the moon became enshrouded with a procession of heavy dark clouds being blown across the sky. The night had become coal black.

Just then a darkened car shot from the alley between the restaurant and the adjacent building.

Hearing the roar of the motor, Lane wheeled around, his gun hand extended as the car rocketed toward him. Lunging to one side and falling to the wooden platform, he rolled over and over. The car, nearly hitting him, went screeching by. Lane bounded to his feet, firing all six shots at the distant outline that now had disappeared out of the lot.

Trembling and shaking his head, he started for his car. Headlights were bearing down on him as a car came screeching into the lot. He was dead center in the middle of the lot—the headlights streaking toward him. He took aim at the driver's side of the blinding lights, pulling the trigger in rapid succession. No shots echoed in the night this time—his gun was empty.

The car came skidding to a halt. Lane could see the outline of a man rushing toward him. It was Ernest!

"Ernie! You crazy bastard! I coulda killed you! I told you to nail any car that came outta here!!"

Ernest, shaking, stood before him. *"Goddamn it,* Lane! I heard shots; I thought you were hurt," he shouted in a mixture of anger and relief.

Lane was quiet for a moment, took a step forward, and held Ernest's face between his two hands, kissing him on the cheek. "Love ya, pal."

"Now you tell me," a smiling, perplexed Ernest muttered.

The view from the John Hancock observatory was magnificent. Sixty stories below, one could see for miles—the sprawling city of Boston. Father Travers and Lane Garrett stood admiring the view as they spoke.

"Father, I appreciate you comin'. I hope I didn't take you away from anythin' important at the hospital."

"No, not at all, Mr. Garrett." Curious, he continued. "I must say I found your wanting to meet me here somewhat unusual."

"It's important that no one know of our meeting. First of all, I want to thank you for the support you've given to Christian."

"You need not thank me. You see, Mr. Garrett, that is my life's work—doing God's will. But that is not why you asked me here. What is it that troubles you?"

"Father, I'm gonna . . . well, lay it on the line with you. The man who raped Christian is a very dangerous person. I don't want him harmed; I just want him stopped. Father, I have narrowed it down to three, maybe four people. You can help me eliminate one of those people."

"How? How can I help you, Mr. Garrett?"

"Dr. Spellie told me he hadn't been to confession in ten years. Father, I know you're bound by your faith not to relate to me anything you hear in the confession. All I want you to say to me is 'continue to investigate' or 'I don't think Dr. Spellie warrants further investigation.' "

"Mr. Garrett . . . I wish I could help you. My prayers are with you to catch this man. However, I cannot breach the sanctity of the confessional . . . not even remotely."

Pausing, Lane saw the finality of Travers's words etched on his face. "I understand. Father, thank you for comin'."

Travers smiled at him. "Mr. Garrett, is there anything that I can do for *you* while I'm here?"

Flustered, Lane answered. "Well . . . er . . . no, I guess I'm in good shape, Father." Lane felt uncomfortable as the priest stared with probing eyes. "Father, what would you do if you were me?" he asked, changing the subject.

"Mr. Garrett, I suspect you're a very good detective. If I were you, I suppose I'd—I'd follow my hunches."

After a hurried phone call to his office, Lane proceeded to place another call to Jonathan Prendergast at Wilmington General Hospital. He asked for a list of names of persons who had been at the hospital for eight years or longer. There were four, including Prendergast himself—and Spellie.

Again and again his mind's eye pictured the four men—racking his brain for something—anything that would bring him a step closer to this maniac. His thoughts kept intermingling with the aspect of the case when Garcia was alive: Damn it, that won't do any good—Garcia's dead . . . it's not him. He thought of Merguson: Someone she knew, that she was close to—a husband, no—a son. Sixty-three . . . yeah, she was sixty-three. Her son would be in his mid-forties . . . less. Spellie . . . Prendergast . . . they fitted the age. Spellie fits in some other places. The bug—he had the know-how, the opportunity—motive? Christ, what do you do when a shrink flips out—who do *they* talk to? Prendergast . . . age, opportunity, what else? The other two—not much chance. I gotta check 'em out . . . all of 'em.

At his office, Lane labored over the eight-by-ten photos of personnel leaving the front door of the hospital. Damn it . . . what did Dennis think he'd find in these? His eyes filled up as he thought of Gina and Don's call that morning saying she hadn't come home last night. How many . . . how many gotta die before this ends? She *has* to be okay . . . she's gotta be. His attention again focused on the pictures—over and over he sifted through them. Picking one up, he paused. His head whirled. Travers's words sprang into his mind: "If I were you, I'd follow my hunches." You're right, Father, sometimes all you got in this business is a hunch—sometimes that's enough.

He proceeded to Virginia Merguson's home. Pulling into the driveway, he glanced around. He was undetected as he got out of his car and went around to the rear of the house.

The back door was padlocked. His eyes searched the rear of the house—no one. He took one step back and kicked the door in.

Slowly, methodically he searched the house—closets, drawers, under beds, sofa cushions, everywhere. Nothing. Walking into the bathroom, he opened the small linen closet, medicine cabinet. Nothing. Down the cellar stairs and into a musty, cluttered basement, he went directly to the washer and dryer. The washing machine was empty. He opened the dryer door; a hard smile crossed his face as he withdrew a man's shirt, pants, and underwear. Now I know how big you are, my creep friend, he thought grimly. He took the stairs back up two at a time, back into the kitchen, and out the rear door. Turning to leave, his eyes were caught by a storage shed. Walking over to it, he opened the door—lawn mower, yard tools, trash cans, and garbage bucket. Slowly, painstakingly he sifted through the trash cans: a bottle of aftershave lotion; an empty bottle marked "Valium," prescription made out to V. Merguson; on and on, nothing more. He lifted the cover on the garbage can. The sight of the maggot-covered swill and the stench coming from it repelled him, making him nauseous. Carefully he lifted the can and dumped it onto the ground. Picking up a stick, he poked through it. There! Bingo! Lane reached into the pile, taking the corner of the cassette tape and gingerly lifting it out of the garbage. Taking out his handkerchief, he wiped it off, then threw the handkerchief to the ground and put the tape in his pocket.

After getting into his car and pushing the tape into the recorder, he listened. The voice of the rapist burst forth as he spoke to Christian, then went silent without her replying.

Why, Lane pondered, why did he keep this one? He took a deep pull on his cigarette. Mother of Jesus! That's it!

Just one more person had to be questioned—to make sure, before heading for Christian's.

chapter 25

It was late afternoon as Teddy hurried down the front steps and across the street. He waved to the man clipping the Dawsons' hedges, secretly hoping the man would not tell his mother he'd seen him leave. Quickly the boy reached the field, thinking he'd be wise to buy his candy before Mr. Katz closed his store.

Teddy was too engrossed with reaching the store to notice Jack Reardon, Lane's operative, following him.

Reardon stood on the sidewalk opposite Katz's corner market. He was beginning to ask himself what was taking the boy so long. He strained to see into the store window from the distance, when he wasn't glimpsing at his watch. Twenty minutes is long enough to buy out the store, he decided as he sprinted across the street.

Jack peered cautiously through the window that reflected the gray, cloud-filled sky. It was like trying to look through a pair of mirrored sunglasses from the wrong side. He opened the door as inconspicuously as possible but the bells above it inside jingled. Jack didn't know why, but he half expected to see little Teddy sitting on a stool with a mouthful of candy, pointing at him and laughing as if to say, I tricked you; I fooled you.

But he didn't see Teddy—or the owner, for that matter. His eyes skirted the room. To "Hello, anybody there?" came no response. Maybe they had gone into the back room. He hurried toward the back of the store only to discover that the rear delivery door had been left ajar. Looking out, he saw an old, dented Ford that he knew belonged to Mr. Katz parked in an alley leading to a back street. He puzzled for a moment, wondering if the boy had gone home out the back door for the first time. But then where was Mr. Katz?

Jack raced through the store room, searching and yelling out, his apprehension rapidly becoming panic. He charged down the basement steps and knocked over cartons that blocked his view. The mere fact that he had had to flick on the light switch was indication enough that the two were not down there.

He bounded up the creaky wooden steps and returned to the grocery store. Once again he ran to the back door, frantically looking down the alley—no one! He charged back through the store and out the front door into the street—there wasn't a single solitary soul! Wildly he flung the door open and reentered the store. The realization suddenly struck him and for one breathless moment he was paralyzed by it: Teddy George was gone. He spun around as if trying to turn his back on the idea that he could have actually lost a mere child. He stared at the worn linoleum floor, shaking his head in disbelief. His only hope was that Teddy had gone home. But when he spotted Mr. Katz coming from the door of his walk-in cooler, moaning as he rubbed the lump on the back of his head, Jack Reardon knew immediately that he was deluding himself. The kid had been snatched . . . and right from under him.

Christian had been sitting in the kitchen trying not to notice her mother's eyes glancing over at her every few minutes. Mrs. Day finally opened the refrigerator, took out the milk, and poured a glass. Looking at it, she decided it was not palatable enough, added some chocolate syrup, and mixed it. Still not satisfied, she piled several cookies onto a plate and started from the kitchen, the food in her hands.

"Where are you going, Mother?" asked Christian.

"Teddy's playing in his room; I thought I'd share my cookies with him," she said, winking.

Christian rose from her chair and smiled. "I'll get him, Mom."

She skipped up the stairs calling to Teddy, eager to grasp him to her and hold him. She flung his door open only to be greeted by an empty room. She walked from room to room, calling out his name and looking under the bedcovers and in the closets, thinking he might be playing a game with her. He never popped out at her gleefully yelling at the last minute, "Surprise, mommy!"

Panic suddenly gripped her. She started to yell Teddy's name and retraced her steps, this time looking under the beds in search for him.

"Mother!" she screamed, stumbling down the stairs. "Teddy's not here!"

"Did you look in the basement?" urged Mrs. Day, already halfway down the cellar steps. She soon reappeared, her face white, her eyes reflecting her fear. "He's not there."

"Oh, my God," cried Christian. "He's gone . . . he's gone."

"He's probably only gone to the grocery store to get some candy," suggested Mrs. Day, trying to calm her daughter.

"Maybe you're right," Christian agreed, hurriedly starting for the door.

"And where are you going?" her mother asked.

"Out to find him."

"Wait, I'll go with you. Let me get my sweater."

"No, Mother," declared Christian, "someone has to be here in case he comes home."

She raced out the door and into the street while Mrs. Day stood by the front door, calling to him. "Teddy . . . Teddy . . . Teddy." Oh, where is that little stinker? she muttered to herself. The thought suddenly came to her that he must be at Bobby Bixby's house. She reproached herself for not thinking of it before and started for the kitchen to telephone them. As her hand reached for the phone, she jumped back startled by the ringing. She hesitantly lifted it from its cradle.

"Hello," said Mrs. Day.

A muffled voice spoke. "Is Christian there?"

Mrs. Day's heart pounded in her bosom as she answered. "No—no, she isn't here."

"I'll call back later on. I have her son."

"No! Holy mother of God, no! Please . . . please . . ."

"Listen to me," he hissed, "don't call the police. If you do, I'll kill . . . him."

"Oh . . . please, I won't call the police. Please don't hurt him."

The phone went dead!

Christian frantically searched the neighborhood for Teddy. She half ran to Katz's store. Trying the door, she found it locked.

"Teddy, Teddy," she called throughout the neighborhood, racing back in the direction of her house.

Opening the front door and desperately hoping to find him there, she climbed the stairs and passed into the living room toward the kitchen. "Mom, I can't find him. He's not in the field or at—"

"Christian," her mother said, softly interrupting, "he has Teddy." Mrs. Day put her hands over her eyes and began sobbing.

"No! No! No! He can't have . . . he can't have Teddy!" The sound of her voice became a distant echo as her eyes became glazed, her knees buckling beneath her as she collapsed onto the floor in a faint.

Lane, who was outside the front door, burst in upon hearing Christian's hysterics and bounded up the stairs to her. He picked her up, gently placing her on the couch. Mrs. Day held an ice pack to her head, while she hurriedly explained to Lane what had happened.

Christian was beginning to come out of it. She was mumbling, "No . . . no, no . . . no . . . he can't have my Teddy . . . my Teddy."

Mrs. Day wept to Lane. "He's called twice. He wants to talk to Christian."

Lane nodded silently.

Christian stirred and tried to sit up, but Lane gently held her by her shoulders. "Easy, easy, wait a minute."

"Lane . . . oh, Lane, what are we going to do?"

"Christian, I know who he is. You're gonna hang tough and talk to 'im. We gotta stall for a little time. Do you think you can handle it?"

She sat up. She was pale, her body shivering. "What . . . do you want me to do?"

"When he calls, tell 'im you won't listen to anythin' he has to say until you talk to Teddy. Now this guy might rant and rave, even threaten to do somethin' drastic to Teddy. You hold your ground—don't talk to him until he lets you talk to Teddy. It's you he's interested in. This creep is gonna wanna make a trade, Teddy . . . for you. Agree with anythin' he wants, but you tell 'im that before you leave this house, you'll want to talk to Teddy again."

"Lane, I don't . . . know."

"Christian, you gotta do it and you hafta sound convincin'. I got this guy nailed; I just need a little time."

"Mom . . . please get me two of the tranquilizers in my top dresser drawer." Her voice was quivering as she spoke.

When Mrs. Day returned, Christian was sitting up, cradled in Lane's arms, his hand stroking her head. Lane took the water and pills from her, handing them to Christian while Mrs. Day took a seat opposite them.

Lane's voice was soft but confident as he spoke. "Now I want you both to listen to me. That man isn't gonna harm Teddy until he's sure he has Christian. Christian, I'm gonna get Teddy back. You just gotta do like I tell you and it will turn out all right. Now listen, I don't care how mad he gets or how he threatens Teddy, you're not gonna begin to negotiate with 'im until he lets you talk to Teddy."

The tranquilizers had taken effect, calming Christian somewhat. They sat there and waited and waited. Lane was again going over the strategy that Christian must use when the phone rang.

The noise of the ringing was frightening to the two women. To Lane it was a sound of relief as he counseled Christian, "Remember what I told you." He gave her a quick hug and hurriedly added, "Now, go get this guy . . . buy me some time."

"Hello."

"Hello, Christian," said the muffled voice. "Christian . . . I have your little boy. It's time for you to come with me."

"I'll—I'll do anything you want . . . just don't hurt Teddy. I want to talk to him."

His angry voice spewed at her. "You listen to me, you whore! You'll talk to him when you come to me."

She drew a deep breath. "I'm not coming to you until you let me talk to him."

He screeched into the phone. "I'll kill him! If you don't listen to me, I'll kill him!"

Lane was listening. He gave Christian the signal to hang up. Her eyes were wide and she was shaking her head no. Lane grabbed the phone from her, slamming it down.

"Lane!" she screamed, terrified. "He said he would kill him!"

He was holding her, hugging. "No . . . he won't. He wants you, not Teddy. He'll call back."

"Lane, what if you're wrong! What if he doesn't call back?" There was desperation and agony in her voice and eyes.

The phone began ringing. Lane held her firmly by the shoulders. "You hear that! We got him! Now you do what I asked you to!"

"Christian . . . don't hang up," the voice implored. "I'll let you talk to your son." His voice had quieted considerably.

"Momma."

"Oh, Teddy, Teddy darling . . . are you okay?"

"Momma, he said he was taking me to Lane's house."

"Teddy, are you all right?" she asked, trying to stifle her sobbing as she clutched the phone.

"I'm okay, Momma, I'm just hungry."

The man's voice replaced Teddy's. "Christian . . . see, he's all right. I won't hurt him. It's time for you to come with me."

"What—what do you want me to do?"

"Christian . . . I have some responsibilities to take care of. I'll call you tomorrow morning. You pack your clothes. I'll tell you where to meet me . . . and Christian, if you call the police, or if your lover tries to interfere . . . I'll kill him . . . I'll kill Teddy."

Each time she heard the words "I'll kill Teddy," it sent waves of horror through her body. "Before I come to meet you. I'll want to talk to Teddy again."

"All right, Christian, all right. I'll call you tomorrow."

She hung up the phone weakly and nearly collapsed in Lane's arms. He patted her on the back, trying to console her as she sobbed freely.

"Christian, you did it . . . you did fine." Lane looked around at Mrs. Day, saying, "Sweetheart, you got any liquor in this house?"

"Lane," the tearful old woman managed to reply, "we have some whiskey."

"Would you get it? I could use a drink."

Christian's eyes pleaded as she looked at Lane. "Lane, if you know who he is, why can't we go now . . . why can't we go get Teddy now?"

He kissed her softly on her tearstained cheek. "Christian, we have to wait until he leaves the hospital in the morning. I checked and he's still there. I can't take a chance in callin' in the law—they'd go to the hospital, maybe arrest him—maybe spook him. We gotta wait till morning when I can follow him to wherever that secret pad of his is."

Mrs. Day returned with Lane's drink. "Here, Lane."

"Thanks, sweetheart." He gulped it down, announcing "You two are gonna have a house guest for tonight."

"You can stay in the spare room," said Mrs. Day.

"I'm really not tired. If you'd just put on a pot of coffee that would be great."

Mrs. Day, deciding to go to her room, kissed Lane and Christian good night and went to bed. She promised she would set the alarm for four-thirty A.M., as Lane had instructed.

Lane called Ernest and advised him to be at the George home at five A.M. He also advised Captain Ray Tiernan of the situation. Tiernan, speaking off the record, advised Lane that he would stand by but would deny any knowledge of the kidnapping.

After the calls, Lane and Christian were seated on the couch in the den. The hot coffee steamed from the cups before them. He kissed her lovingly on the forehead.

"Christian, I promise you I'll get him back . . . and he'll be okay."

Her head was resting on his shoulder. "Lane . . . maybe you should get some help, the police, the FBI."

"Don't you think I'll bring him home?" asked Lane.

"It's not that, Lane. When you leave . . . to find him . . . I'm afraid for you, like I'm afraid for Teddy. I couldn't bear it if anything happened to either one of you."

"Christian, I can't take that chance. He might smell a rat. If the Boston cops or the FBI get wind of this, the guy is bound to smell somethin' comin' down. He's dangerous. I can't risk it. Believe me when I tell you I'll bring this guy down. You gotta believe me, it's important. I need to know that you're with me . . . that you know I'll come through for you—for us."

She looked up at him. "Lane"—she bit her bottom lip, tears overflowing from her eyes and running down her cheeks—"I—I know you'll bring Teddy home."

He kissed her softly on the lips. She sat there and fell asleep in his arms. He watched her sleeping, the diamond-studded heart around her neck sparkling in the light. He rested his head against hers and dozed.

After a five-hour fog delay in Los Angeles and a missed connecting flight in Chicago, Tom O'Brien had landed at Boston's Logan Airport. It was 6:15 P.M. as he dialed Lane's home. Not getting an answer, he tried locating Gina and Ernest, both without results. With the newspaper clippings, complete with pictures, he headed for home.

chapter 26

It was four-thirty A.M. Lane was already up when he heard the alarm go off in Mrs. Day's room. Christian lay on the couch in a fitful sleep, while he was at the kitchen table nursing a cup of coffee, an aching head, and smoking a cigarette. Mrs. Day came into the kitchen in her bathrobe.

"Good morning, Lane."

"Good mornin', sweetheart."

She looked at Lane. His eyes were bloodshot. He had a weary look to him as he reached up, rubbing the dark whiskers on his face.

"Do you want a razor, Lane?"

"Yeah," he said as he smiled tiredly.

Mrs. Day left the room and brought back an electric shaver. "It was Ben's," she commented, handing it to him.

"Thanks," he responded, lighting a new cigarette.

"Lane, how is Christian?"

"She's sleepin' on the couch. She's gonna make it. We're all gonna make it."

He got up, kissed the old woman on the forehead, and went into the bathroom. He had been there about fifteen minutes when he heard the doorbell. Mrs. Day answered it. Hearing the voice of Ernest Hampton, Lane thought: Good old Ernie, right on the button. He finished washing and went into the kitchen.

"Morning, Lane," Ernest said solemnly.

"Mornin', pal."

They were seated at the kitchen table, sipping coffee, as Christian awoke and came into the room. They all fell silent—she the bereaved and they the mourners. Lane broke the awkward stillness.

"Good morning, sleepyhead; have some coffee."

"I will," she answered almost sullenly. "Just let me freshen up."

She went into the bathroom to wash her face. Dark circles stood out under her eyes. She was listless as she feebly brushed her hair and put a touch of lipstick on. Her insides were knotted thinking of Teddy. Feeling herself on the verge of breaking down, she rushed out into the kitchen and sat beside Lane. Her mother put a cup of coffee in front of her and offered her some toast.

"No . . . no thanks, Mom."

The four of them were silent, sitting there drinking their coffee. It was raining out, and a feeling of doom hung heavily in the air. The torment, tragedy, and sorrow were etched on their faces. It was Lane who finally spoke—softly and yet with confidence.

"I'm gonna leave here in about five minutes. I want you all to know the next time you see me come through that door, I'll have Teddy with me. Ernie is gonna stay with you until I get back. If I get the chance, I'll call and keep you all posted. If I don't, that doesn't mean that things ain't goin' right—it just means I can't leave what I'm doin'. You can all help me by stayin' here and buyin' me as much time as you can when he calls again. I know it ain't easy waitin', but some of us gotta wait and some of us gotta do. You people got the toughest part . . . the waitin'. We're gonna come out of this okay, and after today, this guy'll only be a bad dream."

Lane got up to leave and Christian stood up with him. She looked at her mother and Ernest.

"I'll be right with you," she said as she walked into the hallway. "I'd like to see Lane alone for a moment."

She looked at him, her eyes glassy, her lips trembling. "Lane . . . I know you'll bring Teddy back to me. I want you to be careful. I have to let you know something before you go. No matter what happens today . . . no matter how things go"—she swallowed as her eyes released the tears—"I want you to know you've given me a new life. I want you to know that . . . I love you."

She put her head against his chest and cried. He held her there, his cheek wet from his own tears that shamelessly trickled from his eyes. He kissed her.

His voice was cracking and filled with emotion as he spoke. "Christian, I gotta tell you, for the first time in a lotta years I've been a really happy man. You made me feel like a kid again. I guess I'd be lost . . . without you. Lemme go get Teddy, and we'll finish this when I get back—okay?"

"Okay, Lane," she murmured softly.

"Wait for me . . . I'll be back," he said, holding and kissing her.

Lane walked right past the kitchen, not saying good-bye to Ernest or Mrs. Day. The tears still slipped from his eyes as he blindly put the key into the ignition of the rented car Ernest had brought. The street was hazy in front of him as he drove away, brushing the tears from his eyes.

Lane had pulled into one of the side streets that faced the main entrance to the hospital. He thought about Gina and, sensing her fate, was filled with remorse. Dennis Raskin was lost indirectly because of this maniac. And now Christian, he wants Christian. Lane was overwhelmed with bitterness. Not for himself or the two attacks on his life, but for Christian and the agony the freak had put her through.

He waited the better part of two hours before it happened. He saw him at the same time the beeper on the portable radar screen attached to his dashboard alerted him. His car had just passed the side street where Lane was parked.

All right, friend, let's get this over with, Lane thought. It seems like I been waitin' for you all my life. Besides, I got a lady that wants her little boy back. Not yet . . . not yet, get just a little farther away. There, that's far enough, Lane thought as the beeping sound started to weaken. Lane viewed the screen in front of him. The car was traveling north, straight ahead of him. He accelerated the car, keeping nearly a mile between him and the car he followed. He continued to glance at the screen as the car shifted north by northeast. The tiny dot marked the car's location between the two black lines. Lane was behind him for fifteen minutes as the beeping started to grow louder. The man had stopped!

Lane pulled over for several minutes, making sure the man

wasn't stopped for gas or checking the flow of traffic behind him. Lane proceeded cautiously, fearful that the man was seated in his car waiting for the traffic to pass him by. The beeping sound began to grow much louder and his monitor told Lane the car was dead ahead. Lane's eyes strained to see it before he came to it. There! Squarely ahead on the left. Lane wheeled the car into the next street on his right, got out, and quickly walked toward the car.

It was empty—parked in front of a rooming house. He glanced around, making sure the man wasn't still on the street. He walked into the rooming house, checking the names on the mailboxes. His name wasn't listed. He scrutinized all the initials on the boxes. He found the name was different but the initials were the same. Sucker, he thought, he's basically like the others. The name on the mailbox was on the fourth floor. He took his shoes off, leaving them at the foot of the stairs, and cautiously started up the first flight with gun drawn.

The phone at Christian's home was ringing. Christian, in her haste to answer it, nearly tore it from the wall.

"Hello, Christian. It's me. We're leaving today."

"I want to talk with Teddy."

"In a moment, Christian. Are you packed?"

"Yes . . . yes, I'm packed."

"Good . . . that's fine. Christian . . . tell me you're all mine."

"I'm all yours . . ."

"Christian . . . tell me you want me . . . to make love to you again."

Ernest and Mrs. Day stood by her as she spoke to him. Mrs. Day's heart was breaking as she heard Christian's sobbing voice.

"I want you . . . to make love to me again."

"Christian, now tell me . . . you haven't called the police, have you?"

"No," she answered. "You know I wouldn't do that."

"Good . . . because if you do . . . I'll have to kill your son."

"I want to talk to Teddy . . . now."

"You can talk to him later. Good-bye for now . . . Christian."

"No! No! Don't Hang Up! You promised I could talk to Teddy!" she screamed.

The buzz of the dial tone filled the room.

Lane Garrett was right outside the door as the man was completing his phone conversation. Lane shook with the growing tension. He aimed his eyes at the old wooden door, stepped, and kicked it viciously in the center. The door flew open as Lane burst into the room, his gun raised before him.

The man froze as Lane released his hatred. *"Go ahead! Please* . . . please move . . ."

Lane quickly glanced around the room. Teddy was lying on the floor, blood spilling from his mouth. He was motionless.

The man was laughing as he snarled, "He's dead! I killed him! He's dead!"

The hate welled up in Lane. He glared at the man as though in a trance as he seethed in a deadly tone, "You shouldn't have done that . . . you really shouldn't have done that."

Lane walked toward him as the man screamed out, "You Stay away from me, Lane . . . you stay away from me!"

Moments later, outside the rooming house, a man's voice could be heard screaming as he fell through the air, four floors to the street. A huge tractor-trailer jammed on its brakes as the big truck came screeching to a halt, its front wheel resting on the man's head.

Lane was still in the man's room, staring zombielike out the open window to the crowd that had gathered below. He could not bear to look at Teddy. He just stared, dazed, out the window. Over and over in his mind he struggled with how he would break the news to Christian. He continued to look out the window as though hypnotized by the crowd below. He watched the first police cruiser pull up, thinking: First her husband, then she is raped . . . now . . . her son is dead. Suffering Jesus, how much can one person be expected to take?

He remained at the window, looking but not seeing anything as he thought of Christian and how he must tell her of her son's death. Someone touched his hand. He turned slowly. It was Teddy! He was alive!

Lane grabbed him up, hugging and kissing the boy, oblivious to the pandemonium on the street below. Teddy looked quizzically and asked, "Lane, why are you crying?"

"I ain't cryin', I got a cold. What happened to your mouth?"

"I got off the couch to call Momma. The man hit me, and then I think . . . I don't know, I think I went to sleep."

Lane was showering the boy with kisses, holding him, hugging him, as the boy managed to squeeze out the words, "That man has a lady in his closet."

Lane's heart skipped a beat. Gina!

"Teddy, you wait here while I take a look."

He opened the closet. She was in there, gagged and bound. Lane leaned down, his heart racing as he took the gag from her mouth. He continued to untie her hands then feet as she sobbed and tearfully spoke to him.

"Lane . . . I can't believe it was him. He was going to kill me when he went to get Christian. He told me . . . he was . . . going to bury me with the Summers kid . . . behind the hospital."

He pulled her up from the floor and into his arms. "What!"

"Summers saw him go into Christian's room and tried to blackmail him . . . it backfired. I—I thought . . . I was gone." Frightened, she continued, "Where is he?"

Lane, stonefaced, looked toward the window. "He jumped."

Gina looked at him with a trace of doubt, then smiled softly. "It couldn't happen to a more deserving guy."

Lane dialed Christian's number and handed the phone to Teddy. Christian thought it was the man calling her back.

"Hello," she answered nervously.

"Hi, Momma."

"Teddy! Teddy, are you all right?"

"Yes, I'm with Lane and the girl he found in the closet, and momma, the bad man, well, he jumped out of the window and—"

"Teddy . . . Teddy . . ." Christian said, laughing and crying at the same time.

The dingy room suddenly filled with policemen. Gina pulled Teddy off to one side while Lane found himself encircled by several men in blue. He showed a burly officer his identification. "If it's okay with you, I'd like to take these people home."

"I'm sorry, I still have to take you and the girl downtown," came the reply. "A man was killed here; we're going to need a statement."

Lane protested, an angry edge to his voice. "For Christ sakes, this guy jumped out the window. These people have been through enough. Let me go with you and send the boy home with my operative."

The officer hesitated, looking at Gina and young Teddy. "Sorry, Mr. Garrett, but we gotta take you both in. I can send the boy home with one of our teams."

"Listen," replied Lane, puffing on a cigarette, "Ray Tiernan is a very dear friend of mine. Call 'im . . . he'll vouch for me."

"Captain Tiernan?" the big man quizzed, his eyes sizing up Lane.

"Yeah, Captain Tiernan. Maybe you could take the *two* of them home together. They can take her statement in the car."

The officer looked at Gina and Teddy. He nodded in resignation, saying "All right, but *you'll* have to come with us."

Gina and Teddy had just started out the door, following a police officer when she turned. "Lane . . . I—I—"

"Hey."

"What?" she asked.

"Later." He smiled.

Two hours later, when the detective finally decided to believe his story, Lane stepped into the first phone booth outside the police station.

"How's my number-one agent?" he said as Christian answered the phone.

"Oh, Lane . . . we were all so worried about you. We didn't know where you were. Are you all right?"

"Christian . . . I've never been more all right in my life."

"Lane, I want to be with you," she murmured softly.

Filled with emotion, he replied, "I'll be there in about forty-five minutes. Make that thirty-five."

"Lane, we're all fine here. Teddy's in bed and Mother's watching television. I'll meet you at your place—give me an hour."

He wanted to hold her, to feel her next to him. His voice was soft as he answered, "You buyin' the wine?"

"Yes," she replied warmly, laughing.

"See you in an hour."

chapter 27

The moonlight filtered through the glass doors onto the waterbed. They lay there naked, kissing and touching, bonded together from the pain of suffering and the terror of her ordeal. They filled each other with love. The world seemed to explode, sending them floating, drifting, almost beyond their mortal bodies.

They rocked softly on the mattress, trembling in each other's arms. The two half-filled snifters of Courvoisier sat on the nighttable beside the bed. Lane reached over, taking one in his hand, and gently tilted it toward Christian for her to sip from. Returning the empty glass to the table, he reached for his cigarettes, lighting one for both Christian and him. There was no past or present, only this . . . only now. He propped himself on his elbow, gazing at her. He kissed her tenderly on the lips as she said very softly, "Lane, I love you."

He drew back, his lips inches from hers, stroking her face and caressing her moist lips. Her soul was bathed in love as the moonlight caught her white breasts, casting a shadow where their valley lay. His voice was deep as he spoke.

"Christian . . . Christian . . . I love you too."

Their lips met . . . a kiss of love, of promise to each other. He lit another cigarette for both of them. They talked of dreams, of plans for days yet to come.

"Lane," she whispered, "if—if that hadn't happened to me in the hospital, we would never have met."

He smiled. "Oh, I don't know about that. I woulda found you."

"Lane . . . tell me who it was. Tell me why. Make me understand what made it all happen."

He blew a smoke ring from his mouth—its bluish-white haze shimmering in the moonlight. "I talked with Tom just before I got here. He filled in a lot of empty spaces."

"Please, Lane," coaxed Christian, "tell me about the man."

"As far as our weirdo friend is concerned, it all started ten years ago when he walked in on his wife and her lover. They were both in the sack . . . why don't I skip the details? Let's just say he killed them both. Get this, the night nurse at the hospital, Virginia Merguson, was his mother. After the killings, they both came east. Merguson got a job at the hospital and within a short period of time, he was right there with her. She never tipped her mitt that it was her son . . . nine years workin' together, seein' each other every day. What a con job she pulled. No one ever knew that she even had a son.

"Now, when the old witch knew what happened to you at the hospital, she tried to put a leash on her son. She kept him stuffed with tranquilizers and other stuff like that. But he blew his lid anyway. Junior figured he didn't want to listen to Mama's religious ravings anymore and decided to kill her. That's when we got lucky. I found a picture on her bureau that looked exactly like you. It later turned out to be his murdered wife. . . ."

"Lane, what about the bug he sent to my house?"

"According to Tom, the guy was formerly with army intelligence *communications.* The idea about the bug, the mind games, talkin' through a filtered cone—all those little games, he learned in the service. When he saw you in the hospital shortly after you were admitted, he flipped out, seein' his dead wife all over again. That's where he kept comin' up with that jazz 'You're mine, you know you're all mine.' When you kept tellin' me that you knew the voice, I figured you heard it the night you were raped. But you didn't remember it from then, you remembered it from earlier when he first spoke to you in your room. Dennis Raskin spotted him in a picture with Merguson, and Gina had the same hunch on the guy that was in the same picture."

Lane stopped speaking for a moment, then looked at her, saying, "You know . . . I really love you."

"I really love you too, Lane," she replied, snuggling to him, her face buried in the hollow of his neck, feeling his throat vibrating as he continued speaking.

"You see, Christian, the man was an impostor, posin' as somethin' he wasn't. The reason why we kept lookin' right past him, the reason we never gave him a thought, the reason he wasn't on the employee's list—and it was a million-to-one shot we'd spot him. His mother, Merguson, gave him the perfect cover—he was posin' as a priest—the good Father Travers!"

Christian's head jerked up off his chest, facing him. "Father Travers! Lane, it couldn't be. He was with me one day when the man called."

He took a long pull on his cigarette. "Christian, the guy was clever. What you heard was a one-sided conversation—just him talkin' to you—he had it electronically relayed when he knew he'd be with you. He knew Teddy was in school and either you or your mother would answer the phone—a fifty-fifty shot. And if your mother got the call, you'd just figure that he thought it was you. I found the tape in a garbage bucket at Merguson's house."

"Lane, you just spoke to Tom after you went for him. How did you know it was Travers?"

He leaned over kissing her softly on the lips. "When I talked to him about what Spellie had to say in confession, the man wouldn't budge. I learned a long time ago, it's not what someone necessarily says, it's a look, a twitch—it's somethin' in their eyes, face. Two things bothered me about our conversation. First he mentioned 'God's will.' That's a term his mother used when I interviewed her. Then it was like he was tryin' to tout me on Spellie, givin' me that line, 'if I were you, I'd follow my hunches.' And then there were the pictures—Travers was in three different shots with Merguson. It started to hit me—the Jesus freak and the priest, a likely duo. When I called Prendergast at the hospital, he gave me four names that had been there eight years or more—himself, Dr. Spellie, Father Travers, and a ninety-year-old man on the board named Aaron McFarland. I went to Merguson's house and found men's clothes in the dryer. They were much too small for Prendergast and the waist was too big for Spellie. I automatically discounted McFarland, so all that was left was . . . Travers. I went to Prendergast and asked him how Travers came to work at the hospital. He told me he was assigned to Saint Mary's and had been given permission to devote his time to the hospital—and Travers figured who the hell is gonna doubt the word of a priest. Well, he was almost right. I went to Saint Mary's—they never heard of the bum. Whenever the hospital wanted to reach Travers, they called a number that turned out to be an answering service. It never dawned on them the guy could be a phony."

Sinatra's voice could be heard softly drifting across the moonlit room as Christian whispered, "I think I'm going to keep you."

He brought his lips gently down on her yielding mouth. She reached down between his legs, touching him. Breathlessly their lips parted as he hoarsely murmured, "You talked me into it."